Outsider

by

Klaire de Lys

Chapters

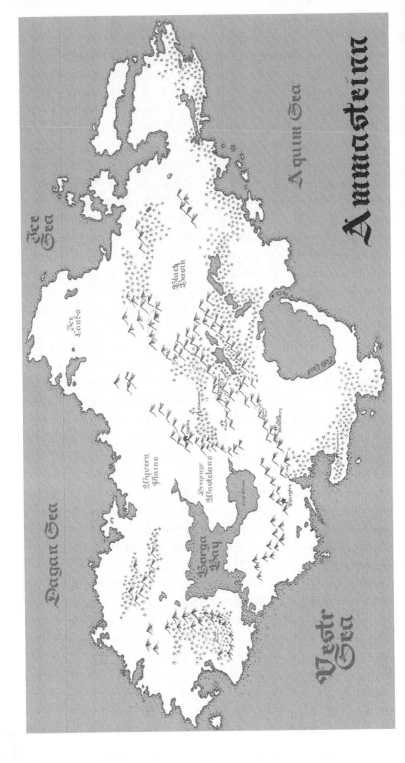

Glossary

Axtī (Elvish):

Frǫðleikr: Magic People
Korro: Stunted
Mātīr: Mother
Mewa: Dirty

Mál (Dwarven):

Agrokū: Goblin Leader
Blanda blóð: Mixed blood
Brojóta burðr: Rape Child
Faðir: Father
Fé: Dwarf money
Goðgá: Blasphemy
Heit: Rare dwarf money
Miðsumar: Midsummer
Ósómi: Disshonoured
Sváss: Beloved

Feoh: Human Money

Astrid didn't say anything.

Knelt on the ground with her eyes half closed, tears streamed down her face. She tried not to sob out loud but couldn't stop herself releasing the repressed pain she felt at seeing her old home after so many years.

Once again she was a small child, helpless and terrified. It had been forty years since that warm day in the middle of the summer; forty years of struggling to kill that frightened child inside of her. Scar after scar, and one reckless adventure after another, to try and make herself tougher and stronger. So many years of tenacity only to become completely unravelled the minute she stepped into the glade.

Before her lay the crumbled remains of an old stone building built around a pine tree. The stairs that circled the trunk were charred and covered with ivy, the roof had collapsed and barely a whole stone wall remained. Even the two small rooms that had been built high up in the tree tops were concealed by the fast growing tendrils that snaked around the entire tree and the ruins surrounding it. Although the plant had destroyed her old home, it also held it together. She lifted her eyes to one of the rafters being held in place by a curtain of green, which hung down like hundreds of small arms from the branch above it and swung side to side in the wind.

Another ten years and it would all be hidden. The ivy would slowly grind its teeth through the stone and beams until nothing remained.

It had been a day much like this; calm and sunny. The sounds of birds and wildlife; Arnbjörg and Sylbil laughing inside the house while she tried to catch a butterfly outside. Sylbil's quiet song-like laugh was so different to Arnbjörg's. His was deep and bear-like; like the rumble of a thunderstorm trapped under a mountain.

Even then, as a child, it would have been impossible for her to not notice the striking differences between her parents.

Sylbil was a good two heads taller than Arnbjörg despite being short for an elf, with poker-straight hair the colour of charcoal and bright forest-green eyes. Arnbjörg's hair was a coppery brown, which at times in the sunlight looked blonde. It was thick hair with tight stubborn curls, which he would often tie back tightly in a thick braid to keep it from falling in front of his face. He often threatened to cut it all off and wear his hair like the humans apparently did, short and manageable. His grey eyes sparkled every time he said this, and Astrid and her mother would laugh, knowing he would never do it. Long hair was important to the dwarves. Short hair was not only a sign of immaturity, but in an adult it was a sign of shame. And Arnbjörg was far from ashamed of his choices.

Being just seven years old at the time, and a half dwarf, Astrid did not have the height of her mother, taking more after her father in terms of stature and physical strength. But her ears were pointed like an elf's, and she had the mannerisms of an elf. Her hair was a raven black like her mother's and fell around her full cheeks in wild and untamed curls. One of her eyes was grey like Arnbjörg's, the other was a bright forest green like Sylbil's. She was a half-blood.

Before she saw them, she had heard the loud thunder of their iron hooves on the ground and the shouts of people approaching. Loud angry voices.

She remembered being frightened of the noise and had accidentally crushed the butterfly's delicate wings in her hands as a loud holler made her jump. Quickly letting it go as she ran towards the house, the butterfly fell to the ground and fluttered its crushed wings pitifully on the dirt.

In the house, she had jumped into her father's strong, dwarf arms. Sylbil had grabbed her bow that hung by the door and hurriedly pulled an arrow to the string before rushing outside. Arnbjörg had reached for his hammer axe and lowered her to the floor, telling her to stay inside. His deep, gravelly voice had tried to sound calm and reassuring but Astrid saw the fear in his eyes. He had squeezed her small, pudgy hands reassuringly before rushing out after his wife, closing the door behind him. The steel latch fastened with a firm click.

It was over; they had been found.

The last eight years had been kind to them; almost perfect. When her parents had left their people they had believed that the Aldwood was far enough away from both the elves and the dwarves to be safe from retribution.

Both the dwarves and the elves were afraid of the forest. Fables in both their kingdoms told of Haltija and Frøðleikr spirits living there - spirits that had once been caring and peaceful but had turned vengeful and angry after an old war, centuries ago. A war too long gone for anyone to remember.

Nobody would look for them. Not here...

Or at least that was what Arnbjörg had told his wife every time he saw the familiar, worried look shroud her face when she had held Astrid and had rocked her by the fireplace in the chair he had made for her, staring vacantly into the red flames.

'We are hidden here!' he would say. 'Don't worry sváss! Both our people have better things to do than to look for us!'

Astrid would look up at her parents, ask them what was wrong, and they would both force a smile and tell her it was nothing, that everything was fine.

Arnbjörg pretended to think his wife was foolish and teased her constantly for it; Sylbil pretended to be annoyed by him, but secretly enjoyed it. As long as he teased her then at least she could pretend that her fear was unfounded.

Pretending was their way of coping with the worry that haunted their every dream.

Had they just been a simple healer and a common guard they would have been left in peace. Shunned, but left to live their lives. But a union between a high ranking dwarf noble from Lǫgberg and the would-be elf queen was not just a rejection of cultural tradition, it was an abomination. A death wish.

Astrid looked up again at the ruins and another sharp stab of emotional pain burst from her chest. Each time she thought the pain couldn't get any worse, another wave hit her, a numbing pain that transformed into a sharp stab, as if a fine needle was being pushed into every single nerve.

Barely six feet in front of her, a forty year old thistle bush grew, its prickly coarse flowers half smothered by a white jasmine that had grown with it. The small, delicate flowers surrounded the tough green and red thistle bush and covered it with white blooms. Both plants had their roots knotted over what had once been her parents' crude graves. Now, barely a small mound remained, her parents' bodies having long since been claimed by nature. The sweet jasmine scent filled the air and images of her mother laughing with the flowers entwined in her hair flashed through Astrid's mind. The flowers of the house of Jīkkā.

Astrid had stayed by the door at first and had heard the horses and ponies thunder into the clearing, their hooves making the ground shake. The animals' braying was almost as loud as their riders' voices as they shouted obscenities at Sylbil and Arnbjörg in Mál and Jaxetī. She may not have known what the words meant, but she understood the hatred behind them.

She had heard shouting;   steel clashing against steel. Strangers screaming. But what scared her enough to make her run outside was the roar of her father's voice as he yelled her mother's name.

'Faðir?' Astrid had whispered, terrified.

Without even thinking, she had rushed up to the table and dragged a chair towards the door. Struggling to move it, she had pushed and pulled with all her might, the heavy chair only moving a few inches with each step she took.

Finally, she had shoved the chair into place and scrambled onto it, slipping at first and scraping her knee on the edge. Ignoring the pain, she frantically reached for the lock and pushed it up. The door swung open a little, and almost falling from the chair, Astrid threw it open and ran outside. But barely a few steps past the doorway she stopped abruptly and stared in horror.

The elves and dwarves, interrupted by her presence, turned to look at her, their faces twisted in anger and disgust.

Sylbil and Arnbjörg had gazed up at her from the ground, their faces pained as they struggled to smile at her. The elves and dwarves encircled them and Sylbil tried to hide her severed hand, the bleeding stump clenched against her chest. Arnbjörg held his wife tightly against him, his strong arms wrapped protectively around her to shield her from further blows.

They hadn't said anything despite wanting to tell her so badly that they loved her, to not be afraid, that everything would be alright. But they couldn't. Astrid saw the words forming in their eyes but they said nothing. She saw them slump to the ground, something impaled between them and glinting in the sunlight.

Screaming their names, Astrid had raced towards them, not caring about the large she-dwarf who stood between her and her parents. She just wanted them to hold her and tell her everything was alright.

Snarling in disgust, the dwarf had kicked her hard enough to knock the wind from her lungs and Astrid fell back. She saw the flash of a blade pass across her face and something hot ran down her lips. A bitter, coppery taste filled her mouth. Reaching up, she'd stared in shock at the bright red blood on her fingers, and holding her mouth she had scrambled away. But the dwarf had laughed and followed her, her sword raised, her grey eyes glinting under her helmet.

Astrid ran her fingertips over her lips and felt the dent in her skin where the blade had cut through. The wound was healed now, just a delicate, faint silver scar remained.

She was a child who had grown up secluded in a forest. She hadn't understood hate, she had never experienced it. But she knew the people walking towards her that night had wanted to kill her. She had screamed for her parents, and screamed louder as she saw the trickle of dark blood staining their clothes between them. Sylbil's eyes had closed first, her father being the last to die. Looking up, his grey eyes had fixed on her, his half elf daughter. Both of them had tried to say so much in that split second, but their eyes had frozen and glazed, the light behind them fading.

'Come back!' Astrid said out loud to the memory re-playing in her mind.

The pain in her chest grew, a hollow burning fire threatening to consume her. She fell to her hands and knees as she remembered the deep, death rattle of her father's voice before the light at the back of his eyes dimmed and vanished. 'Please! Please don't die for me!' she begged to the silence. Falling to the ground, she curled up like the lost little child she was inside.

Their faces blurred in her memory. She could *see* the way she had felt so clearly. The love and safety. The earthy smell of her father's cloak and the scent of the jasmine flower in her mother's hair. But she couldn't see their faces. Like a smudged oil painting, each time she tried to remember clearly even just one of their features, their faces just became more and more hazy. But *their* faces, the faces of the people who had destroyed her life...theirs she remembered perfectly. Every tiny detail was burned into her mind to haunt her. The elf, tall, almost as tall as her mother. His face uncovered like the other elf soldiers he had around him. Pale porcelain skin, pure black hair and cold green eyes staring down at her in disgust.

The she-dwarf, her hair a light blonde and tied into several elaborate braids, which hung down from the opening in her helmet. Grey eyes like her fathers.

Hunched over on the ground, Astrid sobbed, unrestrained. The loneliness and fear of the years she had bottled up rushed from her in an unrelenting deluge.

'Please Faðir! I'm scared! I'm so scared! I don't know what to do!' she cried, reaching for one of the thistles, a jasmine tendril wound around it. She ran her fingers over the plants, trying to imagine they were her parents' blurred faces.

One of the soldiers, an elf, had stopped the she-dwarf walking towards her, had stepped in front of her with his long curved sword raised, ready to strike her first, ready to cut across her neck like he was cutting grass, with not even a flinch of hesitation on his face. To him, Astrid was *Mewa*: dirty, a blight of nature who should be eradicated.

The sword came down...

Like the sound of wind rushing through the trees, a black cloud had risen from the dirt around Astrid. Time seemed to stop, the air stilled, and even the horses silenced for a brief moment. The black dust looked almost like two long, thin hands stretching up around her.

Then with a shrill roar, the cloud had closed around the elf, circling him like a whirlpool at a terrifying speed, and the elf within shrieked in terror. Flecks of blood splattered Astrid's face. The sound changed from a sharp whistle to a screech, like thousands of sharp little blades being scraped over a smooth rocky surface.

She could still hear his terrified, gurgling screams in her mind, see the cloud dissipating, the torn, bleeding pile of pulsating flesh that remained on the ground. Even his armour and swords were torn to pieces. Skin, bone and armour.

The other elves and dwarves had stood in stunned silence, staring at her. A look of rage crossed their faces and a dwarf ran forward in anger only to meet the same fate. Astrid screamed, soaked in their blood, the ground around her flecked with red. The black cloud circling her like a snake would not allow any of them to approach her without ripping them to shreds.

Without a single word, they had suddenly left. The elf spat on the bodies of her parents as he turned to go. After mounting their horses and ponies, they rode off in silence, with the horse of the two who had been killed by the black cloud following them.

For a few moments she had done nothing, fear paralysing her. Then, after several minutes, she had crawled forward with blood trickling down her neck from her split lip. She reached out and laid her hand on her father's face. His body was still warm.

'Faðir? Mātīr!'

Nothing. Crawling closer, she noticed the blood spreading through the fibres of their clothes over their chests. First she shook her father, begging him to wake up. After a few vain attempts , Astrid crawled over to her mother. She grabbed her shoulder and shook her. Sylbil's body slid back a little, exposing the double ended dagger which was impaled between both of them, the blades piercing their hearts. Astrid had stared with wide-eyed horror as her parents' blood settled in the deeply carved runes etched in the handle. A blue glow circled the blade.

'Faðir! Mātīr!' she had screamed again. Her tiny little voice was high pitched and panicked as she shook her mother's head as hard as she could before she finally resorted to hitting her. She prayed with all her might that she would wake up and yell at her for being so rough. Anything, anything but this!

There was nothing. Silence. The air had seemed to be getting colder and Astrid's eyes had darted around in fear as she weaved her fingers through her mother's hair. Grasping it tightly, she'd looked around at the empty glade.

She was alone.

Agrokū

A few months ago...

'Are you sure about this?' Halvard asked quietly under his breath. 'You know Áfastr is just going to try to mock everything you say.'

Jarl nodded. 'I have to! I have to try!'

They had been waiting for over an hour now, the line in front of the gates already long before they had arrived. Dozens more filed up behind them and Jarl leant patiently against the wall, his arms crossed, and stared vacantly at the floor. Halvard, far less patient, paced up and down, grumbling that they should have been let in earlier.

Behind the great stone doors of the hall, Jarl could hear the court guards moving to open them, and he quickly straightened his tunic. He was tempted to leave his tattered cloak with Halvard but decided against it. They should see the cloak, see where the Dip wolves had torn and sliced their claws across it. Maybe in some small way it might influence them to see sense.

With a loud creak, the great stone doors swung open and Jarl's name was called out, echoing down the hall towards the throne of the King. The throne, embellished in gold, stood out against the black granite of the rest of the hall. Torchlight lined the walkway that ran alongside the hall, and it caught in the hundreds of gems that where embedded in the solid gold throne, making it sparkle and glitter.

Jarl felt the eyes of every courtier and noble as he walked forward, but he kept his eyes fixed firmly ahead of him. The hall echoed with whispers and Áfastr Gull's distinctive laugh rang out above the muttering as soon as he saw Jarl.

Clenching his fists together, Jarl approached the throne. Old King Hábrók slumped pitifully in it, an old tired man who looked like he had lost the will to live a long, long time ago. His hair was pure white and his bright blue eyes looked quite terrifying under his thick, bushy white eyebrows. His deformed legs were hidden beneath a red velvet blanket draped over his knees.

Finally reaching the bottom steps of the throne, Jarl bowed, slowly taking a deep breath before he lifted his head to speak.

'King Hábrók, I -'

'Let me guess! The goblins are coming!' Áfastr's voice rang out, interrupting him. Jarl winced at the sound and loud chuckles echoed through the throne room. The King's eyes barely moved as if he had not even heard what had just been said.

'My Lord, when Knute Villieldr was slain in the northern hills, I reported to you what he told me before he died. He told me of a young goblin king, barely in his twentieth year but with the bands of over ten tribes wound into his hair. I do not think it is a coincidence that the attacks around Bjargtre have been increasing.'

'You believe that a young goblin boy has somehow united enough of the northern tribes to become a threat to us?' Áfastr mocked. 'My King! Jarl Vǫrn has never fully recovered from the death of his friend or his family. The last of a once great house desperate to scramble together a small shred of dignity!'

Jarl's face set as hard as stone. He was raging at what Áfastr had said but knew that any violent reaction would weaken his position.

'My concern is that while we pretend to be blind, the goblins, whether they are led by Ulf or not, are growing stronger.'

'I'm utterly terrified!' Áfastr laughed. 'A few more useless and untrained goblins will throw themselves against out walls...the end must be coming!'

'I believe that the goblins have an Agrokū,' Jarl bellowed. There was a sudden hush in the hall; even Áfastr was silenced for a few seconds. The King stirred slightly and looked up at Jarl.

'Why...would you believe that?' he rasped, his old eyes fixed on him.

'The attacks on the traders from Lǫgberg are far too frequent. Soon they won't trade with us at all. Our patrols are being attacked almost daily now, and by goblins in numbers far greater than we have ever seen before. Not goblin swarm, but organized planned attacks! Before long the farms will suffer and we will start to suffer! Knute Villieldr's warning cannot be ignored!'

'The patrols have suffered because of the hard winters. The goblins just took advantage during the storms. Besides, Knute was dying and in pain. If he had said he had seen a griffin dancing with a goat you probably would have believed him!'

'I am not wrong!'

'What...would you... have me do?' the King asked, between violent coughs. A servant dashed up to him and helped him drink from a golden goblet. The King took a long sip, and Jarl watched as some of the water dribbled down the sides of his mouth, his abnormally large jaw making it difficult for him to close his lips against the goblet.

'I would ask that you send word to Queen Vígdís and ask her to send her armies here to help us push back the goblins to Lake Krewa. We do not have the men to push them back. We must ask for help.'

'Ask...Vígdís...for help? Can we not fight our own battles?'

'Today, my Lord, I do not believe we can,' Jarl said firmly. Several people scoffed from the walkway. 'There is no dishonour in asking the High Queen to assist her people.'

'Dishonour...no. It is the Queen's duty to answer to her people. But our pride?'

Jarl paused for a second. He knew how he had to reply but also knew how badly it would be received.

'Our pride will serve for nothing when the city is under siege. It will not feed us or protect us when they break through the Mad Gate.'

To Jarl's surprise, King Hábrók suddenly burst out laughing, his frail body looking like it might snap in half from the movement. Jarl wasn't sure exactly what he was laughing at.

'I'm afraid I do not believe we are in danger!' the King finally said, and Jarl inwardly cursed. 'The city has never been taken, the goblins are far too unorganized and chaotic to possibly allow an Agrokū to rule them, let alone a young goblin as Knute described. No, I think whilst well intentioned, your worries are misplaced. I will not request that Vígdís send us aid.'

There was no point in arguing. The King had made up his mind, and any attempt to disagree with him would be seen as a sign of disrespect. Though he did his best to hide it, Jarl felt his face, along with his heart drop, as Áfastr Gull smirked down at him.

Bowing, Jarl slowly turned and left the throne room, and the guards opened the great stone doors to permit him to leave.

Halvard knew how it had gone as soon as he saw Jarl's face.

'So... I guess we're leaving?' he said, flexing his shoulders as they walked back through the palace grounds, passing the now hundreds of dwarves who were waiting in line outside. Guards at every corner watched them and Jarl was anxious to get back home as soon as possible.

He didn't like the palace, everything about it made him nervous. From the enormous granite pillars which towered above, to the black, polished marble floors, as slippery as ice, that forced everyone to walk slowly or risk falling over. Everything was built in true dwarf fashion of being far too big and grand, and made anyone who entered the city - elf, dwarf, or human - feel utterly insignificant in comparison to their gigantic surroundings.

'We should leave first thing tomorrow. If we take a few ponies we should be able to make it to Einn within a week.'

'Provided we don't get caught and killed,' Halvard muttered.

Jarl laughed. 'Always the optimist!'

'I was being optimistic!' Halvard protested. 'If they capture us it will be far worse than death!'

Jarl breathed a sigh of relief as they left the palace and stepped out into the much smaller and busier tunnels of Bjargtre, where the ground wasn't polished till it shone like glass, and where he was able to walk without slipping.

It took them another half hour to cross the many tunnels of the city and reach the academy. Neither of them said another word as they walked, both deep in thought and worried about the journey they were about to embark on.

Even if they succeeded, it would probably be the last time that Knud and Halvard would see Bjargtre for a good few months. As for Jarl, if he succeeded then he had no doubt that Áfastr would drag what remained of his family name through the mud, having gone against the wishes of his King. At the very least he would become an ósómi and have his hair and beard cut in front of everyone . He'd be a disgrace to Bjargtre.

As they walked through the academy, Jarl gazed up at the statues that lined the halls like stone guards watching over them. Several of his ancestors were within their ranks and he stopped for a moment to stand in front of the statues of his grandfather and grandmother.

Whomever the stonemason had been, his name had been long since forgotten, but his work was without a doubt exemplary. The carvings were so lifelike that in a certain light they almost appeared alive. The pale marble had an almost skin-like quality in the glow of the lamps.

Jarl's grandparents had both been great warriors, honoured guards of their current King back when the house of Vǫrn had been respected. So much had changed since then, and in a way Jarl was glad they were not here to see it. From what little he remembered of them, he knew they had both been fiercely proud, proud of their house and their accomplishments. It would have broken them to see its reputation crumbled and the line reduced to only Jarl. It was better that they were dead.

'I still think you look more like your grandfather,' Halvard muttered. 'The same face. Okay, you're shorter than he was, but you still have the same face.'

'I am not shorter! They make the statues bigger!' Jarl retorted.

Turning away from the statues, they strolled down the hallway and out onto the sidelines of the training arena. Several boys were fighting in pairs with the masters circling them, watching their every move and barking out orders.

Jarl watched proudly as Knud practiced his sword fighting with the other boys. His wild, red hair was tied in a braided top-knot above his head and a few stubborn strands had come loose and stuck out like curly, red grass.

As Knud moved to attack far too quickly, the other much larger boy dodged his blow and tripped him. Halvard chuckled, but Knud instantly picked himself back up and continued to fight, always preferring to attack relentlessly. The other much older boys had quickly picked up on his method and continued to dodge him until Knud wore himself out. Jarl had tried to teach him several times that he needed to be patient and observe his enemy, but the minute he had a weapon in his hands everything Knud had been told vanished from his head.

A loud gong echoed through the tunnels announcing the end of the hearings, and Jarl and Halvard shuffled restlessly. It wouldn't be long until the nobles, Áfastr especially, would make their way to the academy for their next round of amusement. Lately, the hearings had been getting shorter and shorter. Jarl remembered when King Hábrók's father, Hastein, had held hearings that lasted for days on end.

'You'd think they'd learn,' Jarl said, gazing up at the royal box. Several people shuffled about inside as King Hábrók was carried in on his litter, his two sons walking alongside him. Their eyes were as blue as their fathers, but both had abnormally long, heavy jaws which jutted out at a painful angle. 'At least he never had a daughter. I wonder what poor cousin is going to be forced to marry them?'

'One of these days someone is going to hear you!' Halvard said, irritated. 'You shouldn't say things like that out loud.'

'Nobody is around to hear,' Jarl replied calmly. 'Besides, now it's just a matter of time till they make me an Ósómi',

'Maybe they won't,' Halvard suggested, his tone implying he did not believe a word that he was saying. 'If you're right, you will have saved the city.'

'I think you believe that just as much as I do,' Jarl said, raising an eyebrow. Halvard shrugged his shoulders and looked back down at the ring.

Jarl noticed King Hábrók, up in the stands, watching curiously from the box, his old eyes following Knud intently. Jarl looked back at Knud who was panting, his face almost as red as his hair.

'Come on Knud!' Jarl shouted over at him as he fell. Knud flashed him a smile and instantly threw himself at his opponent again. The boy stepped aside and tripped him but Knud was instantly on his feet and lunged again, only to fall a short moment later. Jarl growled frustratedly but said nothing. He had told him enough times to be patient. Knud would just have to keep falling until he learned the hard way.

Finally, Knud fell for the last time, barely having the energy to lift his sword. When his opponent knocked the weapon from his hand, Knud was forced to surrender, with a blunt sword tip pressed against the side of his neck.

With his head hung low, Knud trudged from the ring, the sand from the training ground covering his knees, boots and sleeves. He climbed the stairs to where Jarl and Halvard were waiting for him with the spectators politely clapping at his performance.

'I lost,' Knud mumbled, kicking at the floor.

It wasn't about the fight, Jarl knew that. Today was a bad day. Even if he had won the fight, he would still be downcast.

'You miss him too, right?' Knud asked suddenly, and Jarl's mouth pressed into a tight line.

'Every day,' he whispered.

'Good! I don't want anyone to forget him!' Knud said, looking over at Jarl's cloak, the Dip tears in it clearly visible, and Jarl's crude stitching making them all the more noticeable.

For all his good intentions, Jarl was no tailor. His sewing, especially whilst studying, was aesthetically of a very poor standard. Not that it really mattered. As a fallen house, the only people who cared what he looked like were the Gulls. Even then, he could be dressed from head to toe in gold and jewels and they would still find a way to mock him.

After walking for over half an hour through the many grand tunnels, they finally reached the Vǫrn halls. Knud's cheerful face had returned and they raced up the tall stone staircase and pushed open the sturdy doors that led to the hall.

The halls were unpretentious compared to the other houses, especially the Gull's, whose love of ostentatious gold filigree on pretty much every surface was renowned. The Vǫrn halls were simple: great grey stone pillars that were hewn with knotted patterns, an axe and a long thin dagger, the emblem of the house of Vǫrn, carved into the top of each one.

'What's this?' Jarl asked, taking a seat opposite Knud at the long pine table that ran down the centre of the hall, and staring at one of the many contraptions Knud had been making. Kindling was splayed out across the table, and string, wire and wood shavings were everywhere. Knud tied another thin twig to the frame, his tongue protruding from his lips in concentration.

'Not sure yet, Uncle,' Knud replied, looking at it intently. 'I was thinking of trying to make a weapon so we could shoot goblins before they come near. But I can't get it right,' he said frustratedly, pushing the contraption aside and scribbling wildly over the sketches he had drawn.

Goblins...of course he would make something like that today!

Jarl patted Knud reassuringly on the shoulder and headed to his chambers. Once there, he hung his cloak on the peg on the wall and closed the door to his room behind him. Three bags were propped next to his bed. He sighed. They were packed and ready to go. All they had to do now was tell Knud.

There was a gentle tap on the door and Halvard walked in, took his packed bag from the line and slung it over his shoulders.

'I assume we're leaving now?'

'Just a few more hours. Let Knud play with his drawings a little longer.'

'Have you told him the plan?' Halvard asked, raising an eyebrow so high it almost disappeared into his hairline.

'No. I don't think I want to tell him till we reach Lǫgberg.'

'*If* we reach Lǫgberg!' Halvard laughed, and Jarl grinned, shaking his head at him. He could always rely on Halvard to give a cynical reply to almost anything he said.

'I'm just hoping the journey will toughen him up a little. Make him a little tired of me and wanting some space of his own.'

'I doubt that! The boy idolised you long before Knute died. A few months on the road isn't likely to change that!'

Rolling his eyes and slinging his bag onto his back, Jarl strode out of the room.

As much as Jarl enjoyed Halvard's company, having known him almost as long as Knute, at times his constant pessimism really wore him down, especially on topics that worried Jarl, when he just needed someone to listen and let him reach his own conclusions.

Knute had never been like that. He'd been his best friend and was fiercely optimistic. He was also a determined prankster and Knud was so like him at times that Jarl found himself doing a double take, thinking for the tiniest of moments that his old childhood friend was standing in front of him.

Hiding his bag in the hall so Knud wouldn't see it, Jarl made his way to the servants' quarters and knocked on the door. Four voices called out from inside for him to enter and he walked in to the smell of food wafting through the air. There was chicken, meat and more meat. A few token vegetables were strewn across the stone sideboards and several pots bubbled over the fireplace. The oldest of the women, Holmvé, whose hair had long since lost its colour, cooed loudly at him.

'Jarl! Have you finally come to acknowledge my wisdom and beauty and take me as your wife?'

Jarl grinned at her fondly. Eilíf, Gísla and Hlín laughed out loud.

He had known Holmvé since he was a child; in fact he was pretty sure she had been the midwife who had helped his mother deliver him before she was appointed stewardess of the household. She had always been a grandmother figure to him and only became more so after the death of his family.

He had known all of them since he was a young boy, and even then they had been old. The teasing had originally been initiated by his mother as a plan to bolster his confidence as a young dwarf.

He had been a quiet boy, his grandfather mistaking his stoic silence for weakness. Vidar had constantly tried to put him in the company of other young female dwarves but Jarl had been completely at a loss as to how to behave around them. Although he would not admit it, he was slightly terrified of them. Holmvé, Eilíf, Gísla and Hlín joked with him afterwards to make him feel better and pretended to be young silly girls themselves in an attempt to make him more used to the irritating giggling and shameless flirting he would have to endure.

Over the years the habit had stuck, the tradition making Jarl smile still, and remaining an enjoyable hobby for them. Each of them always tried to outdo the other in their ridiculous impersonations of silly young girls in awe of him.

Not that it wasn't warranted; far from it. Jarl was an extremely attractive dwarf with long, dark brown hair that looked almost black, and with pale blue eyes, which at times looked slightly green, especially in the firelight.

'Oh, I do think I might pass out!' Holmvé laughed, pretending to be flustered and fanning herself. 'Jarl, will you catch me if I faint?' she cackled.

'He'll catch you no doubt, but you might just break him, you old hag!' Eilíf chuckled.

'What are you on about you crazy old woman? Look at those healthy strong arms! Why, I think he could easily carry all of us if he was so inclined!'

'Well if he is, I won't say no!' Gísla giggled.

'Ok stop! The lad probably has something to say,' Holmvé shouted over them. 'He might be here to finally pick one of us, so be quiet, and if he picks me I'll bite the first one of you who protests our love!'

Laughing, Jarl cleared his throat, his face quickly turning serious.

'I'm here to say I have to leave, Holmvé. With Knud and Halvard.'

The women glared at him. 'What? Why?' they asked in unison.

'I want to take Knud to Lǫgberg. I'm worried about all the goblin swarms, and no Holmvé, I'm not just saying that because of Knute. You've all noticed it, I have heard you talking about it and I know I'm not the only one worried.'

'Will you be coming back?'

'Of course I will! I'm hoping to convince Queen Vígdís to send her armies to help us.'

'And if she won't?'

'Then Halvard will stay with Knud in Lǫgberg and I'll come back for all of you.'

For a few moments none of them uttered a word.

'I'll be leaving you in change, Holmvé,' Jarl said. She walked to him and held his heavy bearded face in her wrinkled hands, smiling at him worriedly.

'You take care. I'm not having the last Vǫrn die before me.'

'I'll do my best,' Jarl smiled. He leaned down to kiss her on the forehead, then turned and left the kitchen, closing the door behind him.

'See?' Holmvé chuckled, trying to lighten the mood. 'He picked me! My charm is just too much to resist!'

Picking Up The Pieces

40 years ago...

Dag smiled as he strolled through the forest, the thin rays of sunlight making their way through the canopy above and warming his face. It was one of those glorious days of late spring, right before the heat of summer, when the weather was just perfect. A pleasant breeze swept down from the Riddari, cooling the air that was warm enough to warrant not wearing a cloak. Despite being so high up in the mountains, the Aldwood valley could get surprisingly hot in the summer, so hot that Dag had sometimes returned to find forest fires had scoured large parts of it. The trees would always grow back though, and he had never known the fires to reach the southern side of the Aldwood.

Dag sighed contentedly at feeling the sun on his skin and his bones slowly warming. He leant his head back and eased out the knots in his neck, feeling less stiff than he had during his trek across the freezing

Riddari. The thick fur coats he had worn only that morning were draped over the pony's back.

Behind him, the pony snorted loudly, butting its head against his arm. Dag laughed and pulled an apple from his bag, which he had been saving for the last stretch of the journey. The dappled pony happily munched on the apple whilst they walked. Looking almost as old and tired as he did, with its white, grey and black spots faded and coarse, it slowly plodded along behind him and ignored Dag as he pulled gently at the reins, urging it to move faster.

After the grueling week it had taken to cross the Riddari, the pony was in no mood to obey its warlock master, and stubbornly stood still when they stepped into a small clearing. Dag frowned at it.

'Come on Felix! It's not far now! You can rest when we get there!'

Almost like it could understand what he'd said, the pony shook its head and snorted loudly, bent its knees and slumped down heavily on the grass. It peered up at Dag as if it was daring him to try and make it move.

'Fine then! I'll walk ahead and you can just follow me later,' Dag snapped, letting go of the reins and storming ahead. The weather was too lovely to be annoyed with his pony for long, and he quickly calmed, enjoying the sunshine.

Ahead of him, he could see the old pine trees which led to the glade, their trunks and some of the canopy covered in jasmine flowers. When he had first led Sylbil and Arnbjörg through this place, they had decided to stay as soon as Sylbil had seen the beautiful flowers on the pines. She had wept quietly, and Arnbjörg had comforted her, reminding her once again how much they had given up to be together. The jasmine was the symbol of Sylbil's family house, the house of Jīkkā. A house she was now a pariah to.

Strolling past the trees, Dag plucked a few of the vines and began twisting them into a garland , being careful not to crush the delicate flowers as he wound the tendrils around in a circle, in and over each other. He had made a garland for Sylbil and Arnbjörg's wedding day, and since then, each time he had come to visit them in the Aldwood, it had become a tradition to make one for her.

Reaching into his bag, Dag winced as his hand brushed across the red thistle plant he had carefully packed inside. Its roots were tightly bound with several strips of sackcloth he had used to keep the earth in place, the cloth moist from when he had submerged the plant in a river for a few moments earlier that morning.

There were no red thistles this side of the Riddari Mountains, in fact there were no thistles at all in the valley. With so many jasmine around, Dag thought Arnbjörg might appreciate having a reminder of his old home and family crest.

Chuckling, Dag laid the jasmine garland carefully over the thistle plant. It was quite amusing how much the two plants reminded him of Sylbil and Arnbjörg's personalities. Both so completely different, but somehow so perfect together. A coarse prickly plant, which many people overlooked as weed, and a seemingly delicate but fiercely tough, white flower.

Next to the plant, and in a small pouch sewn into the side of his bag, were two small rings, expertly made to fit together like a jigsaw, but which could be separated to be worn separately.

When he had married them, they had been in the middle of a storm, the rain hammering down on the cave above them and thunder making the whole mountain shake. They'd had no gifts or rings to exchange, nothing but each other to offer. Dag was determined that that not always be the case.

It was then that he heard the animals; at first just a few yelps, like pups play fighting over the tidbits of food their parents had brought home. Then he heard the snarling - loud angry snarls - and a small voice shouting; panicked. Another loud yelp echoed through the trees.

Dag's heart raced as he quickened his step, the hairs on the back of his neck starting to rise. He had no idea what was happening, no idea what to expect, but a sixth sense picked up on it before he could see it for himself and warned him something was very seriously wrong.

Pushing his way through the bushes, not caring how they whipped across his face and arms, Dag stumbled into the clearing, tripped over a root and fell awkwardly to the ground. The wild dogs turned to look at him and a few padded towards him before sensing that despite his elderly appearance, this old man was not to be meddled with. The air around him tingled with magic.

Glancing up, Dag felt his heart drop into his stomach and time seemed to stop. He stared in horror at the scene before him.

Sylbil and Arnbjörg were lying on the ground a few feet from their house with blood staining the grass around them. The flies had already started to move in, circling their bodies like hundreds of little back clouds. The door to their house swung to and fro in the breeze.

Standing beside them, Astrid was holding the end of her mother's long black hair in her hand as if it was a leash. With an arrow in her other hand, she was stabbing at the air to fend off the wild dogs, which were almost as tall as her. Screaming and shouting at them, with dried blood all over her hands and shirt, and the end of her arrow glistening with fresh blood, she looked wild; terrified. One of the dogs was limping, a deep wound prominent above its front left leg, and whimpering in pain. Two dead dogs lay on the ground near Astrid, their faces shrivelled and twisted as if the fat from their flesh had been sucked away at an incredible speed.

Astrid didn't even notice as Dag stood up, her eyes completely focused on the dogs. She turned swiftly to hit at the cloud of files that swarmed around her parents' bodies, before turning back and whacking one of the dogs as hard as she could across its face, cutting its nose and puncturing its eye, as it tried to move towards Sylbil's feet.

Sensing their window of opportunity was closing, two of the four remaining dogs closed in and leapt towards the bodies, their teeth bared.

Dag stared in horror as Astrid dropped the arrow and lunged at the nearest animal. She grabbed its face with her bare hands and screamed as she pulled the life from it. The other dogs yelped in fear and scuttled away. The air prickled with static as Astrid's hands glowed red. The dog shrieked in pain and clawed at her wrists but Astrid refused to let go. The animal went limp, its face shrivelling like a prune, the skin cracking in several places. Astrid kicked its body away, screaming at the other dogs to stay away, and picked up the arrow again, not even noticing that her hands were bleeding. The wild dog had clawed her skin off and blood oozed down her arms.

Dag quickly conjured a small burst of blue flame and hurled it at the dogs, who rapidly scattered, yelping in fear. He edged towards Astrid, praying she would remember him from when he had visited the previous spring.

'Astrid! Astrid it's Mossi! Do you remember me?' Dag asked, his hands raised and his palms extended as he knelt on the ground.

Astrid glared at him, her eyes wild and frantic, appearing far more animal that human. She was filthy, her hair matted with dirt and blood, and her eyes and cheeks sunken.

Shuffling a little closer, Dag reached out for her, but stepped back as Astrid lifted the arrow and pointed it at him, snarling and moving her other hand over Arnbjörg's face protectively. She winced as she felt the cold skin under her fingers and lowered her head to look into her father's stone grey eyes, which stared blankly ahead at his dead wife.

'Astrid! Astrid please! It's Mossi! Remember me? I made the flame flowers!'

Her face was blank, emotionless, and taking a deep breath, Dag turned his right palm up and raised it in the air. A small swirl of light circled under the skin of his hand and slowly formed above it, twisting and curling in the air until it took on the shape of a thistle and jasmine. Astrid's eyes slowly focused, her breathing quickly turning into an hysterical rasp, then she crawled forward, tentatively at first, before suddenly throwing herself into Dag's arms, screaming like a wild animal.

'Shhh! It's ok, goldheart! It's ok!' Dag whispered, gently stroking her hair, his fingers getting caught in the hundreds of knots which riddled it. Even with just one arm around her, Dag could feel how much weight she had lost. Her bones jutted out from under her skin and her twig-like arms held barely a thin layer of fat. For a young girl who was growing, the lack of meat on her bones was worrying. Judging by how she looked and the state of her parents' bodies, it had barely been two days since they had died, but not enough time for her to shrink so drastically.

Dag held her close and looked down at Sylbil and Arnbjörg, noticing for the first time the dagger impaled between them. Tears filled his eyes and he quickly rubbed them away.

'Astrid! Goldheart, tell me what happened,' Dag asked. Astrid shook violently and she slipped to the ground, her legs finally giving way from exhaustion.

'They killed them! An elf, he had green eyes like Mātīr. And the dwarf, she had grey eyes like Faðir! I don't know why! Did...did I do something wrong? Why are they dead? Why...Mossi, why did they kill them?'

Astrid, panicking, tried to pull away from Dag and swept her arms around Arnbjörg, disturbing the flies that settled all over him. She clung to her father's body, refusing to let go. Dag tugged at her gently, coaxing her back into his arms, but Astrid held on even tighter as the flies began to resettle around him.

Behind them, Dag's pony appeared in the clearing and Astrid, hearing the sound of its hooves, looked up, the last spot of colour draining from her face. Utterly terrified, she screamed as loudly as she could.

Dag ran to the pony, led it out of the clearing and tied its bridle safely around a tree. He muttered a few words under his breath and waited until a small protective circle of blue flames encircled it. The wild dogs watched from a safe distance but quickly scattered when Dag tossed another ball of flames at them. Satisfied that Felix was safe, he raced back to Astrid.

She was crouched on the ground with a glowing hand on Arnbjörg's limp body. Her heart thundered in her chest, strained and exhausted, as she tried to transfer the energy she had absorbed from the dead wild dogs to her father. The skin she touched glowed with life but quickly returned to its dead, grey colour the minute she removed her hand.

The tears slid down her cheeks as again, she lowered her hand to his chest.

'No Astrid! You can't!' Dag said, grabbing her arm to stop her. 'There is nothing you can do!'

'Please! Please I've done it before! I've healed animals before! Just let me heal them!'

'You can't, goldheart! You can only heal the living. They're...they're not here anymore!'

'But I can! Just...just let me try!'

'ASTRID!' Dag shouted, grabbing her firmly and shaking her as she tried to push past him and touch her father's skin again. 'You can't! They're gone, there is *nothing* you can do!'

Shrieking, Astrid tried to fight him. She kicked and scratched and pulled at his long beard in an attempt to get away. Dag held her hands tightly and refused to let her go, now realising why she looked so sickly thin. It was lucky he had arrived when he had. Another few hours of trying to revive dead bodies and she would have drained the last bit of energy from her own.

How she had learned to absorb the energy from the wild dogs, killing them, Dag did not know. Sylbil was a healer, he doubted even she knew how to absorb energy, despite her three centuries of knowledge, and even if she had, it was not something she would have taught her young daughter. Jakkito powers were not something to be taken lightly. Without proper training it was very easy give too much energy and either severely damage or even kill oneself. In fact, Sylbil would not have begun teaching Astrid magic at all, was it not for her natural ability.

Dag had been there the previous spring when Sylbil had accidently crushed a small mouse in the door as she closed it behind her. The tiny animal had made a run for the gap but had narrowly missed. With its ribs and organs crushed, and squeaking helplessly on the floor, Astrid had raced to it and scooped it into her hands. Dag had been sitting at the table carving something, what he couldn't remember, but both he and Sylbil had stared in shock, Sylbil's expression being closer to horror, as Astrid's hands had started to glow a pale blue before turning completely ashen. She had lost consciousness for a brief second and fell to her knees as the newly healed mouse leapt from her hands and scuttled under the stairs to safely. Arnbjörg had heard Sylbil shouting and had dashed from the tree room above in a panic. At the bottom of the stairs he saw Sylbil cradling Astrid in her arms, saw her run her hands over Astrid's face to revive her.

After that, Sylbil had had no choice but to show Astrid how to use her Jakkito gifts. It was rare for such a young child to be gifted so early; Sylbil had only realised her own gift in her ninetieth year. It had terrified them all.

Fortunately, Astrid's powers were weak and undeveloped and she did not yet know enough to put her full strength into attempting to heal her dead parents.

Picking her up, Dag led her away from them and held her tightly until she stopped struggling. Her breathing was heavy and pained and the little energy that remained in her frail body was barely enough for her to fight him.

'Please Mossi! Please! I can help them!'

'You did, goldheart. You did. Now let *me* help them.'

Astrid nodded reluctantly and dropped to the floor, her hand pressed over her heart and head in pain. She was physically and mentally drained.

Dag walked over to Sylbil and Arnbjörg. He bent to close their eyes and muttered several words under his breath. The ground beneath them rumbled and moved and he watched as their bodies slowly sank into the ground. A mound of earth built up over and around them and Dag's hand glowed brighter. Tears streamed down his face. Astrid watched, her eyes glazed and distant, her shoulders slumped as she finally resigned herself to the terrible truth.

Pausing for a moment, Dag lowered himself to the ground, rubbing the tears from his face. Between them, he could see the hilt of the dagger glinting, but congealed in blood. He glanced to his left and saw a pile of rotting flesh a few feet away from him. The wild dogs had devoured most of it and the flies covered the splashes of blood that covered the ground. Small pieces of blood-soaked armour were strewn around. Elf armour.

'Looks like you were right, Sylbil,' Dag muttered under his breath, his eyes red and swollen from the tears. 'Don't worry. I'll take care of her. I promise.'

In that moment, Dag could have sworn he heard a low sigh behind him. He turned and saw a small cloud settle back into the ground as the wind picked up slightly through the trees.

He considered moving the bodies so that they were lying side by side and not how they had fallen. But he couldn't bring himself to do it.

Curled up against Arnbjörg, Sylbil's arms were clenched to her chest, her good hand cradling the stump that remained of her other one. Dag had a horrible feeling that one of the wild dogs had probably taken the severed limb but he scanned the area around him in hope, seeing nothing but a large splatter of blood and some unrecognisable flesh on the ground next to him. He looked back at Arnbjörg holding Sylbil protectively in his arms, his large calloused fingers brushing the side of her face so gently. It almost felt disrespectful to move them. They had had such a short amount of time to be together, had fought so hard to live in peace. The very least he could do was to leave them together in death. The sight of the old, thin, red scar around Sylbil's neck that peeked out from under her collar made the tears in his eyes well up even more.

Dag reached into his bag and placed the jasmine garland he had made between them, before moving the piles of earth over their bodies. The mud swirled down into the hole like it was water, twisting and twirling until it finally covered them.

'Faðir? Mātīr!' Astrid whispered behind him, repeating the words over and again as if in prayer.

Dag pulled the thistle plant from his bag and carefully unwrapped the cloth strips surrounding the

45

roots. He dug a hole with his hands in the dirt and placed the thistle roots inside it, firmly pressing the soil tightly around it.

Standing up, he raised his hands and closed his eyes. The rocks in the ground around him pushed their way up through the earth like moles, slithering towards the mound and piling up around it; sliding around the newly planted thistle and securing it in its new home. Each stone carefully slotted against the one beside it forming a beautiful, knotted pattern. The final stone rolled up the stony mound and fell into the last open space with a loud chink. Dag lowered his hand and returned to Astrid.

'It's ok, goldheart,' he said, picking her up in his arms. 'You're coming home with me.'

Walking into the hut, Dag looked around. He knew they couldn't stay there; it would be haunted forever now to Astrid, but the thought of pulling her away from the only home she had known was almost as bad as the realisation that Sylbil and Arnbjörg were dead.

He had been there when the first foundations were laid. He had helped them erect the solid stone walls and had returned the following spring to help them build the rooms in the trees' branches. Behind every stone, rafter and plank, there was a story, but now he had to leave it to let nature tear it down.

Dag lowered Astrid to a chair and told her to wait for him as he climbed the stairs.

In the far corner of the room next to Sylbil's and Arnbjörg's bed was a low table holding several wood carvings. Various sharp knives and carving tools littered it, and in the centre was a small, carved house, an almost perfect replica of their home. Alongside it was what must have been the last of the figurines Sylbil had been working on before their murderers arrived, Dag thought. Arnbjörg's distinctive long hair and beard was carved into the pine wood, and its hollowed out eyes stared up at him. Only Arnbjörg's feet remained uncarved. The figurine's body appeared to have grown at random from the small pine block, although the whittling knife beside it told otherwise.

Dag stepped away and headed to Astrid's room, a tiny room decorated with an abundance of things that had been unearthed in the forest. Several old birds' nests lined the rafters and a wind catcher hung over her bed with hundreds of feathers attached to it. Magpie, crow, pheasant and woodpecker feathers, and even some of the more exotically coloured eggshells, which Arnbjörg must have recovered from the forest floor when he went hunting for food, had made their way into it.

The upper walls of the second floor were all constructed of wood and Astrid had carved her name in Mál and Jaxetī in the boards several times, no doubt the previous summer when Sylbil and Arnbjörg had decided

47

it was time to teach their daughter to write in their native languages. Dag knew that Astrid struggled with Mál in particular, the elven language. Jaxetī had come a lot more naturally to her.

Dag made a mental note to keep on teaching Astrid; it would have been what her parents had wanted. She was a child of both worlds; it was only right that she continued to be taught about her rich, mixed heritage.

Dag grabbed the quilted blanket from her bed and opened all of the hand-made drawers in Astrid's room, carefully moving her clothes and belongings into the centre of the blanket. Felix would only be able to carry so much, the old creature was worn and tired, but Dag was determined to take everything he could.

The following months would be hard on her, having to readjust to her new life, and the least he could do was take as much of her old life with him as possible.

'Can we stay?' Astrid's voice whispered from the doorway. Dag turned around and saw her staring up at him with one of Sylbil's arrows held loosely in her hand.

'We need to leave, goldheart,' Dag replied, kneeling down in front of her and resting his hands on her shoulders. 'Those people might come back. We need to leave.'

'I could fight them,' Astrid whispered, tears filling her eyes. 'You can help me fight them!'

'I can't, goldheart! I can't protect you here,' Dag said.

'Please Mossi! Please!'

He shook his head. 'It's not safe. Take anything you want, but we have to go.'

Astrid turned and padded back into her parents' room, climbed onto the bed and buried her head under the blanket. The familiar smell made her feel safe and warm for just a few moments. Pulling it around her like a cloak, Astrid walked back to Dag who had collected the last of her things. He took her hand and slung the rough sack made from her blanket over his shoulder and headed downstairs.

'Is there anything else you want?' Dag asked her as they ambled outside.

Astrid glanced around her and then walked over to the grave. She picked up Arnbjörg's hammer axe and Sylbil's bow and quiver.

'I want these,' she said firmly, trying to lift the heavy axe but failing. Dag picked it up for her.

'Ok, goldheart. We can take those.'

After loading up Astrid's belongings onto the pony, Dag cupped his hands under her arms to lift her onto Felix's back, but she quickly stepped away, her face terrified.

'I don't want to ride!'

'Astrid you must! You can't walk. Just ride Felix for a while. He's nice!'

49

'No!' Astrid yelled back, staring at the pony, horrified. Felix mashed his hooves into the ground, sensing Astrid's magic, her anger making him agitated.

Again, Dag tried to pick Astrid up and settle her onto Felix's back, but she screamed and tore herself away from him, her hand pushing against the pony's neck, her palms glowing. Felix shrieked out in terror as a burning brand-like pain shot across its back. The skin Astrid had touched curled in on itself, as if it had been burnt.

'Astrid!' Dag shouted in shock, dropping her to the ground. Felix bolted and Astrid crawled away from them, frightened, yelling again and again that she would not ride the pony. Her hand glowed and she wrapped her parents' blanket closer around her.

'Ok! Ok!' Dag conceded, coaxing her closer. He took her hand and held Felix's bridle in the other. 'You don't need to ride him, you can just walk.'

As they headed through the trees, Astrid turned several times to look back at the house and watched as it slowly disappeared from sight. Grasping Dag's hand tighter the further they walked away, her breathing quickened, and although she tried to calm herself, she felt nothing but panic.

Everything was gone.

Leaving

'Knud! Knud! Wake up!'

Knud rubbed at his eyes, the warm blankets feeling so much more comfortable in the fogginess of his awakening.

'What's wrong?' he mumbled, slightly alarmed at the sight of his uncle's attire. His bleary eyes swept over the hundreds of small metal plates held together by leather binding, the light armour that allowed Jarl to move more easily than the full, heavy steel armour which was worn in battle.

'Nothing's wrong,' Jarl said quickly. 'We're leaving Bjargtre.'

'Why? Where are we going?'

'Lǫgberg.'

'Lǫgberg!' Knud exclaimed, his whole face lighting up. 'Why are we going there?'

'I have friends I want to see there,' Jarl lied, 'but we're leaving now. I've already packed everything we need, you just need to get dressed.'

Jarl left the room, and even before he'd closed the door behind him, Knud leapt from his bed and changed into the clothes Jarl had left for him, not even noticing that his old coat had been replaced with a newer one with rabbit fur lining. Pulling on his boots and nearly toppling over in his excitement, he headed into the hallway.

In the great hall, Jarl ran his hands along the wall, praying that this would not be the last time he spent in his family home. Holmvé and Halvard were waiting for him, Holmvé slouched at the table and doing her best not to cry.

'You'd better send for us soon, you hear?' she sniffed, getting to her feet and striding up to him. Her old brown eyes glared at his. 'If you don't, I'll have some serious words to say.'

Jarl reached into his pocket and passed her a sealed scroll. His face was serious as he pressed it into her hand.

'Don't open it till we're gone,' he said, and Holmvé nodded and tucked it into the large pocket at the front of her apron.

'I made some food for you, I packed it in your bag. Knud would eat it all if I'd put it in his!' Holmvé laughed and brushed a tear from her cheek.

Jarl kissed her on the forehead, smiling at her, and she held him tightly like she had when he had been just a young dwarf.

'Maybe you'll find someone in Lǫgberg?' She smiled and Jarl rolled his eyes at her, shaking his head. 'And if you do she'd better be better than that vain cow Yrsa! I'll never know what on earth your father was thinking. She was never suited to you!'

'Who would you pick then?' Jarl asked, grinning, the disgust on her face amusing him.

'I would pick someone brave and smart. You're not the brightest star in the heavens, so she would have to make up for that,' Holmvé replied. Halvard chuckled behind her. 'And kind, she would have to be kind, just like you.'

'She won't have to be beautiful then?' Halvard said, and Holmvé turned and flashed him a withering look.

'Take it from the old; all faces lose their beauty with age,' Holmvé replied.

Knud strolled into the kitchen and picked up his bag. Smelling the cakes Holmvé had packed at the top of Jarl's bag, he opened it inquisitively.

'Stay away from those!' Holmvé barked, and smacked him playfully across the head. She turned to Jarl. 'You'd better go now,' she sniffed, rubbing at her old eyes and pushing Jarl towards the large, oak door, 'before I decide to make you stay.'

Halvard and Knud walked through first and Jarl turned to Holmvé, taking her hand in his and holding it firmly.

'I'll send for you as soon as I get there,' he said, smiling at her reassuringly. But his eyes looked just as worried as hers.

'I know you will lad, now go on! And find yourself a wife if you can! Soon you'll be as old as me!'

Jarl turned and walked with the others down the stone street, the lamps that lined the walls glowing red.

Holmvé closed the door and took a deep breath, then rubbed at her eyes once more before reaching into her apron pocket. She carefully opened the scroll Jarl had given her and took a few moments to read it. At first confusion washed over her face before shock replaced it. She ran to the door and opened it, desperate to run after Jarl, but the road was empty. They had gone.

Holmvé sat down on the ground, dazed. She read through the scroll one last time with tears streaming down her face.

* * *

Knud was exited, trotting alongside Jarl on his pony and driving him slightly mad. Every several minutes Jarl had to shout at him to not canter so far ahead, even though he knew the goblins would not be a problem until night

54

fall. They had grown daring but not yet so daring as to attack in broad daylight.

They hadn't taken the old road, but one of the many winding paths over the hills and mountains, some of which had been unused for such a long time that they were barely more than dirt trails for animals. Tall pines surrounded them for miles and fallen pines constantly blocked their way.

'He's going to wear himself and that pony down if he carries on like that,' Halvard muttered. Jarl grinned and nodded his head.

'Let him! Let him enjoy himself while he still can.'

'You mean before he realises how dangerous this is?'

Hearing them talking, Knud turned his pony around. 'Are you talking about me?'

'Course not,' Jarl lied, his face expressionless.

'How long will we be staying in Løgberg?' Knud asked, still jumping up and down on the pony's back.

Jarl's patience finally snapped. 'I'm not sure. A few months or so. And can you please stop doing that and ride properly?'

'What are you going to do there? Are you going to become a guard? Or maybe the Queens guard!'

'I don't know!' Jarl laughed. Knud's optimistic enthusiasm was endearing and Jarl secretly prayed he would not have to leave Knud in Halvard's charge, knowing the dwarf's constant pessimism would eventually affect him. He already had so much to be sad about and the last thing Jarl wanted to be taken from Knud was his positive, though admittedly naive outlook on life.

'And what about me? What will I do?'

'You could train with the other nobles. They have better teachers in Lǫgberg; you would become a great warrior.'

'But I can become a great warrior now! I mean, we'll be traveling through the wild for months! There will be Frǫðleikr and goblins! I'll be a great warrior by the time I get to Lǫgberg!'

Laughing, Jarl shook his head, trotted alongside Knud and ruffled his hair. 'Ride to the ridge up ahead and look out for goblins.'

'When are you going to tell him?' Halvard whispered when Knud was out of earshot. Jarl's smile disappeared and he pressed his mouth into a hard line.

'I'll tell him when he's ready, or when I have to.'

'He's got a lot of growing up to do.'

'He's done a lot of growing up as it is,' Jarl snapped back, irritated by Halvard's constant attempt to strip Knud of his childhood. 'Let him enjoy his youth while he still can.'

* * *

Knud was tired, sore, grumpy, and hurting in places he didn't know could hurt. After three days of riding during the day and sleeping with one eye open during the night, any romantic notions he had had of travelling through the wild were well and truly buried. He rode silently alongside Jarl, with Halvard scouting ahead of them.

'Tired?' Jarl asked grinning, amused at seeing him so quiet.

'Yes. When will we get there?'

'It'll be another three days. Only a few more hours on the road and we can take some of the human river boats to Einn. They'll be safer than the road. We can trade the ponies for passage.'

'Humans? I get to see humans!' Knud exclaimed, a little of his enthusiasm returning.

'Yes. But you will stay near me, understand? And I'll do the talking, not you! If you see any other dwarves, do not talk to them. And you mustn't tell them your name.'

'Why?' Knud asked, confused.

'If you outrank them, they could try and use it to shame you in public. Especially if someone like Áfastr Gull was to find out.'

'Why do the Gull's hate us so much?'

'I don't know,' Jarl said. 'I think it has something to do with my father, I never got to ask him before he died.'

'And why is it bad to trade with the humans?' Knud asked, barely waiting for Jarl to have answered his first question.

'It's not bad. In fact I think it's stupid that we don't trade with people closer to our borders. Lǫgberg is too far away; it would make a lot more sense to trade with Einn.'

'Don't tell him that!' Halvard snapped, riding up next to them. 'Knud, the reason we only trade with dwarves is because you can only trust your own people. The humans, they're different. Different ways, different customs. When you're not the same it causes problems. It's safer to trade with dwarves.'

'But what about the elves? Why don't we trade with them?'

'Don't ask stupid questions!' Halvard snapped. Jarl shook his head, praying that if he did have to leave Knud with Halvard it wouldn't be for long.

'It wasn't a stupid question, Knud,' Jarl said quietly under his breath. 'We haven't traded with them since the Rojóða wars.'

'That was a long time ago, wasn't it?'

'At least three thousand years. Nobody knows exactly how long ago it was.'

Jarl stiffened his back and pulled on the reins, bringing his pony to a halt. 'Hold up, Halvard,' he said, reaching into his bag for his flask. He popped the cork from the top and raised it to his lips.

'Do you think you'll ever get married?' Knud suddenly asked and Jarl, nearly choking on his water, spluttered loudly.

'Do you think you'll find a lady to marry in Lǫgberg?' he went on, grinning like an imp.

'A lady? Haha! No, Jarl will end up marrying a servant or a shield maiden! He's far too simple for a lady!' Halvard laughed but quickly wiped the smile from his face when he saw the dark look flash across Jarl's eyes. There were a few things that Jarl would not tolerate being teased about and this was one of them. He turned his pony and trotted on ahead.

'Vard told me you were courting his mother once,' Knud said, knowing he could get away with asking things Halvard could not.

'Yrsa Gull? Yes. Once.'

'Why didn't you marry her?'

'I didn't like her.'

'So, who would you marry?'

Jarl chuckled. 'Why are you in such a rush to marry me off?'

'I'm not. But if you do, I was wondering what my aunt would be like.'

'I won't get married, Knud.'

'Why?'

Jarl sighed. 'Because if I marry a woman who is not a noble, then I will lose you.'

'What? Why?' Knud said, his eyes widening in horror.

'Look, there's nothing to worry about. It's not going to happen. But if I marry lower than my rank, I can't raise you. It's the law.'

Knud was silent for a moment as they trotted ahead, but then he turned his face to his uncle. 'Please don't get married,' he begged, only partly joking.

'We're there!' Halvard yelled, riding back towards them. Jarl dismounted and helped Knud from his pony. The poor boy, quite unused to riding, was sore all over. The inside of his legs felt like the skin had been peeled clean from them. He swore he'd never ride another pony again.

'You...you are evil, you know that?' Knud hissed at it. It shook its head and snorted loudly as if in agreement.

They strolled to where Halvard was waiting for them. Ahead of them, through the clearing, was a small cluster of houses by the riverside, five in total, the fifth so small it could technically be considered a shed. A feeble stone wall surrounded them that looked like an attempt to re-build it was underway, the newer part of the wall not much better than the old one. Two small barges were docked at the small pier.

'What do you want?' a voice bellowed from behind the wall, and several tall humans stood up behind it, longbows in their hands and aimed straight at them.

'We're here to trade for passage on the ferry,' Jarl replied, his hands raised slightly and his palms extended. The humans eyed him warily.

'You're not a goblin are you?' one of them called out, and Halvard snorted.

'Look, I know he's ugly but he's nowhere near ugly enough to be mistaken for a goblin, you fool! Halvard retorted. The humans lowered their longbows slightly and Jarl stepped forward.

'We're just here for the barge to Einn. We can trade the ponies for passage.'

Cautiously, one of the humans emerged from behind the wall, looked them up and down and inspected the ponies.

'Lower your bows!' the human called out. 'They're not goblins.'

'Oh well done! Capital observation there!' Halvard said. Knud grinned and Jarl flashed him a look to be silent, worried at how agitated the humans were.

'The ponies aren't enough; we need a Heit per dwarf too,' the man said, his eyes peering over their shoulders towards the forest. Halvard turned to see what the man was looking at, but there was a disturbing lack of noise coming from the trees, with not so much as a single bird chirping.

Jarl reached into his bag and passed three gold Heit to the man, then grabbed Knud's hand and climbed over the wall towards the barge. He had been cheated, he knew that, just one pony should have been more than enough for passage to Einn. But they could not risk another night in the forest and were not in a position to argue.

'That one's too shifty for my liking,' Halvard whispered .

Jarl nodded. 'I don't think I'm the only one to notice the goblins have gotten more daring.'

Halvard shook his head. 'Nah! If the goblins had come this far, nobody would be alive here.'

No sooner had the words left his mouth, a third barge further out in the river came into view, half burnt and half submerged. The side that was still above the surface of the water smouldered gently.

'What happened?' Jarl asked casually.

'Goblin attack last night. We were just about to leave when we heard you. Thought you were them coming back,' the man muttered. 'Come on,' he said, beckoning them. 'Get on. We're leaving now.'

They filed onto the barge. The deck creaked in protest as they stomped past the peeling painted walls to the rough seats built into the sides. Looking up, Jarl saw the roof had collapsed.

The four remaining humans took the second barge along with the ponies, having to coax the nervous creatures onto it.

The barge they were on was old, and Jarl worried that it was slightly too old to be carrying so many of them. But the humans seemed to feel safe enough as they crowded onto the top of the barge and pushed away from the pier. Two men at the rear turned the hand-wound paddle and the barge gradually moved forward.

'Uncle...can you swim?' Knud asked worriedly, as they passed the smouldering remains of the barge.

'Don't worry Knud. The goblins don't attack in daylight.'

'I'm not worried about the goblins, I'm worried about drowning!'

'Knud! Don't worry!'

'Well *you* look worried.'

Throwing his arm around his nephew, Jarl kept his other hand as close to the hilt of his sword as he dared, with the humans watching him suspiciously.

It doesn't make sense, Jarl thought. *Why would the goblins destroy one of the barges, but not the houses?*

'Would you mind not pointing that at me,' Halvard growled at the human who was standing alongside him with his eyes on the shoreline, his bow still drawn.

Without a word, the human strolled further down the deck, barely noticing that Halvard had even spoken.

Other than the rhythmic slapping of water against the side of the barge, and the occasional bird-call, there was silence. But suddenly, a flock of birds rose up swiftly from the forest floor near the bank. The black crows shot over them, their piercing screeches almost deafening, and flew into the distance before everything returned to a deathly silence.

'Uncle?'

With a loud thud, an arrow shot up from the bank, hitting the third human squarely in the centre of his head. Three more arrows followed and hit the two humans who had been pedalling before they even knew what was happening.

Without saying a word Jarl dropped to the floor, pulling Knud down with him, and placed his hand over his mouth to stop the young dwarf from screaming in fear. Halvard followed suit, falling to his knees, and flashed Jarl a worried look.

'Don't make a sound!' Jarl whispered. He let go of Knud and began to crawl cautiously down the centre of the barge. The ponies on the second barge screamed as three more arrows found them, and judging by the terrified sounds the animals were making, the arrows had not been as well aimed as for the humans. Knud covered his own mouth and tried not to whimper in fear as the ponies continued to screech and squeal then finally gurgle as they began to choke on their own blood.

Reaching the small porthole at the end of the barge, Jarl looked down at the three dead humans lying on the boards next to him. Their eyes were glazed and staring up at the grey cloudy sky, and small pools of blood puddled around them.

At least they didn't suffer, Jarl thought to himself. If they were caught, they would be lucky if their deaths were as quick. Goblins were not known for acts of mercy.

Peering through the porthole, his breath caught in this throat.

Lining the bank were at least thirty goblins, all of them with their arrows raised and aimed at the second barge. The screams of the ponies were cut short as the arrows rained down, puncturing every square foot of surface.

We're next!

He motioned at Halvard and Knud to join him, and as they crawled forwards, Jarl pushed the body of the nearest human towards them.

'Get underneath!' he ordered. 'Quickly!'

Knud stared at him, aghast, but Halvard did what he was told without question.

Hearing a goblin shouting a command on the bank, Jarl grabbed Knud and dragged him to the floor. He took hold of the closest human body and heaved it over them both, just as the arrows rained down on them. Within seconds, the entire deck was speckled with arrows, and Jarl inhaled sharply as one of them pierced straight through the body of the human and protruded right between his fingers, which were holding the body up.

'Don't say a word!' Jarl whispered. 'Don't move an inch!' He could feel Knud trembling beside him as the goblins shouted and hollered from the riverbank.

Everyone waited tensely, not daring to breathe, not sure if the goblins would try and board the boat or not. They prayed that the river's current would keep the barge in the centre of the river and not let them drift back to the bank.

After what seemed like an eternity, the voices on the shore diminished and eventually disappeared. Jarl crawled out from underneath the human but instructed Knud to stay where he was. He inched his way to the side of the barge, maneuvering around the dozens of arrows that riddled the deck.

Peeking through the porthole, he saw that not only was the bank clear of goblins, but that the barge was being carried firmly down the centre of the stream by a strong current.

'Are they gone?' Halvard asked as Jarl crawled back.

'I think so, but we should wait till we're a few miles downstream. I don't want to take any chances.'

'Agreed!' Halvard said, shuffling a little to try and get more comfortable. He lay back as if he were taking a nap, the fact that he had a dead body on top of him not bothering him in the slightest.

Knud, however, was not so comfortable, with the open eyes of the man on top of him clearly upsetting him. Jarl reached over and tried to close the man's eyes but they sprang back open.

'Why are they doing that?' Knud whispered, his voice shaking.

'Some people just die like that.'

'Please close them! He's looking at me!'

Ripping a thin strip off the human's tunic, Jarl tied it around the man's eyes like a blindfold, and Knud breathed a sigh of relief.

'There, you can't see them now,' Jarl said. 'Now stay there. I'm not risking anything until we're at Einn.'

* * *

Knud awoke with a start when the side of the barge slammed into the riverbank. Jarl jumped onto the grass and held the ropes taut as Halvard clambered from the deck with their bags, Knud's being the only one lucky enough to have avoided being decorated with one of the goblins' arrows.

'Come on, Knud,' Jarl called. 'We haven't got all day!'

They had decided to sail the barge downstream overnight, and Jarl and Halvard had pedalled quickly, stopping and dropping to the floor the minute they heard any kind of noise coming from the forest.

Knud got to his feet and rubbed the sleep from his eyes. Yawning, he watched as his uncle tied the mooring ropes to an old, wooden post on the side of the bank, as Halvard, on his knees, splashed water onto his face from the river. And then as he turned, he saw it: the second barge drifting slowly towards them. From where he stood, Knud could see the limp bodies of the humans and ponies sprawled across the deck, pools of dark red blood encircling them and staining the planks. There was a stream of red flowing from the side of the barge into the water, where one of the humans had tried to crawl over the side having been struck with an arrow through his neck. His body was bent in half, slumped over the side like a sack. A second arrow protruded from his forehead.

'Jarl!' Knud shouted. 'Look!'

Jarl looked up and saw the barge, lapping in the current and drifting towards him.

'Halvard!' he said, shoving the mooring rope into his hand. 'Get this tied up!'

Halvard got to his knees, saw what the others were staring at, and shook his head. 'We don't have time for pleasantries,' he growled.

Jarl ignored him, and with Knud's help, they pulled the second barge to the riverbank.

The next twenty minutes were spent pulling arrows out of the humans and respectfully laying them on their backs. Next they removed the arrows from the ponies.

Knud watched Jarl at work and nervously copied what he was doing, but he gagged several times as each arrow came away in his hand, the horrible squelch of the arrow being pulled from flesh, and the stream of blood that followed, making him nauseous. He worked slowly, unable to look at what he was doing, each tug of the arrow and the resistance against the flesh making him urge. Halvard shook his head at him. The boy needed to toughen up.

Jarl collected all the remaining arrows from the deck and handed them to Halvard. 'I'll be one minute.'

He jumped from the barge onto the bank, leapt back onto the one they had travelled on, and knelt down to remove the blindfold from the human who had protected him.

'Jarl! We don't have time for this!' Halvard snapped.

'One minute!'

He worked quickly, removing arrows and dragging bodies to the middle of the deck so they rested alongside each other. He moved their arms so they crossed peacefully on their chests. Finally, he gathered the humans' bows and the goblins' arrows and joined the others.

Halvard glared at him.

'Come on, it only took a moment,' he said, sliding the arrows into his bag.

'I don't care!'

'They deserved at least a little dignity!'

'They are not our own!' Halvard yelled. 'We care for our own!'

'If it wasn't for them we'd be dead! This was the least we could do!'

'I swear, one day your ridiculous sensibilities are going to get us killed!' Halvard snapped, taking off down the path and kicking at the ground.

Jarl let out a breath he hadn't realised he'd been holding and slowly unclenched his jaw.

'How far are we from Einn?' Knud asked quietly. Jarl turned to him and for the first time noticed he had splatters of blood on his face.

'Only a few hours. A few hours and then you can have a nice warm bath, some warm food-'

'And a warm bed!' Knud finished, smiling. 'Forget the food and the bath. I'll settle for just a pillow if I have to.'

Both Afraid

39 years ago...

Dag watched Astrid cautiously out of the corner of his eye as she slept. She moved every few seconds in her sleep, wincing, flinching, holding her parents' blanket tightly around her with one hand, and loosely grasping her father's hammer axe in the other. Sylbil's bow was standing ceremonially behind her. She had been like this for the past three weeks, trying to sleep, but every few minutes jolting awake, screaming from the nightmares. The only thing that seemed to calm her were having her parents' weapons close by. She held them as lovingly as if they were her favorite dolls.

Felix whinnied, nervously switching hooves as Astrid stirred again. The pony didn't trust Astrid any more than Astrid trusted the pony; the skin on its neck where she had touched it was now shrivelled and wrinkled in the shape of a small hand.

Dag still did not know what to think.

He had never, in all the thousands of years he had lived, seen anything like what he had witnessed in the Aldwood. To be so strong so young; to be able to take energy whilst still a child; it terrified him. He had seen others, many centuries ago, who had been as able and strong as Astrid was now, but not at her age. And their stories had all ended violently. The thought that Astrid could be travelling the same road terrified him almost as much as the realisation that he now had a child to raise.

Getting to his feet, Dag pulled an apple from his bag. He held it out to Felix who promptly began munching it from his cupped hand.

'Don't worry boy, it's ok,' Dag muttered. 'She didn't mean to hurt you. We'll be home in a week, I promise.' Finishing the apple, Felix settled back down onto the grass and Dag growled to himself as it started to drizzle. He strolled over to Astrid, muttered a few words under his breath and raised his head to the treetops. The branches creaked and cracked as they twisted above him, and although they looped around on each other to create a thick covering of leaves, he hoped they were adequate enough to shield Astrid from the rain.

Dag tucked the blanket around Astrid more tightly as she shivered in her sleep, the temperature having suddenly dropped several degrees with the rainfall. He sat down next to her and stroked her head fondly, gazing at his glowing palm, the magic circling beneath his skin like a neon fish swirling in his hand.

He had always planned to teach Astrid how to use magic when she was older, but after today, he didn't think that would be possible anymore. She was too broken, too angry. Teaching her magic was out of the question. To master magic one required self control, especially control of one's emotions. It was something Astrid didn't have.

Waking with a start, Astrid peered up at him, the fear in her face quickly diminishing as soon as it registered he was there.

'How long till we get there?' she asked.

'Only a few days now, goldheart.'

Nodding her head, Astrid stared blankly into the middle space between herself and the trees, her eyes vacant and lost. Dag racked his brain for something to say, tired of seeing that look in her eyes, wishing he could think of a way to bring back the excitable and innocent goddaughter he had once had, rather than struggle with this hollow shell of a child.

'I'm going to build a room just for you! It'll be as big as you want! And I'll make you your favourite meal when we get there. Do you still like rabbit pie?' Dag asked.

Astrid said nothing, but eventually realised he had asked her a question and nodded vaguely, still gazing blankly into the distance.

'What do you want me to make for your room?' Dag asked, hoping to coax just a little conversation from her.

'Nothing,' she said. And then for the first time in days, she sat bolt upright and looked at him, her green and grey eyes shining with a sudden intensity in the firelight.

'I want you to teach me how to fight,' she said firmly, her jaw set in a tight line. 'That's what I want! Teach me how to fight!'

'Fight?' he said, part of him overjoyed that she had finally spoken, but feeling totally unprepared for a response.

'Yes. I want to be strong.'

'You are strong, goldheart!'

'No! No I'm not! I couldn't help them! I...I need to be strong!' The tears slid down her cheeks and Dag pulled her into his arms, holding her close to his chest. He rocked her gently back and forth, over and again, whispering in her ear that everything would be alright, until finally she slept.

Astrid was exhausted, her feet red, swollen and blistered from all the walking she had done over the previous few days. Her fear and stubbornness had prevented her from riding Felix, and even when the skin of her heels had begun to crack and bleed, she had hobbled on determinedly.

The fire spluttered slightly, and Dag let go of Astrid for a second and moved his hand across it, muttering some words under his breath. The fire roared into flames again, despite the lack of wood to burn.

Pulling the blanket back over Astrid, Dag rocked her gently for a few moments before finally attempting to lay her gently back down on the ground. She awoke instantly, her eyes wide, her arms wrapping around his neck in a panic.

'Teach me to fight!' she said, her eyes closing. 'Teach me to fight.' Her voice trailed off into sleep again and Dag raised his head to the sky.

'What am I going to do?' he whispered, a sudden dread overwhelming him. 'What on Ammasteinn am I going to do?'

*　*　*

Dag sighed with relief as he saw his small cabin come into view. Astrid looked up to see what had made him start, her feet so numb she could barely feel them, but she did her best to hide the limp that had been bothering her for the past few days.

Dag had often told her about his cabin; he had even used his magic to paint an image of it in the air. But to see it was quite a different thing.

Built between four tall oak trees, the cabin was made of large pine logs laid over each other to create thick, wooden walls, the gaps between them filled with a reddish clay. The two large chimneys built at either end of the cabin appeared to be the only parts of the building that were not made of wood. The roof was carpeted with a layer of lush, green grass and an ivy plant climbed up the four trees that the cabin was built around, spreading over parts of it. Tendrils cascaded over the porch like a curtain and Dag swept it aside, tying it to one of the posts that held up the porch roof. A flurry of butterflies fluttered away from it and Dag looked back at Astrid for a moment in the hope that the sight of them may have made her smile. She loved butterflies; Sylbil and Arnbjörg had forever been telling her off for trying to catch them each time Dag had visited.

Astrid flinched as they swarmed around her, and she raised her hand and roughly brushed one away as it settled on her head.

'Come in goldheart. I'll show you your room.' Dag smiled, holding his hand out to her, and Astrid reluctantly took it and followed him inside.

Dag sat her down at a small table in the corner next to the only window in the cabin, which stretched across almost the entire wall. Each tiny glass pane between the leading was a slightly different colour and sent a cascade of rainbow beams across the floor and the walls.

A floor to ceiling bookcase took up one wall at the far end of the cabin and a large oak table stretched from one side of the room to the other, strewn with inks and manuscripts.

'Where would you like your room, goldheart?' Dag asked. 'You can have it anywhere you want!'

Astrid took a few moments to look around. She felt dazed, like her mind was about to float away from her body. Dag's forced cheerfulness made her nervous, like there was nothing to worry about, like her parents were not dead. Though she wouldn't tell him, part of her wished he would just show how sad he was, even wail and cry if he wanted to. At least that way she could stop feeling like she was walking through some kind of horrible dream.

Looking up, Astrid saw an old bird's nest - a swallows mud nest - built in the corner of the roof at the far side of the room.

'Up there,' she whispered, pointing. 'I would like my room up there.'

'Ok, just give me one minute,' Dag said.

Stepping forward, he clapped his hands together making Astrid jump at the sound. The cabin shook as if a burst of thunder had ripped through the building. Dag slowly separated his hands and as the oak floorboards and the rafters at the far end of the room shuddered, his fingers glowed an electric blue.

Despite how she was feeling, Astrid couldn't hide her amazement as two long sprouts burst from the ground, twirling in spirals until they wrapped securely around one of the rafters. Branches grew from it, twisting together, to create stairs leading upwards.

Up on the rafters, several more branches emerged like threads, weaving together so tightly they created floor boards, the surface texture knotted. The branches at the edge of the rafters climbed up and connected to the ceiling, this time winding together to create a beautiful screen of woven patterns, which loosened as they reached it.

Dag Picked Astrid up in his arms and carried her up the stairs and into the new room, setting her down on the floor. He pulled the blanket from her shoulders and folded it carefully.

'I'll make you a mattress tonight. I'll make some new clothes too! Ragi makes some beautiful green silk; I'll get him to give me some and I'll sew you a pretty dress.'

'Ragi?'

'He's my friend. He's a hobgoblin.'

Nodding, Astrid stared around her. She reached over and took the blanket back from Dag and pulled it around her, hugging her knees to her chest.

'Do you want some food?' Dag asked, unsure of what to do next. Astrid nodded and Dag nearly fell down the stairs in his rush to get to the fireplace.

There were two in the cabin, one of which had a roasting spit spread across it. Old wooden cupboards were built into the wall beside it, crammed with glass and clay jars containing various nuts, flours, and oils. Dag pulled a few of them from the shelf and mixed their contents in a large clay bowl.

Up in her new room, Astrid studied her surroundings. Everything about the new place made her feel displaced. The smell, the feel, everything was alien to her, the smell being the thing that scared her the most. Her old home had the aroma of wood shavings, wax and a roaring fire. It smelt warm and safe. This place was new; it smelt of moss, mold and plants. There was nothing remotely familiar about it.

Overwhelmed by the feeling of abandonment, Astrid rolled onto her side on the ground and pulled the blanket over her head like a tent. She pressed it against her nose and inhaled the familiar smell, closing herself up under it, in the old, safe world it reminded her of.

Worried by the lack of noise coming from her room, Dag covered the pot of meat bubbling over the flames and headed back upstairs.

'Astrid?'

Curled up like a squirrel in hibernation, her blanket wrapped around her and only her nose and eyes exposed, Astrid was fast asleep. For the first time in days she looked at peace.

Dag pulled out two fresh blankets from one of the cupboards lining the wall opposite the window, walked back up to Astrid and tucked one of them underneath her head like a pillow. The second blanket he placed over her and he stroked her head fondly before leaving her be.

* * *

Dag watched as Astrid dug her fork into the rabbit pie, raised it to her mouth and began to eat, the overcooked crust cracking loudly against her teeth.

'Do you like it, goldheart?' he asked nervously.

Doing her best to hide her disgust, Astrid nodded, even managing a smile. The look of contentment on Dag's face was almost worth eating the revolting food for.

'Do you want some more?' he asked excitedly, and moved to scrape some more of the pie onto her plate. Astrid quickly shook her head.

'No thank you. I'm not very hungry,' she lied.

'But you've barely eaten anything!'

'I'm fine,' she said, finishing up the last of the pie as slowly as she could. Her stomach growled for more but she ignored it.

For the next few minutes Dag ate in silence and Astrid did her best to keep her eyes fixed on her plate, not wanting him to have any reason to try and talk to her. The last few days had been a relentless monologue of conversation and Astrid felt like she might start screaming if she heard so much as one more word come from his mouth.

More than anything else, Astrid wanted peace and quiet. But Dag, meaning well, had given her the opposite. He had talked to her constantly whilst she had helped him make the furniture for her room, but he had avoided the only topic Astrid cared about. Any mention or even a reference to her parents' existence had been brushed away; forgotten. It was just another constant reminder that they were gone.

'Is it alright if I take a walk outside?' Astrid asked, pushing her plate away.

'Of course, goldheart!' Dag said. 'Just let me get my cloak.'

'No! No...can I just go by myself?'

'Oh...ok...yes. Of course you can,' he said hesitantly. 'But don't go far.'

Astrid left the table and strolled out of the cabin, eyeing Felix distrustfully as she passed him. Spotting a gap in the hedge to her right, she headed towards it, breathing a loud sigh of relief as soon as the house was out of sight. What soon followed was a flurry of tears, the bottled up sadness and frustration from the last few days hitting her like a wave. The clouds above her rumbled threateningly, and the first few drops of rain began to fall, mixing with the tears on her cheeks.

Glancing at her reflection in a puddle, Astrid stopped and knelt down next to it. She moved her fingers to her mouth and touched the deep scab across her lips, shocked at her appearance.

Moving her fingernails to the edge of the scab, Astrid began to pick at it. She winced, but felt a strange sense of relief, the pain distracting her from the horrible hollowness she felt inside. She peeled the scab on her upper lip away until she felt the warm, metallic blood in her mouth, then reached to the scab on her lower lip and began to pick away at that.

'What are you doing?'

Astrid yelped in shock and turned to face the tall thin figure who had crept up behind her. Her hands glowed blue as she held them up in front of her defensively.

Even though she had never seen a goblin before, she knew almost instantly what the creature in front of her was. Its skin was pale but with a distinct green undertone and it was shorter than Dag but much taller than her. Its nose was flat and the tip of it connected to its upper lip. Two sharp front teeth protruded from beneath it, the ends as sharp as needles. Its huge green eyes stared at her in shock and it raised his hands towards her, the long, slender fingers looking almost like spider's legs, they were so thin and gangly.

'What are you doing?' the goblin repeated, this time more gently. Crouching down onto its knees, it eyed her worriedly. Astrid was surprised to hear the kindness in its voice.

'Who are you?' she finally asked, noticing how the goblin's long, pointed ears flinched like a cat's in the rain.

'Ragi. And you are?'

'Astrid.'

'Astrid...Dagmar's goddaughter?' Ragi asked surprised.

Nodding, Astrid lowered her hands and the blue glow faded. *This must be the hobgoblin Dag told me about* she thought.

For a moment they just looked at each other curiously as the rain became heavier, the drizzle turning to a downpour.

'Listen, I don't like rain and I don't think you do either. My hut is near here. You can come inside if you'd like.'

At first Astrid didn't move. After her last encounter with strangers, she was more than a little nervous. But something about the goblin made her feel sure that he didn't mean her any harm, even though his appearance suggested otherwise. Perhaps it was his eyes, the large eyes that held just as much fear of her as she had of him. It was much like how she imagined a spider would look at someone who was about to squash it.

Astrid stood up and slowly followed the goblin, keeping a safe distance away from him. Before long, she spotted a round hut ahead of them with smoke billowing from a small metal chimney in the centre of the roof. A large tarp of animal skins shielded the entrance from the rain and the door itself was made of two more skins that overlapped and hung across the door.

Ragi pushed one of the skins aside and stepped through, but seconds later his head emerged between the flaps.

'Want to stay out here?' he asked.

Astrid sat down in front of the door and nodded.

Ragi's head disappeared again and she heard him cluttering around inside the hut. Her curiosity goaded her to follow him, but her common sense prevailed.

Astrid was surprised to see how orderly the forest around the hut was. From the stories her parents had told her of goblins, she had expected to see everything broken and in disarray, but everything - the washing basin, the log hut and the outdoor fire - were all meticulously maintained. The walls of the hut were made of neat tiles of tree bark, measured and cut to perfectly match the triangular tiles beside them, and overlapping each other like scales. Not so much as a single tile was out of place or different to the one beside it.

Ragi appeared and sat down a few feet away from her, placing a bowlful of food in front of her. Astrid peered down at the selection of nuts, dried and fresh fruits and some bread, and quickly moved her hand to her stomach to try and hide the loud rumble her insides made. After four days of Dag's food, she was desperate to eat something that didn't crumble to ash in her mouth, or that didn't have the texture of slime.

Leaning forwards, Ragi took hold of one of the apples, raised it to his mouth and took a large bite, his eyes fixed on Astrid as if to say: *'see...it's safe to eat!'*

Barely able to stop herself from cramming everything she could into her mouth, Astrid grabbed a handful of nuts and began chewing them furiously, almost swallowing them whole and grunting happily at the taste of them. She moved onto the dried apples and shoved as many slices as she could into her mouth. Ragi took a few more pieces of food from the basket and ate slowly, his long fingers picking at the food in his palm before eating it whilst he observed her with interest.

'You should slow down. You'll be sick,' Ragi said worriedly. He pulled the bowl away from her until she had finished chewing, only giving it back to her when she had taken a few seconds to swallow what was in her mouth.

'You've been eating Dagmar's cooking, haven't you?' He grinned, the shape of his mouth making it look more like a snarl, but his eyes lit up the way any elf's or dwarf's would when they smiled.

Nodding, Astrid took another handful of food, this time taking her time with each mouthful. When she hiccupped loudly, Ragi laughed.

'Told you! You should have a drink, it will help stop the air bubbles,' he said, pointing to a nearby well.

'I'll wait,' Astrid replied, not wanting to go out in the rain.

'How long have you been with Dagmar?'

'A few days,' Astrid replied, focusing only on satisfying her need to fill her stomach and completely forgetting that she had not intended to talk to the goblin.

'You must be starving! The man can't cook!' Ragi cackled. He pushed the bowl of fruit closer towards her. 'Take it, you need it more than I do!'

Astrid was so busy eating that she didn't even notice Dag's voice in the distance calling for her. Ragi heard him and looked over at the forest, his long pointed ears turning outwards and quivering at the sound.

'You should go,' he said kindly. He stood up and walked into the hut, then returned a moment later with a large leather pouch. He swept the food from the bowl into it and passed it to her. 'Take this, it should last you a day or two. When you can't take his food anymore I have plenty more here.'

'Thank you,' Astrid said, surprised. She reached for the bag and flinched as her hand touched his accidently, his skin much like the texture of a toad; lumpy and clammy.

Astrid strode through the forest towards the sound of Dag's voice and hid the bag of food underneath her tunic. The rain, heavier now, started to seep through it.

Reaching Dag's cabin, Astrid saw him on the far side of the glade, his face twisted in panic as he ran his hands through his long, white hair. Hearing the snap of twigs as Astrid stepped into the clearing, he turned and raced towards her.

'Goldheart! Where did you go?' he asked, his ice blue eyes darting around wildly.

'I just went for a walk,' Astrid replied, surprised at how alarmed the old warlock was. Her hand pressed over her side to hide the bulging bag of food Ragi had given her.

'Ok..ok...just, just let me know next time you want to wander off.'

'I met your friend.'

'Friend?'

'Ragi. The goblin.'

'Oh Ragi, yes...Ragi...he's a hobgoblin,' Dag clarified, stepping back and running his hands through his hair again as he tried to calm himself. 'Come inside, goldheart. You're soaking wet!'

Following Dag inside, Astrid felt the cord around the bag of food come loose. A few of the dried fruits dropped out and slid down the inside of her tunic, dangerously close to spilling out onto the floor. Hurtling past Dag, she ran up the stairs to her room in the rafters, reaching it just as the fruit clattered onto the boards. She lifted up the straw mattress Dag had made for her and tucked the pouch of food underneath it, then crawled over to the food which had fallen and scooped it into her hands just as Dag walked up the stairs, his old eyes worried.

'Goldheart? What's wrong?'

'Nothing!'

'Don't lie Astrid, please don't lie!' Dag begged, tears suddenly filling his eyes. 'I know I'm not doing very well, but you need to talk! Tell me what I'm doing wrong!'

Out of nowhere, Astrid felt a lump jump into her throat and unable to stop herself, she burst into tears. She wasn't entirely sure what specifically she was crying about, but knew she needed to satisfy this overwhelming urge.

She was tired of the dodging around every mention of her parents. The pain in her chest had built up each day until it just felt like everything inside her had been hollowed out, leaving a gaping burning hole inside that only crying could relive.

Astrid buried her head into Dag's robes, and the old warlock cried with her for several minutes. The rain pattered down on the roof like thousands of small stones falling from the sky, then cascaded like waterfalls and splattered down on the ground. There was a faint sound of thunder in the distance.

'I'm scared, Dag,' Astrid sobbed, her voice almost lost against the rainfall.

'Me too, goldheart,' Dag whispered back, fondly stroking her head. 'Me too.'

The Knot

Jarl's spirits lifted as he finally saw the gates of Einn in the distance.

Worried by the silence of the forest, Halvard walked gradually backwards, facing it, as Jarl and Knud ran towards the city wall. Several guards hollered as they approached, and spotting the tip of an arrow glinting in the fast approaching sunset, Jarl grabbed hold of Knud and stepped in front of him, raising his hands in the air in peace. A crow cawed noisily behind them in the forest and Halvard raised his axe, his eyes scanning the trees.

'We're from Bjargtre! Don't shoot!' Jarl shouted.

For a moment there was silence. Jarl noticed that three arrows were pointed directly at him, two from the top of the stone wall and one from the small opening in the wooden gate.

'We can pay for passage!' Jarl yelled, trying not to turn and look at the forest as he heard a flock of birds flying up from the forest floor.

'We need to get inside!' Halvard hissed.

The large, heavy locks clunked behind the side door in the wall, and Jarl took a step forward with Knud close behind him. A human appeared in the doorway shortly followed by a second, an archer, with his arrow lowered but ready to raise at a moment's notice.

Only ever having seen dwarves in his lifetime, Knud couldn't help staring at the humans. They were so tall, a good three heads taller than Jarl. Their skin was dark, the colour of ebony, and they were draped in thick furs, the hems of which were embroidered with shapes of birds and trees. Brightly coloured threads of red, green, orange and blue stood out against the dark browns and blacks of their clothes. The buttons of their tunics were made of bone and had been carved to look like knotted rope. Rabbit fur topped their worn, leather boots, and Knud stared at the patchwork of leather pieces and the small, sharp studs sewn into the points of them.

'What are you willing to pay?' the taller human bellowed.

'We can pay one Heit per dwarf,' Jarl said quickly, painfully aware that they still had dried human blood on their clothes. He felt the hair on the back of his neck rise, his senses telling him something was watching them from the forest. 'We don't have any more than that,' he lied, knowing he had a purse stuffed with coins in his bag.

Nodding his head, the human glanced over at the forest warily and held out his hand. Jarl reached into the pouch that hung from the back of his belt and pulled out three Heit. Each coin was thick and hollow through the centre, almost resembling a belt buckle, with various letters and runes stamped upon it. Jarl pressed them firmly into the human's hand and walked forwards, beckoning the others to follow. As soon as they were through the door it clunked heavily behind them, and Halvard lowered his axe, his face relaxing.

'The inns are that way,' the guard snapped, pointing ahead. 'Take the second street on your left.'

Nodding his head in thanks, Jarl marched down the street with Knud and Halvard close behind him. The humans stared at them in surprise, many of them never having seen a dwarf before.

As they followed the human's directions, the sun set over the mountains and the temperature dropped at an incredible speed. The street had no paving and the ground beneath them was hard from the cold. They shivered as they walked, passing rows and rows of wooden and stone houses with sharp, angled rooves, a thick layer of thatch covering each one. A warm yellow glowed from the square leaded windows and thick knotted patterns were carved into the door frames of each house.

They reached the second street and Jarl turned into it.

'If I don't find a bed soon I'm going to start using this thing,' Halvard grumbled, waving his axe in the air, 'They'll probably try and overcharge us again. Three Heit was far too much!'

'Quite frankly I'd have given them all the Heit we have if it meant we could get out of that forest,' Jarl replied. 'Something was watching us.'

'Well, I'd rather have a good fight than be robbed in broad daylight.'

Shaking his head, Jarl said nothing. It was no use arguing with Halvard when the cold made him grumpy, lack of a decent sleep made him worse, and not having warm food for a few days made him borderline murderous. He could never be reasoned with in this mood.

Ahead of them at the far end of the street, several inn signs lined both sides, each with the inn's namesake painted on it. A knot, a red barge and a rising sun were the first three images that Jarl saw, the red barge being the smallest of the three. The Knot was easily double the size of its competitors and took up the entire end of the street. It had a second floor and a stable built beside it.

He glanced across at The Red Barge. Skad had mentioned he would be staying there and Jarl decided immediately that although he had to see him, he would avoid the place for as long as he could. The man was absolutely insufferable to be around.

Jarl strode up to the large oak door of The Knot, straightened his back and pushed it open firmly, his head held high. The many people crowded around inside stood aside to let him through. Knud stared up at his uncle, amazed at how he could command the attention of the room without so much as saying a word. It had been a long time since he had seen Jarl exercise this ability; in fact he couldn't remember him having done it since Knute died. Something inside of him had disappeared with the death of his best friend.

Striding up to the counter, Jarl cleared his throat loudly, and the innkeeper turned around, looking up at the space above Jarl's head before looking down and spotting him. His eyes seemed to linger on the bloodstains on Jarl's clothes and Halvard swallowed hard, his steel blue eyes glaring up at the man.

'How much for three rooms?' Jarl asked.

'How long will you be staying?'

'A week,' Jarl said. Halvard glanced at him, one eyebrow raised, but said nothing.

'That'll be five Feoh,' the innkeeper finally said, and Halvard stiffened, positive they were being charged double the normal rate.

'I only have Fé,' Jarl lied, wanting to conserve the remaining Heit he had.

'That'll be ten Fé,' he replied, and Halvard growled behind them. Jarl, scared that Halvard was about to ask the man to step outside, quickly pulled the money from his pouch and passed it to the innkeeper. He took the money and reached below the counter for the keys, then lifted the counter door and led them through the crowd to the stairs. The humans who were sober enough to notice turned to stare at them and one, who was too drunk to see their beards, bellowed out from the crowd.

'No children allowed!'

Jarl grabbed Halvard by his arm and stopped him from lunging at the man who had said it.

'Calm down!' Jarl muttered under his breath.

At the top of the creaky, pine staircase, the innkeeper opened three of the many doors lining the hall, and passed each of them a key.

'Food will be served for another hour, then it's only ale. If you want, the maid can bring up hot water.'

'Yes!' Jarl said, his bones desperate for a nice warm bath. Halvard, seeming not to have heard what the innkeeper had said, lumbered into his room and slammed the door behind him. There was a loud thud from behind the door, the sound of Halvard falling to his bed, and then silence.

The innkeeper walked back down the stairs, managing to resist the urge to turn around and stare at them. It was not the first time he had seen a dwarf but it was the first time since he had been a little boy. No matter how close they were, the dwarves of Bjargtre kept to themselves. To see a dwarf was rare, something to be discussed with friends for weeks afterwards. Normally they just passed through and left within a day or two. But whatever was happening up on the mountains seemed to be pushing more than just the occasional dwarf down into Einn.

In his room, Knud headed straight for the bed and practically fell into it. He kicked off his iron-capped boots, dropped the key onto the floor and grabbed the edge of the blanket, rolling over in the bed so that it wrapped around him. He looked more like a worm than a dwarf, with his bright orange hair stuck out of the end.

Jarl stumbled into his room, locked the door and placed the key on the bedside table. Like an invisible wave, the tiredness from the last few days hit him and he dropped his bag to the floor and kicked off his shoes. He pulled a clean outfit from his bag, desperate to get out of his filthy clothes, and as he slipped off his tunic, he noticed the mud and blood speckling it. A large patch of dried human blood covered the shoulder area from when he had hidden under the dead bargeman.

'No wonder they were wary,' Jarl muttered.

Just as he was about to tumble into his bed, he heard a faint tapping on the door. Irritated, he opened it, and instantly any thought of sleep disappeared when he saw a maid standing timidly in the hallway with a steaming jug of water in her hands.

Jarl beckoned her into the room with an outstretched arm, and without speaking, she poured the water into the wooden tub at the far end of the room. She opened the tap on a large tank of cold water then hurried back to the hallway, returning a second later with two more jugs.

'I think your friends are asleep, so I figured you could have these instead,' she said cheerfully, trying not to stare at him.

'They're tired, it's been a long few days.'

'If you want, I can take your clothes down and have them washed.'

'No! No, thank you, I prefer to clean them myself,' Jarl said quickly, worried about how the humans would react if they saw just how much blood was on his clothes. They were already drawing attention just by being here. The last thing they needed to do was make anyone think that they might be dangerous. The bargemen who had died would no doubt have friends or family who lived in Einn, and three dwarves arriving with blood on their clothes that wasn't their own would raise questions.

The woman left and Jarl locked the door behind her. The tub was almost half full and he closed the tap to the tank, undressed, and stepped into the water.

The water could have been straight from the cold tank and it would have still felt warm to Jarl. His body was so cold it felt like ice had managed to make its way to his bones and into the marrow, freezing him from the inside. At first it felt as if his skin was burning, but once he became accustomed to the sudden temperature change, the warmth slowly seeped through to his insides.

Against his better judgment, Jarl leant his head against the back of the tub and closed his eyes. The exhaustion crept over his body as a dark mist descended on his consciousness...

* * *

It was so cold, and the air bit at his exposed face and turned his skin a mottled red. Pulling his fur cloak tightly around him, he trudged forwards through the snow. It was a slow, exhausting haul forwards and each foot felt as if it were made of rock, becoming heavier by the second. He was tired from the two hours it had taken to walk so far, and when he turned to see exactly how far he had come, he saw the tracks behind him had disappeared, the falling snow having covered them in seconds.

Halvard had decided to stay in Bjargtre; he had not been terribly enthusiastic about stepping out into the spring storm. The snow would not last for long, at most a day or two before it melted, but that did not stop the cold, and Halvard hated the cold.

Knute should have been back hours ago, and no matter how much Halvard had told him it was absurd to go looking for him along the Austr road, and that the snow storm had probably just slowed his patrol down so there was nothing to worry about, somehow Jarl had not been able to shake the strange feeling inside of him, a hollow sense of foreboding urging him to leave the city and go in search of his friend.

The road was nothing more than an endless stretch of white and he was barely able to feel the stone road under it.

Knute had only left with his patrol to escort the merchants from Lǫgberg back to the outpost, which was barely an hour's walk away. When they had left, the storm had not yet hit the mountain and there had been nothing more than a heavy cluster of clouds slowly creeping towards Bjargtre against a clear blue sky. They would have reached the outpost before the snow became a hindrance, but even so, he should have seen them by now. He could see the tall towers of the outpost in the distance but not a single figure was nearby.

The wind blew yet more snow down onto the ground, and the air became so thick with snowflakes he could barely see more than six feet ahead of him, the outpost towers now little more than a blur.

Suddenly, his foot hit something in the snow, something soft and fleshy. Jarl crouched down and scraped away at the snow with his fingertips.

With a shudder, a half dead donkey whinnied in pain, and as Jarl frantically pushed away more of the snow, he saw a deep stab wound to its neck, the snow around it a crimson red. The donkey had belonged to the merchants from Logberg, he was sure of it. Its distinctive, shaggy red-brown coat had looked like hundreds of long hair cords; it's snout completely white.

His heart jumped into his mouth and Jarl looked around him, suddenly noticing small mounds in the snow nearby. He stumbled to his feet, raced to the nearest mound and scraped away at it in a panic. He stared down in horror as he uncovered the merchant's face. The man's throat was cut open and his eyes, lifeless and grey, stared up at him, a look of shock and fear embedded in them.

A few feet to his right, Jarl suddenly saw one of the mounds move. He ran to it and dug at the snow as fast as he could. At the sight of the hem of Knute's cloak, Jarl burrowed his fingers into it even faster, his hands having lost all feeling long ago . He clawed the snow away from his friend's face just as Knute reached up and grabbed his hand in a vice-like grip, shaking uncontrollably.

'Knute!' he cried, as his friend yelled out in pain, panting and terrified. His face, or what was left of it, was a patchwork of torn and shredded skin; his left eye was sliced wide open whilst his right flinched wildly and stared up at him.

Jarl didn't need to ask what had happened; the marks on Knute's face told him all he needed to know. The claw marks had not just torn the skin, they had burned it, and the wounds had been cauterised seconds after the claws had ripped it open. There was only one *animal that Jarl knew of that left marks so identifiable: the Dip wolves of the northern plains. Any Dip this far west could only mean one thing: the goblins were raiding a lot further than Lake Krewa.*

Shoving his arms beneath Knute's body, Jarl pulled him up out of the snow and onto his feet, all the while Knute wincing in pain.

'Jarl! Jarl, put me down!' Knute groaned. Jarl let him go and he fell to the ground, his hand pressed tightly over his stomach. Dark red blood oozed between his fingertips, his entire hand was swathed in it, his clothes soaked with it.

Even if they had been at the gates of Bjargtre, there would have been nothing they could have done. This much blood loss was fatal. Knute's skin was deathly pale and his breathing a hollow rattle. At most he would live for another few minutes.

For a few seconds Jarl said nothing, feeling like he had been disemboweled himself. Moving to try and help Knute, he pressed his hands tightly over the slice across Knute's stomach but knew deep inside that nothing could be done. His best friend was about to die in front of him.

Taking a deep breath, Jarl forced himself to talk.

'What...what happened?'

Knute stared up at him, his good eye darting around like a madman's. Jarl pressed his hand harder over Knute's stomach urging him to hang on, to not let go.

'Goblins! There were goblins!' Knute said, his voice panicked. A small trickle of blood gathered at the corner of his mouth. 'You have to warn them, tell King Hábrók the goblins have an Agrokū!'

Jarl didn't know what to say or do. A part of him thought that maybe he could carry Knute back home, that it was still possible to save him; he was horrified at the thought of a life without his best friend. He had known Knute since he was a child; they had grown up together. He had been at his wedding, he was his son's godfather. Knud...oh dear God...what would he say to Knud? He had already lost his mother to the red plague barely a year ago, how was he going to tell him that he had lost his father too?

'Jarl!' Knute shouted loudly, and Jarl's mind snapped back. 'You need to tell them! He was a young goblin. He can't have been much older than fifteen or twenty, but he had so many rings in his hair! I heard them call him Ulf.'

'How many rings?'

'I don't know,' he choked. 'I only saw him for a few seconds before he cut me. But he had at least twenty. Twenty, Jarl! If this goblin has managed to control over twenty tribes while he's still a boy...you must tell King Hábrók!'

'I will!' Jarl promised. Knute gripped Jarl's arm more and more tightly, his breathing getting worse by the second. A horrible pained gasp escaped from his mouth as his life began to ebb away.

'Knud...take care of him! Take care of my boy!'

'I will! I promise!'

Knute pushed Jarl's hands away from his stomach, knowing he was just delaying the inevitable, but Jarl instantly pressed them back over the open gash.

'It doesn't hurt any more Jarl,' Knute said, smiling, bright red blood seeping between the gaps of his teeth. 'I miss Lína, it will be good to see her again!'

'Can't you wait a little bit?' Jarl asked, knowing that Knute would prefer for him to joke in the situation, but he couldn't hide the sadness and rage in his voice.

'No, don't think I have a choice this time!' Knute laughed, looking up at the sky where the snow was falling less heavily now. 'Ulf made sure of that.'

'I'm going to kill him!' Jarl growled, his hands shaking. 'I'll kill him!'

'Feel free! He made my boy an orphan. I'm a little annoyed about that,'

Half laughing, half crying, Jarl held Knute's hand tighter.

Knute had always been like this. No matter what the situation, there was always a joke to be made, usually at his own expense. It was just like him, joking till the very end.

Closing his eyes, Knute breathed out slowly, his fingers curling inward and tightening for a second *before folding outwards. His eyes glazed over and his whole body relaxed as his head rolled back against the snow.*

He stared blankly up at the sky.

* * *

With a start, Jarl woke up, his head dipping below the surface of the bath water for a moment. He panicked as the water made an attempt to fill his lungs and he sat up quickly, panting heavily, rubbing his face to wake himself.

'Idiot!' he muttered. He climbed out of the tub and furiously dried himself, then shivering, got back into his clothes.

The last time he had had to revisit that terrible day in his dreams had been months ago, and he had prayed with all his might that it was the last time, despite knowing that the dreams would haunt him all his life.

Jarl pulled on his boots and unlocked the door to his room. Within seconds he was hammering on Knud's door, desperate for him to answer. There was a shuffling sound and then footsteps from within.

It was always like this after the dreams; a deep but irrational fear washing over him that something had happened to Knud. He always had to check, to make sure. He would never forgive himself if...

The key turned in the lock and Knud stood in the doorway, his sleepy brown eyes looking up at him.

'Are we going?' Knud asked, slightly worried.

'No. No...I just wanted to check you were sleeping alright,' Jarl replied. 'Go back to bed and lock the door.'

Groggily, Knud shook his head in confusion and closed the door, and Jarl waited until he heard the key turn in the lock before heading back to his room.

'What the hell are you doing?' Halvard snapped, and Jarl turned to see a pair of furious eyes staring at him. 'It's not even bloody dawn! Go back to sleep!'

Jarl nodded, returned to his room and closed the door. He slumped onto the floor and concentrated on his breathing, trying to stop it from getting out of hand. Resting his head against his hands, he took several deep breaths, each one more controlled than the last.

'Come on! You're being stupid! You've got to stop doing this!' he whispered to himself.

He hated this. If the dreams weren't bad enough, the panic that overtook him each time afterwards was in some ways much worse. To become a slave to such a stupid, paranoid fear made him feel too much like he had that day; useless. Helpless.

Jarl got to his feet and fell into bed, pulling the blankets tightly around him. Hopefully this time, the nightmares would stay away.

* * *

Through the small circular window, Jarl saw the sky outside turning orange as the sun began to rise. The edges of the leaded window fogged.

He left the room and walked down the old pine stairs, his eyes heavy, dry and sore from lack of sleep. He half considered dunking his head in the horse trough outside if it would stop him from feeling so utterly exhausted and groggy.

The inn was silent. The innkeeper was asleep by the fireplace on an old couch, the feet of which had been chewed to pieces by various dogs that had come into the inn with their masters. Fresh hay had been strewn across the floor, all of the tables had been wiped down clean, and the fireplace smouldered slightly, a few of the coals still glowing amid the mountain of grey ash which surrounded them.

Being careful to walk quietly, Jarl opened the inn door, groaning as the cold air hit him. He rubbed his hands together and stepped out into the street.

Skad had said last time he had visited Bjargtre that he would be staying in Einn for the two weeks leading up Miðsumar. There were only five days left now, so if Skad had done what he had intended, he would be here by now.

Jarl screwed up his eyes as the sun finally made its way over the horizon, the first few rays catching him in the eye and temporarily blinding him. Shielding his face, he strolled towards The Red Barge and opened the door.

The inn was similar to The Knot, just smaller and considerably dirtier. The paved ground was covered in a carpet of old hay that looked like it had not been cleared for days. The tabletops still glistened with the spilled ale from the previous night.

Next to the fireplace, a large mastiff lifted its head as Jarl closed the door behind him, the animal as poorly groomed as the building. Although it was clearly well fed, its fur was matted with hay and dirt. Jarl eyed the dog warily and it growled at him as it got to its feet, waking the innkeeper who was sprawled on a thin mattress beside him.

'What do you want?' the innkeeper groaned.

'I'm here to see Skad.'

'Skad?'

'Skad Löfgren.'

'Oh, him,' he muttered, slumping back down and reshuffling the hay of his mattress. 'Third hallway, fifth door.' He tossed a log onto the smouldering embers and motioned lazily to the hallway opposite before turning away from Jarl and back towards the fireplace.

Jarl headed down the hallway, finally stopping at the door that had a number five crudely scraped into it.

Skad would be angry if Jarl woke him, but the man was always in a foul mood so it really made no difference if Jarl spoke to him now or later. Making a fist, he rapped firmly on the door and waited.

Throwing open the door, Skad opened his mouth to yell at whatever ignorant soul had dared to disturb him, despite the fact he had been awake for a few hours now, but the words caught in his throat as soon as he saw Jarl.

'And you couldn't wait a few more hours for me to wake up?'

'Don't lie, you've been up for hours,' Jarl snapped back, trying to be civil, but something about Skad had always annoyed him. His perpetual bad temper and cruel remarks to everyone who crossed his path was enough to make anyone dislike him within a few minutes of meeting him.

'Common courtesy, Jarl! Did that die with the rest of your family?'

Jarl clenched his fists and walked into the room, and Skad slammed the door without any thought for the other people sleeping in the rooms adjacent.

'So...you ended up coming,' Skad muttered. He stood by the door and crossed his arms, glaring at Jarl from beneath his thick, bushy white brows. His grey eyes had lost their darker outer ring to age, but they were still as alert as the day he had been born and glistened like those of an animal.

'Yes. You said there would be a human traveller here who could escort us to Lǫgberg if we came before Miðsumar.'

'Huh? Oh...yes, Outlander is here,' Skad replied. 'I'll ask tonight. Where are you staying?'

'The Knot.'

'Right. Then wait there. I'll make sure she's there tonight.'

'She?' Jarl exclaimed.

'That's what I said isn't it?' Skad snapped.

For a moment Jarl said nothing, surprised. When he had spoken to Skad about this before, he had given him the impression that the Outlander was a man.

'Do you vouch for her, this human?'

'Yes I do! And she is the only one mad enough to take you. Now get out and let me sleep!' He stepped aside to let Jarl through and then slammed the door as loudly as he could behind him.

Jarl walked back down the hall, shaking his head, and out of the Red Barge door, being careful to not wake the innkeeper who he was surprised to see snoring loudly by the fireplace.

Not wanting to return to The Knot quite yet, he ambled up the street. He was already nervous about this journey. It would be long and dangerous, and having a human escorting them just made it more unsettling. But the only other options had been to risk the journey on their own or ask Skad to take them, the latter of the two being completely out of the question. One day with the dwarf was bad enough, but months on the road would be hell.

Jarl stopped walking, closed his eyes and took a deep breath, telling himself that they would be alright. If Skad recommended her then there was no doubt she was one of the best. Skad was a proud man and Jarl could not remember him ever vouching for anyone, so whomever this Outlander was, she was the best they could ask for.

A Little Magic

38 years ago...

Astrid opened her hand and focused on bringing her energy to the centre of it. Her fingers glowed blue and the light travelled up them and swirled in her palm like a ripple.

'I'm doing it!' Astrid said, her eyes lighting up.

'No! Don't speak. Focus!' Ragi said. Astrid's face dropped and the light began to flicker and finally disappeared. She clenched her hand into a tight fist and growled in frustration.

'I don't understand why I can't do it!' she said. 'I'm trying so hard! Why won't Dag teach me?'

'Dag...is afraid what magic will do to you.'

'Why? Magic is just magic.'

'That's why! It's not *just* magic. It's your energy, and if you misuse or attempt magic that is too strong for you, it will kill you. You cannot cheat it.'

'I'm not trying to cheat it! I just want to use it!' Astrid yelled.

Ragi raised an eyebrow, his face serious, and she bowed her head.

'I'm sorry I shouted.'

He had been extremely patient with her over the last few months, agreeing to teach her the little magic he knew if she promised to not tell Dag. She had tried numerous times to convince Dag to teach her but the warlock had refused, a terrified look washing over his face every time she suggested it.

'Why is he so scared of it? He uses it all the time, yet he won't teach me.'

'You are angry, Astrid. Magic is extremely dangerous when you're angry.'

'I just want to feel strong, Ragi. He won't teach me to fight, either.'

Sighing, Ragi crouched down in front of her. 'I want you to imagine your head is inside your heart. I don't want you to think; I want you to *feel*.'

Nodding, Astrid closed her eyes and turned her hand over so the palm was facing towards the ground.

'Now, imagine you are moving your heart to the middle of your hand. Feel it, Astrid.'

Slowly at first, Astrid's palm began to glow again and Ragi noticed that once of the quartz crystals he kept on his shelf was trembling. He turned back to her, a thin smile on his face.

'Now, imagine your heart is going back to where it belongs, but it's going to leave a small piece of it behind.'

At first the light in her hand faded, but then just as quickly as it had dimmed, the light picked up again. It rose above the surface of her skin at a painfully slow rate, flickered for a moment, and then fell back again. It rose and fell several times before it finally hovered above her skin like a floating feather.

'Now Astrid...I want you to take the light and move it exactly how you want to. That small piece of your heart has to become what you want.'

No sooner had the words left his mouth, there was a bright flash. The blue magic in her hand transformed into a deep orange with tinges of red around the edges. Astrid opened her eyes and glared down at it. The magic rose and twisted into the shapes of horses with riders on their backs, their swords and axes raised. Astrid curled her fingers and crushed them in her hand. The magic disappeared in a puff of smoke.

'I want to kill them,' she hissed. Her green eye caught in the candlelight and for a moment she looked chillingly snake-like.

Ragi dashed from the hut and returned a minute later with a rabbit in his hands. Its back legs were mangled and it struggled in pain, its eyes wide and terrified. Astrid stared at it in horror and the rabbit stared back at her with a similar expression.

'What did you do to it?' she shrieked.

'Nothing. It was a fox. Now, you're going to take it and heal it.'

'What? No, I can't!' Astrid said, shuffling backwards, but Ragi walked forwards and placed it in her arms.

'Help it. You know you can.'

Flicking her eyes between Ragi and the rabbit, she tried to stop her hands from shaking. She could feel the rabbit's pounding heartbeat beneath her fingers.

You're like me, aren't you? she thought. *You're frightened.*

Taking a deep breath, Astrid smoothed her hand over the rabbit's leg, closed her eyes and tried to picture a memory that would allow the magic to work.

It always started the same. She remembered running into the house crying and her mother racing down from the upper rooms. Arnbjörg had taken her in his arms and explained to Sylbil that she had fallen and cut her knee. Sylbil had taken her, sat her on her lap, and laid her hand over the graze on her knee. When Astrid had felt a warm sensation spreading outwards from the cut, she'd looked down to see that it had healed.

Astrid tried to stay with the memory, to make it stronger, but the faces of the elf and the dwarf filled her mind - the blonde haired dwarf with her cold grey eyes glaring at her through the space in her helmet... The tall, black haired elf with eyes as green as her mother's, his long sword drawn with blood running down the blade...

The rabbit began to struggle and the blue glow turned yellow. The wound on its leg, which had started to heal, suddenly shrivelled.

'Astrid, stop!' Ragi yelled, grabbing her wrists and lifting her hands away from the animal.

She looked down at it - at its eyes rolled back in his head, its breath coming in short, sharp pants. Tears slid down Astrid's cheeks and she curled her finger under its chin and gently stroked it.

'I'm sorry! I'm so sorry!' she whispered.

'Astrid, don't close your eyes this time,' Ragi ordered. 'Just look at it. Don't take your eyes from it.'

In the Aldwood she had always closed her eyes when she had healed something, but she couldn't do that anymore. The memories were always too strong.

She stroked the rabbit repeatedly, rhythmically, trying to calm it, and her hand began to glow again.

'It's ok, I'm going to help you,' Astrid whispered, as the rabbit's leg shuddered and the skin began to move. Its eyes relaxed and its heartbeat returned to a steady rhythm.

Smiling, Ragi watched, relieved to see the frustrated look on Astrid's face transform into a peaceful calm when the rabbit blinked, shook itself, jumped up, and darted out of the hut.

'I did it! I did it!' Astrid laughed, wrapping her arms around Ragi and hugging him.

'Astrid! Where are you?'

She pulled away from Ragi at the sound of Dag's voice in the distance.

'You'd better go,' he said. 'And you'd better take this.' He passed her a small bag of dried fruit.

Astrid ran out of the door, circling and avoiding Dag as he made his way towards Ragi's hut.

Ragi gathered the food he had put out for Astrid, quickly hid it in the cupboards behind him and stepped outside just as Dag appeared in the clearing.

'Have you seen Astrid?' Dag asked, clutching a doll in his hands, the crude stitches telling Ragi it was his friend's latest attempt at sewing.

'I sent her back to the house,' Ragi said, grabbing Dag's arm before he could turn back. 'No, Dag, we need to talk.'

'Talk? What about?'

'I've been teaching Astrid magic.'

In a split second, Dag's eyes turned from distracted to pitch black, the pupils expanding and swallowing his pale blue iris.

'You...WHAT?'

'You heard me,' Ragi said calmly, completely unphased. 'And you need to teach her how to fight, Dag.'

'I will *not* teach her how to fight! She's just a child!'

'No, she is not! Her childhood ended a year ago with her parents' deaths. She's a lost girl looking for some kind of control, and right now, she thinks it's magic.'

'She can't use it! She's too angry! She can't even heal!'

'She did today,' Ragi said, smiling.

Dag raised his eyebrows. 'She did?'

'Yes. We've been trying for a few weeks now, and today she managed it.'

Dag said nothing, but his mouth turned up into a small smile. As he moved to leave, Ragi tugged him back again.

'Dag, you need to take this seriously. One day she will leave, and when she does she will need to learn to protect herself. Please, teach her to fight.'

'I can't!'

'Then find someone who will!' Ragi snapped, his voice a terrifying bark, coarse and guttural. 'She needs it!'

Ragi stormed back into his hut and Dag stared after him for a few moments before looking down at the doll. As he headed back home, Ragi's words echoed in his head.

* * *

'I made this for you,' Dag said, forcing a smile and passing Astrid the doll. His brow was furrowed into a worried knot.

'Thank you,' she whispered, taking the doll and peering down at it. She absently picked at its hair, made from hundreds of thick black threads crudely tied into the doll's cloth head. It had one green bead for the right eye and a grey bead for the left, the thread from the left eye loosening and hanging down across its face.

Dag watched as Astrid ran her hands over it. Her eyes slowly glazed over and her mouth pressed itself into a tight line as she crushed one of its arms in her hand. A faint yellow glow appeared around her fingers and smoke rose from the fabric.

'Astrid!' Dag shouted.

Astrid jumped. 'Sorry!' she said, and placed the doll on the table then held her hands tightly in her lap. She bowed her head, avoiding eye contact with Dag.

'I'm going to teach you to fight,' he finally said, and Astrid looked up at him in shock, sure she had heard wrong.

'What?'

'I have a...friend, he can teach you to fight,' Dag said slowly. 'I'll get him to come here if you promise me one thing.'

'What?' Astrid asked excitedly, her eyes lighting up.

'You must promise me you will not learn magic from anyone else except me,' Dag said firmly. 'I will teach you magic when I think you are ready, but you must not learn from Ragi or anyone else.'

For a moment Astrid said nothing. She peered down at her hand, the centre of her palm a dim glow. Closing it, she looked up at Dag, her mind made up. She nodded and Dag smiled.

'I'm not trying to be cruel, goldheart,' he said softly, moving around the table and sitting down next to her. Astrid flinched slightly as he moved his arm around her shoulders, but she didn't pull away.

She couldn't explain why, but over recent weeks she had started to develop an irrational fear of being touched, yet all the while being desperate for human interaction. She craved it, yet feared it. Each time Dag held her hand or hugged her, she couldn't stop herself from shivering, from flinching, and Dag, hurt by her reaction, had become more and more distant, unsure of how to react.

More than anything else, Astrid wanted to tell him it wasn't his fault. She didn't know why she did it, but she had no control over it. And no matter how much she tried to force herself to tell Dag that it wasn't because of him, she could never find the courage. She was afraid that if she did, he would treat her differently. It was illogical, but she couldn't help it. At times it felt as if she was paralysed, and she had an overwhelming dread that one day Dag would decide he no longer wanted to care for her.

'I'm old, goldheart,' Dag said quietly, stroking her head. 'I've seen magic turn good people into monsters. I don't want that to happen to you.'

'I'm not a monster,' Astrid whispered.

'Of course not, goldheart!' Dag replied. 'I know that, but you're afraid and angry, and magic has a way of taking that and using it to change people. I don't want it to do that to you.'

'I want to kill them,' Astrid said, turning and looking up at Dag. 'I want to kill those people!'

'I know. But they can't hurt you. They'll never be able to hurt you.'

'Yes they can! What if they come back?'

Taking a moment to think about what he was going to say, Dag took her hands in his.

Astrid, you know the black cloud that killed the elf?' he said, and Astrid nodded. 'That was them.'

'Them?' Astrid asked, confused.

'Your parents, goldheart. The cloud was your parents. They...sacrificed themselves to protect you.'

Angry tears filled Astrid's eyes. 'No! I saw the dagger! *They* killed them!'

'Yes they did!' Dag said quickly. But they would have killed you, too. Your mother had a dagger, it's called an Atibiw. It's very old magic. Very powerful. If two people offer up their lives to protect a third person, it protects them. They gave their lives to protect you! They loved you!'

Astrid said nothing, but then a strangled cry escaped from her mouth. Confusion and horror spread across her face. 'So *I* killed them?'

'No! No, goldheart! *They* killed them! But your parents *chose* to die so that they could still protect you!'

Astrid stood up and backed away from Dag, stumbling over her feet. She ran out of the house and into the forest, not caring where she was going, just so long as she was moving. The branches and leaves whipped past her, scratching at her arms and her face, but she didn't care. She tripped several times and fell to her knees as her feet got tangled in the long grass, but she picked herself up and continued to run. Her head felt as if it was detached from her body and spinning wildly, as a series of images flashed through her mind over and again: Sylbil and Arnbjörg lying on the ground, their eyes blank, the glow behind them gone, the dagger they had killed themselves with still between them, the double ended blade embedded in their hearts.

I did that! I did that! They're dead...because of me!

Without warning, almost like she was a spectator watching herself from a distance, Astrid felt her mouth open and a guttural scream rose from her throat. She closed her eyes and released all the rage she felt inside her. She skidded to a stop and clenched her fists as hard as she could. Her scream rose higher and higher until it was a piercing, hair-raising shriek. The air around her tingled and her skin crackled with magic. Leaves on the ground shrivelled and then burst into blue and yellow flames. A circle of fire spread out around her and consumed every plant and animal in its path.

A pheasant that had been hiding underneath a nearby bush screeched as it burst into flames. It ran, beating its wings in a panic, the flames ripping across it until it fell to the ground, twitching in pain. The smell of burning flesh filled Astrid's nostrils and she unclenched her fists and stared around her in horror.

Everything around her was burnt to a crisp. Two pine trees crackled loudly as the bark cracked and snapped from the heat. The burnt grass sizzled and popped, the bugs and insects that had lived in the leaves frying before they exploded. There was a ring of death around her; almost nothing had survived her rampage.

The pheasant twitched, clawing at the dirt, and Astrid ran to it and picked it up. Its feathers had burnt away exposing the pink, throbbing skin underneath.

'I'm sorry! I'm so sorry!' Astrid gasped. She closed her eyes but Ragi's voice echoed in her head. *Keep them open, goldheart!* Looking down at it, she moved her hand over the bird, concentrating, calling up her memory, willing it to live. The skin puckered beneath her fingertips and then slowly regenerated, inch by inch, under her unblinking stare. Astrid smiled as the skin healed completely and she carefully placed the bird back down on the burnt ground. The bird didn't move and its eyes were fixed in an agonised stare.

'Move...I've healed you!' Astrid whispered, poking the bird gently, but it didn't flinch.

She picked it up and shook it, its body floppy and heavy in her hands. Astrid ran her fingers over the bird's chest but couldn't feel a heartbeat. Dropping it on the floor, she crawled away in horror as its healed feathers began to smoke then burn, the flames spreading across them in small ripples. The inside of its body was charred, and Astrid realised she had only managed to heal the outside for just a few moments. Dag's voice rang in her head: *'you're afraid and angry, and magic has a way of taking that and using it to change people.'*

Scrambling to her feet, her knees covered in ash, Astrid gazed down at her hands in horror before glancing around and noticing the other animals that had been caught in the fire ring. Several mice, fixed in their last stance, had been carbonised in seconds.

Suddenly, Astrid felt a horrible pain, and looked to see the skin on her right hand blackening. A cold wave spread over her from the back of her head and she slumped to the ground.

* * *

'Dag? Dag?'

For a few seconds Astrid couldn't see anything. Her eyes were blurry and a horrible itchiness crawled over her right hand. Moving to scratch it, she realised it was wrapped in layers of thick bandages.

'Dag!' Astrid screamed, but heard nothing. Fear washed over her. Where was he? Had he abandoned her? 'DAG!'

'What? What's the matter, goldheart?' he said, appearing at the top of the staircase.

'I thought you'd gone!' Astrid said, her heart pounding in her chest.

'Gone?'

'I thought you'd left me.'

'Don't be silly! I wouldn't ever do that!' He perched on the edge of the mattress and softly stroked her head. For the first time in weeks Astrid was still, not shivering at his touch, but instead she leant her head against him and closed her eyes.

'I won't use magic again, Dag,' Astrid whispered, the fogginess in front of her eyes clearing away. She raised her hand and stared at it. The tips of her fingers were shrivelled and burnt, with a patchwork of red and pink skin underneath the charring.

Dag said nothing. He continued to hold her tightly, stroking her head, and rocked her in his arms. He was happy that she finally understood why he feared magic, but broken-hearted that it had taken such a terrible incident to show her.

'I'm going to stay till you get better and then I'm going to have to leave for a few weeks.'

'What? Why?' Astrid asked, holding him tighter.

'My friend...the one who can teach you how to fight. I'm going to find him.'

'Can't you teach me?'

'I'm too old. Skad will be able to teach you much better,' Dag said. He smiled, amused at the thought of it.

'Skad?'

'Yes, Skad. He's a dwarf.'

'A dwarf...like Faðir?'

'Skad is not like Arnbjörg, goldheart,' Dag said quickly, knowing she would only be disappointed if she expected some kind of reincarnation of her father.

'Nobody is like Faðir,' Astrid said sadly.

'No, nobody,' Dag agreed.

'Can I come with you?'

'No, it's better you stay here. Ragi will take care of you.'

'Ok,' Astrid said finally, forcing herself not to panic at the idea of Dag leaving her. *At least Ragi can cook,* she thought.

* * *

Gripping her hands together tightly, Astrid watched as Dag strode away from the house. The bandages had been removed the previous day but she was still sore, and the skin smarted as she pressed it tightly, using the pain to distract herself from the irrational fear that she would never see Dag again.

Ragi took her hand in his, his clammy skin slightly sticky at the touch.

'Don't do that, you'll hurt yourself!'

'It's helps,' Astrid whispered back.

'Come on. Let's make some food that actually tastes good,' Ragi said, smiling. Astrid had gotten used to his snarl-like smiles now, and she followed him into the house.

Ragi blew gently across his palm and several tongues of fire rippled on his fingertips and fell into the fireplace, igniting the wood. Astrid rubbed her hands nervously and watched as the fire licked its way up the wood and consumed it.

'Astrid?' Ragi asked, recognising the distant look in her eyes. She turned to him, forcing a smile. 'What do you want to cook?'

'I'm not very hungry.'

'Don't lie!' Ragi laughed and hopped onto the sideboard to reach one of the top shelves. 'I've tasted shit with more flavour than Dag's food!'

Chuckling, Astrid walked up to the counter and took the jars from him as he passed them down to her.

She liked Ragi; he made her feel comfortable. Not that Dag made her feel nervous, but he always looked at her like she was broken, and she was tired of feeling that way. Even if it was a lie, she wanted people to look at her like she was strong. Each pitying glance from Dag just reminded her of what had happened. With Ragi she could forget.

For the next few hours they did nothing but cook. Astrid dipped her fingers into everything and almost ate the dough before Ragi had even had a chance to put it into the small stone oven. He pretended to be annoyed at her, but then took a scoopful himself as Astrid laughed happily.

With the small berry pies cooking in the oven and the warm, sweet aroma filling the house, it felt all too familiar to Astrid. Her smile suddenly disappeared as she remembered exactly what it reminded her of. Home.

'Mātīr used to make those,' Astrid said.

'Well...mine will taste just as good,' Ragi said simply, clambering up onto the sideboard and asking her to pass him the nearly empty flour jars.

'How long will it take for Dag to come back?'

'Sick of me already are you?' Ragi joked, grinning down at her.

'No!' Astrid laughed, before a worried look crossed her face. 'I'm just nervous.'

'Don't be! Now let's practice some more Echaim. Tell me: 'Dag's cooking tastes like shit!''

'I can't say it right. It hurts my throat to speak it.'

'That's because you're used to a language where you chew when you speak.'

'I don't!'

'Yes you do! All your words are at the front of your mouth.' Ragi grinned, making a chewing motion with his hand and laughed at her.

Taking a deep breath, Astrid tried to translate what he had said, the words forming so far back in her throat it almost hurt. It was like she was trying to sing in a range which was not natural to her; it grated on her vocal chords.

'You speak too softly. If I heard someone talk like that I would think I couldn't trust them.'

Trying again, Astrid argued with him in his native tongue, at times stopping and racking her brain for the words she needed. Ragi smiled as she became more and more comfortable with the guttural language.

'You're getting better. You just need to practice more.'

'Why is it so hard to speak?' Astrid asked, rubbing at her throat. 'I don't find Mál or Axetī hard. They're easy!'

'They're easy because you're used to them. And they only have one level. I've only taught you the most basic form of Echaim.'

'What?' Astrid gasped, dismayed. Even though she found it hard to speak, she had thought that she was starting to master the language. The realisation that there were still several more dialects to learn made her feel like giving up all together.

'It's a mixture of many languages. Different regions speak different mixtures. Beziickt is the most common.'

'Then why doesn't everyone speak it?' she asked, confused.

'It's a common dialect. The higher the level of language, the more important your rank. It's hard to change rank because people can hear your Beziickt accent. Very few people can master the accents perfectly.'

'Why do people hate goblins?' Astrid asked. She sat down on the floor and looked up to the sideboard where he sat cross-legged on the top.

'Many of us are raiders, so it's not surprising. I would hate us too if I was attacked by goblins.'

'You're not all raiders?'

'No. There are two tribes in the north, two big cities. But they're closed off to the rest of the tribes. Most of the goblins hate them. Think they're arrogant.'

'Are they?'

'No. They're just trying to protect themselves. If they let all the other tribes in, there would be civil war. We look the same but our way of life is too different. It would be like trying to mix oil with water.'

'What are they called?' Astrid asked, resting her head on her hand and listening, fascinated. At first she'd just wanted to distract Ragi from making her speak Beziickt, but now she wanted to know more about his people.

'What are what called?'

'The cities!'

'Oh. One is called Lig and the other Dragh,' Ragi replied, his voice switching to a much harsher tone as he pronounced the names. Astrid repeated the names after him, her tone of voice much softer. Ragi insisted she repeat them again until she could mimic him perfectly.

'What do they speak?'

'I'm not sure, but if I had to guess it would be Xill, or Gurght.'

'Is it hard to learn those?'

'Yes, but they're better. More words, easier to say exactly what you mean.'

'Can you speak them?'

'No, my mother did. I just never understood it.'

'Where is your mother?' Astrid asked, and a pained look crossed Ragi's face.

'I don't know. She re-married,' Ragi spat, and jumped down from the sideboard and opened the oven, cursing as he saw the tops of the small pies were burnt. Astrid wondered if he was more annoyed about the pies or her question.

'I'm sorry I asked,' she said.

Ragi pulled the pies from the oven. 'Well, tell me these are better that that shit Dag cooks, and I'll forgive you,' he said, placing the hot tray down on the floor to cool.

Astrid gazed at them longingly. 'Can I have one now?'

'No. They're far too hot. Patience, Astrid, is a virtue.'

She waited an agonising fifteen minutes before finally, Ragi plucked a pie from the tray and handed it to her. The hot crust warmed her hand and she held it there for a moment before taking a large bite. The berries inside burst into her mouth as her teeth pressed down through the pastry, the sweetness of them mixing perfectly with the buttery taste of the crust. She wolfed down the pie in seconds, accidently spilling some of the sticky berry juice on her tunic and staining it with bright red streaks.

'Good then?' He passed her another one, and this time Astrid ate it slowly, savouring the taste.

'It's delicious!' she mumbled through her full mouth, crumbs falling from her lips in her attempt to speak.

'Good! Let's cook some more! We only have a few weeks, and Dag's cooking is making you far too skinny.'

The Outlander

Knud could tell Jarl was nervous. With his jaw clenched and his body rigid, Jarl's eyes darted around the room like a restless fly. He was wary; on his guard.

'Skad said the Outlander would be here,' Knud said. 'We don't have to wait up. You should sleep.' He hoped Jarl would finally admit how tired he was and go to bed, and leave him to enjoy himself without being supervised.

'You're right. We don't have to wait up, but I'm going to. You, however, can sleep,' Jarl replied curtly, not even turning to look at Knud, his eyes still dancing around the lively room. His sword, hidden beneath the table, was propped between his legs, ready to be drawn at a moment's notice. The room bustled with all sorts of people, mainly dwarves and humans, but a few elves were scattered about. Jarl watched the elves in particular, with more intensity than the rest.

Halvard laughed as Knud protested, as usual his attempts at trying to convince Jarl to do something backfiring.

'But I'm not tired! I want to meet her!'

'Go!' Jarl said firmly.

'But I wanted to-' Knud began.

'Go to bed...now!' he snapped. 'You can meet the Outlander tomorrow.'

Hanging his head, Knud trudged over to the stairs and reluctantly climbed them, hoping that if he made himself look pitiful enough, Jarl would change his mind. He didn't.

Jarl shook his head and took a quick sip of his ale, his eyes still focused on what was happening around him. When an older man walked towards their table, his hair scraped into several tightly plaited braids with sharp, silver tips attached to the ends of them, Jarl put down his flask. Halvard recognised him from Jarl's description. It was Skad.

Skad placed his large flask of ale on the table, pulled out a chair and sat down awkwardly in his heavily embossed leather armour.

'Where is she?' Jarl asked, not even waiting for Skad to have a sip of his ale. Skad rolled his eyes and took a long drink before lowering the wooden flask to the table.

'Jarl Vǫrn?' a soft voice asked, and Jarl turned to see a woman of about his height standing beside him. A strong scent of jasmine surrounded her and her face was hidden beneath a black veil, only her eyes exposed. The veil hung down from her nose and wound around her neck like a scarf. He suspected it was even a part of the sash that was wrapped around her waist, too.

Her eyes! Jarl couldn't help but let a look of surprise cross his face as he saw them. One eye, her right, a piercing bright green. The other, a silver grey. Her lashes were thick and black, which made them stand out all the more. Her right hand was covered in tattoos of white thorn tendrils and small black roses, spreading upwards from her fingertips. The skin beneath was burnt and wrinkled, the tattoos almost, but not quite, hiding it.

Jarl stood up, eyeing her up and down, surprised that she had managed to sneak up to their table without him noticing, but still doubtful that a human woman was strong enough to be able to guide them. Especially such a short human woman! Why, if he hadn't known better, he would have said she was a dwarf! She certainly had the height of one. Unlike the humans, her skin was not a deep ebony black, but an almost ghostly pale. It seemed to shimmer against the veil that concealed her face.

Jarl didn't know what to think. He had heard of pale humans in the far north of Ammasteinn in the ice lands, but it seemed strange that one of them would travel this far.

Her clothing was a strange mixture of dwarf and human, with what he suspected was elven influences.

Her boots, a black leather, were embossed with wave patterns. Her trousers were wide and baggy, except for the parts that reached her boots, where they were tightly bandaged down under them. Her tunic was the same - baggy everywhere except for where the sleeves reached her hands, and where the bottom hem reached the black sash around her waist. Black bandages served a little like gloves, covering her hands to her knuckles.

But the strangest thing was the large wolf-skin cloak she wore over her shoulders, the wolf's head still attached and frighteningly lifelike, its head resting over hers like a hood and staring down at him. The skin was an unusual pattern of black stripes over a reddish- brown fur.

'Where are you from?' Jarl asked finally, sitting down and expecting her to do the same.

'Does that matter?' she replied, still standing and watching him as intently as he was watching her.

'No. But I would like to know more about the person I am trusting my nephew's life with.'

'If you know of me, then you know someone who has travelled with me. Their recommendation should be enough,' the Outlander replied calmly.

'You'd think it would be,' Skad replied, glaring at Jarl, annoyed that the dwarf who was a good forty-five years' younger than he was doubting the Outlander and essentially doubting him.

'I do not mean any disrespect,' Jarl said quickly, realising he had offended Skad. 'But this is my nephew!'

'Since Skad will be coming too, I doubt you will have to worry,' the Outlander replied, her voice emotionless. Jarl had the distinct impression she was repressing a strong urge to let anger seep into her voice, and for the briefest of moments her eyes flashed.

'Yes I am going with you,' Skad said as Jarl threw him a confused look. Barely able to hide the dismay on his face, he racked his brains to think of a way to dissuade the dwarf from joining them.

'Are you the Outlander?' Knud said behind him, interrupting his thoughts. Jarl turned swiftly around and glared at him, but Knud ignored him and darted over to the Outlander and looked up at her with fascination.

'Are you the Outlander?' he repeated.

Jarl watched her curiously as she stepped back a little, a strong flash of emotion crossing her eyes for a second before she cleared her throat and turned to Jarl.

'This is the boy?' she asked, and Jarl and Halvard nodded.

'I'm Knud!'

'Outlander.'

'That can't be your real name. Is it?'

'It's what you can call me,' she replied firmly, turning back to Jarl. 'I'm assuming you want to leave as soon as possible?'

'Yes.'

'Then meet me at dawn by the east gate.'

Before Jarl could reply, she turned and left, easily weaving through the crowded room and slipping out of the door. Knud faced his uncle, ready for the severe telling off he was sure was coming. But to his surprise, Jarl wasn't even looking at him. His eyes were fixed on the door of the inn, a confused look on his face.

'Don't pay her any Heit,' Skad said as he drank the last dregs of ale in his flask. 'She won't want them.'

'What? Why wouldn't she?' Jarl asked, now wary. Nobody in their right mind would refuse to be paid in Heit. It was valuable, not just as money but as a pass to trade with any dwarf. To own Heit meant you were trustworthy. It was a currency that was rarely used but priceless to human merchants.

'Astrid won't use them. She prefers gold coins or human money,' Skad said firmly, calling for the barmaid to refill his flask.

'Her name is Astrid?' Knud interrupted, looking like he was in half a mind to rush after her and ask her every question under the sun.

'Yes it is. Astrid Dagmar.'

'Dagmar? Like the warlock?' Knud said excitedly.

'Yes...like the warlock. She's his daughter,' Skad replied. 'But do not call her Astrid under any circumstances! Call her Outlander, or woman, if that is too hard for you to remember,' Skad said, getting up to go.

'Why?' Jarl and Knud asked simultaneously.

'Because I said so!' Skad snapped, glaring at them.

As soon as Skad was out of earshot, Jarl swore under his breath. Halvard shook his head.

'I knew this journey wasn't going to be easy, but now I know it will be terrible,' Halvard grumbled. Knud looked at him.

'Why will it be terrible?' he asked.

'Knud, go away!' Jarl snapped, and he quickly realised his uncle was not in the mood to be argued with. He scuttled off to the far side of the room.

Halvard ordered three new flasks of ale, paying the barmaid extra to bring them as quickly as possible.

'Knud is not drinking that!' Jarl said, as Halvard pushed two of the flasks towards him.

'They are both for you,' Halvard clarified, and Jarl nodded in thanks. He lifted one of them to his mouth and took a large gulp before venting his frustration.

'There has to be a way for him to not come.'

'It would be safer if he did, though.'

'I think I'd rather face goblins that have to deal with that miserable git.'

'You never did say why you hated him so much.'

'He's just miserable. An old, miserable man.'

Halvard took several large sips of his ale and Jarl growled to himself before doing the same.

'I hope I won't regret this,' he said , slamming his ale firmly down on the table and looking up at Halvard as if expecting him to say something.

'Jarl, you've thought this through a hundred times. It's too late to turn back now!'

'I should just leave Bjargtre and go to live in the human lands with Knud. Leave all the politics and scheming behind.'

Halvard couldn't help bursting into laugher at such a ridiculous suggestion. 'You would go mad! You'd miss Bjargtre!'

'I'd miss Vǫrn hall and Holmvé, but Bjargtre? No, I think I'd be happy without it.'

'You're mad!' Halvard snapped back, unsettled by Jarl's confession. 'Knud wouldn't like it.'

'He'd love it!' Jarl laughed. 'So many new people and places to see!'

'Can you stop talking about it?' Halvard said, practically shouting. 'It's not normal to want to leave! Dwarves should live with dwarves!' He cleared his throat. 'Look, I'm not Knute. I don't know what to say to you, but you're not wrong about Ulf.'

'You're just saying that so I'll shut up.'

'Maybe!' Halvard grinned, the motion looking slightly alien on his face. 'But you know you're not wrong. So finish your drink and get some sleep. We're going to have to get up early tomorrow.'

'I know...more nights on the road,' Jarl groaned, moving onto his second flask of ale. The taste was quite disgusting but the motion of drinking calmed him. 'I'm going to have no back left by the end of this.'

'You'll be lucky to be alive at the end of this,' Halvard muttered.

'Always the optimist,' Jarl retaliated, resting his head against his hand and trying not to dwell on the fears circling his head like crows.

*　*　*

The air was cold, nipping at any exposed skin. Winter had just passed but the weather was unpredictable as was often the case in early Spring. Only yesterday, the sun had been shining brightly, not so much as a single cloud in the sky. But by the looks of the sky today, snow looked imminent, the temperature having dropped at an alarming rate. There was frost on the windows of the inn, a stark contrast to the warm yellow glow emanating from within.

Knud rubbed his hands together and already wished he had slept when Jarl had told him to, feeling so much colder than he should have from tiredness.

'Worn-out?' Jarl asked, and Knud bowed his head and nodded. 'Well...you should have gone to bed when I told you to,' he went on, his voice softening when he saw the apologetic look on Knud's face. 'Don't worry. You can sleep on the pony.'

'We're taking ponies?' Knud said, surprised.

'Yes. Just to the Salt Monasteries, but after that we travel on foot,' Halvard replied from behind him.

'Why are we walking after the Salt Monasteries? Won't that be slower?'

'We need to be able to hide easily; the ponies are too large. And any Dip would catch their scent instantly.'

'Wouldn't they smell you first?' Knud asked Halvard, not realising at first how his question had sounded. He quickly apologised when Halvard glared at him, and Jarl laughed.

'Who's the fifth pony for?' Skad asked, strolling out from the inn. He rubbed his hands together as the cold hit him and pulled his cloak tightly around his shoulders.

'It's for Astrid,' Knud replied cheerfully. Skad flashed him a terrifying glare, and Knud recoiled.

'DO NOT CALL HER THAT!' Skad hissed. 'In fact, it's better if you don't talk to her at all. Take the pony back. She won't ride it,' he growled, pulling out rock salt from one of his pockets and popping a clump of it in his mouth.

'What's she going to do? Run alongside us?' Halvard jested.

'Yes,' Skad snapped back. 'Knud, find out if you can sell the pony back to the innkeeper. We won't need it.'

'I'll take it,' Jarl said quickly, grabbing the reins from Knud and leading the pony gently back around the inn until he reached the stables.

The stable boy was fast asleep by the gate, a thick woolen cloak pulled around him, his breath turning to mist from the cold. Gently waking him, Jarl asked if he could sell him back the pony. The stable boy agreed and paid him back the money before opening the gate and leading it back to its stall, too tired to haggle as he would normally have done. He was sure that the innkeeper would make him pay for his being so quick to agree, but he didn't care. Right now all he wanted was to sleep, and for the infernal headache the previous night's ales had given him to disappear.

Turning to leave, Jarl spotted Astrid on the opposite side of the street, emerging from an inksmith's shop. A tattoo-covered human walked out with her and smiled at her as she covered her arm with a bandage.

Jarl, for a brief moment, caught a glimpse of the extensive black and white rose tattoos - starting at her fingertips and extending all the way up around her arm and, he suspected, all the way to her shoulder. But that wasn't what shocked him. Tattoos were commonplace for warriors in the dwarf culture, in fact it was expected for a dwarf to get a commemorative tattoo after important life events or great victories. No; what shocked him were the scars.

Beneath and above every tattoo were hundreds of scars, slices and tears in her skin. Some of them recent, some of them, he guessed, at least thirty years old. He could see the distinctive burn-like marks of Dip wolf claw on her skin, ugly scars brought about by their poisonous talons.

Standing on her toes, Astrid hugged the human inksmith and then readjusted the veil over her face.

'When you come back, I'll finish off the thorns for you,' he said, smiling at her.

'Hopefully!' Astrid replied, rolling down her sleeve. She tightened the cuff and pulled on her gloves, the tips having been cut off so her fingertips were exposed. 'See you in a few months, Aaren.'

'Be safe,' Aaren said, a worried look on his face, and Astrid laughed, waving him away.

Seeing her turn to walk towards the inn, Jarl quickly turned away, his hood covering his face, and waited for her to pass before making his way to where the others were waiting.

Skad Löfgren

37 years ago...

Astrid stood in the doorway and swept the dirt out onto the porch. The birds, realising how much of the pile was composed of crumbs and tidbits of food, swooped down and started to peck at the pile as it settled on the ground. Astrid turned back to the house, determined to attempt one last sweep before heading back to bed.

It had been almost two months since Dag had left, and each night she had slept with Arnbjörg's hammer axe and Sylbil's bow held tightly to her chest.

Ragi had arrived each morning and had left after dark, happy for Astrid to do whatever it was she wanted. She'd enjoyed the novelty of it, choosing each day's activities. Ragi had even taken her out to hunt. Her quick elven reflexes were much faster than his, and after a while, Ragi had not even bothered to bring his own bow and arrows, but instead had let Astrid take the lead. He had simply tagged along for company. She barely ever missed, nearly every shot hitting the target right between the eyes, killing it instantly and painlessly.

Her Echaim, or rather her Beziickt, had improved greatly. She had even started to dream in the new language, something that curiously made her nightmares stay away. The haunting of her parents' deaths were strongly associated with Mál and Axetī, but Beziickt was a language that had no painful memories attached to it, and her dreams were no more frightening than arguing with Ragi over pronunciations. At first she had found the language coarse and ugly, but she was starting to appreciate its unique beauty; its strong, decisive sound.

Astrid propped the broom against the wall and sat cross-legged on the porch. The early morning birds chirped cheerfully in the branches, the weak wind blowing through the trees not yet strong enough to shift the light morning fog. The sun was little more than a hazy, yellow orb in the sky, but it was enough for Astrid to feel its presence.

She felt content. Happy was too strong a word, she doubted she would ever be blissfully happy again like she had been in the Aldwood, but she didn't feel so afraid. Life here in the Red Mountains had given her a small measure of peace, and she was hugely grateful for it.

Glancing down at the birds, she noticed one of them had a clubbed foot, two of its toes broken and curled in on each other, the skin an off-grey colour. It hobbled along, trying to get to the crumbs on the floor, but the other birds pushed it away and created a wall between it and the food.

Holding out her hand, Astrid fixed her eyes on the bird, making sure to keep her focus only on its leg. The bird turned and looked up at her as if hypnotised, then slowly hopped towards her and leapt up into her outstretched hand.

Astrid's eyes flickered as she focused her energy into the palm of her hand. Within moments, the bird's toes slowly curled out and the skin returned to a healthy pink. It sat for a while and then leapt off her hand and barged its way through the flock, screeching at the other birds loudly. Its newly healed foot stood firmly over the crumbs and the other birds stepped back, allowing it to eat. Astrid smiled at her work.

She thought of her parents, and wondered how proud of her they would have been at having learned so much since they had gone. She closed her eyes and tried to conjure up their faces in her mind.

In the Aldwood, every day had seemed to blur into the next; there were no months or days. Only seasons. But each Autumn her parents would pick an ideal day for her to have a birthday and wake her up early in the morning with an abundance of hand- made gifts.

Like a cold shower of water being thrown over her, Astrid realised again, to her horror, that their faces were blurred in her memory; the faces she knew better than her own smudged in her mind's eye. The more she tried to trace over their features, the more distorted they became. Only the outline of their faces remained defined.

Astrid stumbled to her feet and ran indoors. She grabbed one of the cold, burnt embers in the fireplace and raced up the stairs to her room, fell to her knees and began scrawling on the floor in a panic. Black charcoal covered her hands and flew across the floor, but she didn't care; her only focus was on remembering. She started first with her mother's face before moving on to her father's, the crude drawings only making her memory of them more unclear. Astrid tried again and again to re-draw them, and the floor was soon covered in dozens of failed attempts, not even a single one being close to how she knew their faces to look. She wore the stick of charcoal down to a stub before finally tossing it away.

She pulled her hands and knees to her chest, closed her eyes and tried with all her might to remember them, every single memory that she cherished replaying in her mind in an attempt to grasp a clear image.

She recalled helping Sylbil repair the thatched roof in the upper rooms. The feel of the straw, and how Sylbil's hands had moved when she was tying together thatching was clear to her, but again, when she tried to look up at her mother's face, it was a blank; a painting with the face smudged. Even their voices were a strange muddle of sounds.

Astrid crawled to her bed and curled up beneath her blanket, the panic washing over her. She closed her eyes and inhaled, the familiar but weakening smell calming her. Slowly her heart stopped pounding and the darkness closed in, and she drifted off to sleep in the hope that they would visit her in her dreams.

* * *

With a loud bang, the door to the house was kicked open. Astrid awoke with a start, and hearing someone stumbling through and dropping something large and heavy on the floor downstairs, she got up.

With her blanket wrapped around her like a cape, Astrid dashed over to the stairs, a smile on her face, expecting to see Dag in the doorway. But the stranger she looked down upon wasn't Dag, and when he lifted his head and their eyes met, they both stepped back in shock.

'Who are you?' Astrid asked firmly.

'Skad Löfgren!' The dwarf replied indignantly, as if she should already know exactly who he was.

Astrid felt a sudden pang of pain as she noticed his eyes, grey like her father's. Instantly, she felt a kinship to the strange dwarf and the panic she had felt earlier subsided.

He wasn't a very tall dwarf, in fact from what Astrid remembered he was probably an inch or two shorter than her father. But unlike her father, Skad did not have a particularly warm or kind look to him, in fact quite the opposite. Deep frown lines were etched into his forehead and mouth, undoubtedly from years of wearing a permanent scowl on his face.

His clothes were covered by light armour; hundreds of small metal square plates held together by leather straps.

Dag appeared in the doorway, and spotting Astrid at the top of the stairs, he grinned at her.

'Did you miss me goldheart?' he said, and Astrid flew down the stairs and fell into his arms, hugging him tightly. Neither of them noticed the look of disgust on Skad's face as he saw her pointed, elven ears.

'Skad, this is Astrid,' Dag said, letting her go.

'Just Astrid?' he asked, with the faintest tone of repulsion in his voice.

'Astrid Hvass Jīkkā,' Dag said firmly, his face hardened. Skad widened his eyes and stared at him disbelievingly.

'Hvass?'

'Yes, Hvass.'

'Father?'

'Arnbjörg Hvass.'

Astrid looked up at Skad curiously as he stared at her.

'Mother?'

'Sylbil Jīkkā,' Dag replied, lowering his voice slightly in the hope it would lesson Skad's reaction.

'Sylbil Jīkkā! Tyr Jīkkā's sister?'

'Yes,' Dag replied, nodding.

'Tyr? Who's he?' Astrid asked.

'Nobody, goldheart,' Dag said quickly. He reached into his pocket and pulled out a small wooden box covered in embossed leather, a pattern of thistles and jasmine etched into it, and passed it to her. Astrid flicked the bronze clasp at the front and a broad smile spread across her face as she saw a beautiful bottle inside, the glass a foggy shade of light green. A simple cork top prevented the liquid inside from escaping.

'What is it?' Astrid asked.

'Open it and see!'

She carefully popped the cork off the top, and as a powerful aroma of jasmine filled the room, Astrid's mind flooded with a rush of memories. A clear image of Sylbil appeared in her head: her eyes, her smile, the flowers woven into her hair. Tears filled Astrid's eyes and she blinked, forcing them back.

'Thank you!' she whispered, carefully closing the bottle, then hugged Dag tightly before grabbing another stick of charcoal from the fireplace and rushing upstairs to her room.

With the bottle of oil in her left hand, her right hand drew as fast as it could, the image in her mind already starting to fade.

Finally, Astrid sat back and looked down at the finished drawing with a contented smile, relief washing over her. The final drawing was as clear as crystal, every curve and slant of their faces perfect.

'Hello!' she whispered.

* * *

'What was Bjargtre like?' Astrid asked, trying to use the conversation to distract Dag so she could slip the pie, piece by piece, into her pocket. She planned to ask to leave the table in the next few minutes and dispose of it in the forest, far enough away for the animals to not draw attention to themselves as they ate it. *If* they ate it.

The two months Dag had spent away had somehow made his cooking even worse, if that was possible. The crust of the pie was almost completely black and the inside only half cooked. It was all Astrid could do to not throw up as she swallowed the first few chunks.

'You've never been?' Skad interrupted.

'No,' Astrid replied. 'I've never seen a city.'

'That's probably wise.'

'Why?'

'Because you'd probably get murdered!' Skad replied. Dag slammed his hands down on the table and they glowed perilously, making Astrid sit back in her chair. Skad didn't flinch.

'You can't lie to her all her life, Dag!' he growled. 'She has to know.'

'Know what?' Astrid said. She had never seen Dag look this angry. The air around him seemed to darken and the air crackled with magic, making the hairs on her arms stand up.

'Nothing, goldheart,' he said. 'You don't need to know anything.'

Skad knew better than to cross the old warlock, even though he was itching to say what was on his mind.

'Know what!' Astrid repeated, fixing her eyes on Dag till the warlock turned to look at her. 'What is it Mossi?'

'Nothing! Go outside for a moment,' Dag said firmly, and Astrid rose from her chair and sauntered outside, closing the door behind her.

As soon as she was outside, she dashed around the side of the house, emptying her pocket along the way. The soggy clumps of pie fell to the ground, and she ran up to the tree that grew alongside her bedroom, kicked off her shoes and climbed it with the ease of a squirrel. She pulled away some of the loose thatch and crawled in through the small hole she had made, into her room, sliding forward on the ground until she was as close to the stairs as she could be without being spotted.

'Honestly, what did they think would happen?' Skad hissed at Dag. 'I'm not saying it's right, but it's what people do!'

'She doesn't need to know that!'

'She will one day! She's a Blanda blóð! It's only-'

'Don't...EVER...use that word around me!' Dag warned.

'So...you just want me to pretend to teach her how to fight then? Is that it?'

'No. I want you to teach her how to fight properly.'

'So, now I'm reduced to teaching an elf. If I'd known that was how you were going to insist I pay my debt, I might have let those human raiders kill me instead.'

'I'll kill you myself if you mistreat her!'

'Is that a threat?' Skad stood up and glared at him, his hand hovering over the heavy sword that hung from his belt. Astrid watched, terrified, from the top of the staircase.

'Yes,' Dag replied simply, the wood of the table beneath his hands blackening and smouldering.

'How long do you expect me to stay here till I've paid my debt?'

'Till Astrid is better than you.'

Skad laughed, reached for his ale, and took a large swig.

'So I'll be here a long time then,' he muttered, his voice an angry snarl.

'Not as long as you think. Astrid is smart.'

'Not smart enough! If she doesn't like your food she should just say so!'

'What?'

'You didn't notice? Your pie, Dagmar, is in her pocket. Or it was! I'll wager she's dumped it out in the forest where the birds will eat it.'

Dag looked towards the door and saw a trail of pie sauce that had dripped through her pocket and onto the floor.

Creeping back over to the new hole she had made in the roof, Astrid crawled through it and held her head in her hands, feeling ashamed of herself. She reached into her pocket and pulled out a small piece of the pie that remained. She placed it on her tongue and forced herself to eat it, the hurt look on Dag's face making her feel miserable; worthless.

Hearing the front door close, Astrid walked back over to the stairs expecting to see Dag standing by the table, but instead she saw Skad.

Turning to look up at her, he put down his ale. They could both hear Dag calling for her outside.

'Are you going to go outside?' Skad asked, his sturdy figure and strong stance looking quite formidable against the light glowing from the fireplace behind him.

'Are you going to train me to fight?' Astrid asked, ignoring his question.

'Yes. I am.'

'Are you good?'

'Better than you'll ever be,' Skad snorted, disdain dripping from his voice.

For the first time in her life, Astrid felt something growl angrily inside of her. She did not know what the words Blanda blóð meant, but she knew that for some reason this dwarf did not like her, and she could not explain why she suddenly felt a powerful need to prove him wrong.

Angu Worms

Jarl watched Astrid curiously as she ran ahead, the wolf's head still propped over hers, and the bag that hung from her shoulders under her wolf-skin cloak making her look hunchbacked.

She'd been at this for hours now, since early dawn, and hadn't once changed her pace. It was a slow steady run and her eyes darted around, watchful and alert.

Knud, on the other hand, was as far away from alert as was possible: draped over the neck of his pony with his mouth hanging open and his eyes closed. Jarl had strapped him down to the saddle so that he wouldn't fall from the pony's back.

'We should stop,' Jarl whispered to Skad who was riding next to him. 'She's going to get tired.'

Skad laughed, shaking his head. 'She likes to run. The ponies will get tired before she does.'

The air had gotten warmer when the sun had risen, but it was still very cold. Jarl pulled his tattered cloak tighter around him.

For the first few hours they had ridden through dense forest and followed an old, beaten path. They'd passed several small streams and had stopped to re-fill their flasks and let the ponies drink. But before long, the forest had begun to taper out into eerie rock formations and the trail led them through a deep canyon. The sound of the ponies' hooves echoed against the walls of stone around them. Perfectly circular holes littered every surface, even the ground, and at one point they had to dismount and carefully maneuver themselves across it before finally reaching a slightly less punctured pathway.

'Outlander!' Halvard called. 'These holes. What made them?'

'Angu worms,' Astrid replied.

'Worms? Worms did this?' Jarl asked, never having heard of anything that could eat through stone.

'Stone worms,' Astrid said, stopping for a moment and turning to look at him, her different coloured eyes catching him by surprise again. 'They're not dangerous during the day, they never come up to the surface if the sun's out.'

'You call this *out?*' Halvard mumbled, looking up at the clouds with disgust.

'Any light will hurt or kill them. They won't be a problem till nightfall.'

'And when it comes?'

'Either keep moving or stay near the fire,' Astrid warned, turning and leading them ahead again.

'Have you seen the way she looks at the ponies?' Halvard said, riding alongside Jarl with Astrid walking a good fifteen metres ahead.

'Skad said she didn't like them,' Jarl replied simply, not wanting Halvard to continue the conversation. Something about Astrid made him feel like she could still hear them.

'No. She's afraid of them,' Halvard said. 'Look at her eyes! She's afraid!'

'And if she is?' Jarl asked, shrugging his shoulders.

'What do you mean, if she is?' Halvard scoffed. 'We're being led through the wilderness by a small human woman who is afraid of ponies! I'd say that's a reason to be concerned.'

'If Skad says she's the best, then she's the best,' Jarl said, and Halvard sighed, exasperated.

'Skad is old. And you've never liked him. Why do you trust what he says anyway?'

'Because he trained me, and he was a better warrior than even my grandfather. If he trusts Astrid, then so do I.'

Almost as if she had heard him, Astrid bowed her head and walked a little faster.

'Why do you trust this human?' Halvard said, moving alongside Skad. Arguing with Jarl was getting him nowhere.

'I don't need to say why. Just that I do. That should be enough for you,' Skad snapped, marching his pony ahead to join Astrid. She flinched as the pony's nose almost touched her shoulder and Jarl looked up in time to see her leap to the side away from it.

'They're just animals!' Skad sneered, and Astrid scowled, turning her head away from him so he couldn't see the disgust on her face.

'The same could be said of every being,' she said quietly, her voice deceptively calm. The path thinned and Astrid moved ahead of him.

'How long will it take to get out of this place?' Skad said. The dead rock face for miles around made him feel agitated, and the warm heat and distant sounds emitting from the rock holes made him uneasy. It was like a strange mixture of slow heavy breathing and something soft and fleshy rattling against the stone.

'Only a day.'

'Just a day?'

'Didn't you hear me the first time?'

'Don't speak to me like that! I am your elder!' Skad snarled down at her, completely unaccustomed to being spoken to in such a manner, and worried the others may have heard her.

'Blanda blóð's do not have elders,' Astrid replied, striding ahead.

* * *

If it had been cold before, it was freezing now. A few snowflakes floated from the sky and Halvard quickly unloaded some of the firewood they had salvaged from the forest earlier that morning.

Astrid took it from him and arranged it into a mound, then lit it with one quick strike of her flint. Jarl watched her as he silently brought the ponies a little closer to the fire.

She pulled her bag from under her cloak and tossed it to the ground, a little further back from where the others were sitting. Jarl caught a glimpse of the silver elf bow strapped to the side of it, the metallic surface catching in the firelight. On the opposite side of her bag was a quiver of red-tailed arrows.

Astrid sat down and tucked her hands into her sleeves, her eyes fixed on the flames. The others, closer to the fire, extended their hands to warm themselves, Halvard not even bothering to hide the fact he was staring at her.

'How did you get that?' Knud asked, noticing a deep cut on Skad's knuckles.

'Goblin attack!' he said proudly. He stood up and flexed his hand to make the scar more noticeable. 'Escorting Queen Vígdís back to Lǫgberg!'

'I have this,' Knud said, pulling up his trouser leg to show a deep scar scratched into his knee. 'Fell down the stairs!' he said smugly. Astrid smiled under her veil at how proud he looked to have such a simple little mark.

'Ha! That's nothing! Though it's probably more than Jarl has!' Skad scoffed.

'I'm not competing with you,' Jarl said calmly, refusing to even look up at him. Astrid studied him curiously.

'You wouldn't win anyway!' Skad laughed.

'He wouldn't lose,' Halvard replied, and Jarl flashed him a look which clearly read 'don't.'

'What? Did soft little Jarl trip and scuff his knee too?' Skad mocked.

'He has Sótthringr scars!' Knud said quickly.

'Knud!' Jarl bellowed. His face hardened, his eyes flashed dangerously, and Knud bowed his head. Astrid looked up.

'Oh poor lad. Maybe one of these days he'll get a real scar!' Skad went on.

Jarl's eyes flashed in the firelight; a deep blue. Astrid easily recognised the shielded glare and knew that painful memories floated just beneath the surface.

'This is a real one,' Halvard interrupted. He pulled up his sleeve to reveal a long silver line stretching from his wrist to his elbow. Astrid guessed it had been inflicted by the tip of a sword.

'Not bad! But...' Skad pulled up his sleeve and smiled triumphantly. Most of his arm was covered with battle wounds. Astrid noticed three Dip claw scars.

'What about you?' Knud asked suddenly, and Astrid turned her head and noticed they were all staring at her. She shook her head and got to her feet.

'Keep the fire going,' Astrid said. 'Whatever you do, don't let it go down. If you have to relieve yourself, take a torch. Don't go anywhere where there isn't light.' She pulled the hammer axe from her bag and strode out into the darkness.

'Where are you going?' Halvard called out after her. Astrid ignored him and carried on walking.

'She wins,' Jarl said quietly under his breath.

From a large rock a few feet away, Astrid's grip around her father's hammer axe tightened. Her hands shook as her eyes flicked across the dozens of large holes in the ground.

After checking the perimeter, she returned, pulled her cloak from her shoulders and dropped it over her bag to hide her bow. She tossed another log into the fire and a burst of sparks rose from it. Sitting down on the ground, she held her hands out to the flames.

'Where's Knud?' she asked, glancing around, noticing that the young dwarf was nowhere to be seen.

Jarl looked at the empty space where he'd been sitting and jumped to his feet.

'Knud!' he called. 'KNUD!'

Astrid stood up, grabbed the end of one of the burning sticks from the fire and turned to leave with the others close behind.

'KNUD!' Jarl yelled again.

'Stupid boy,' Skad muttered.

Suddenly, there was a loud shuddering sound, and the ground beneath their feet shook, as if something was moving under the surface. Astrid took off, running towards the sound.

'This way!'

'There!' Jarl yelled, seeing Knud's hand scrambling up from a hole in the ground, his nails clawing at the dirt as if something was trying to pull him down. His scream echoed and he disappeared.

Without a second's hesitation, Jarl flung himself into the hole. Skad and Halvard reached out to grab him but it was too late.

'Do not follow us!' Astrid ordered, quickly tossing her wolf-skin onto the ground and hurtling into the tunnel after Jarl.

Down below, Jarl's torch all but went out as he plummeted at a frightening speed before slowing and hitting the ground. He shook himself off, shuffled himself forward, and looked around to see he was in a large cavern, with the sound of several loud creatures shuddering in the many tunnels leading off from it. Jarl raised his torch. The flame picked up and shone brightly, the light bouncing off the silky smooth stone. Huge shadows backed down the tunnels, away from the light.

'Help me!'

Jarl turned towards the sound of Knud's voice and threw himself into the tunnel to his right. He crawled as fast as he could, Knud's yells getting closer and closer. The tunnel began to slope downwards and he pressed his arms and legs tightly against the walls to stop himself from falling, using the ridges in the stone like the rungs of a ladder.

'Knud! Don't move!' Astrid shouted. Jarl turned and saw her crawling down the tunnel behind him. 'Don't move or they'll crush you to death!'

Astrid grabbed hold of Jarl's leg and yanked him backwards. 'You have to put the torch out!' she hissed.

Using his legs to hold himself up in the now almost vertical tunnel, Jarl closed his hands around the burning torch and the flames hissed as they were smothered by his bare skin. He grimaced but didn't make a sound. Dropping the torch, he let go of his grip on the wall and hurtled down the tunnel, landing with a thump. As soon as his feet hit the ground, he drew his sword and dagger, his eyes flitting around wildly. Something large shuffled towards him, and Knud, to his right, whimpered in the dark.

Astrid dropped to the ground behind him, barely making a sound.

'Knud! Don't move!' she whispered.

It was pitch black and Jarl couldn't see a thing. The creature slid across the ground a few feet away from them both.

'Jarl!' Knud cried out, his voice a deep rasp as he struggled to breathe.

Jarl raised his sword and took a step forward, but Astrid reached out and grabbed him tightly around his neck, pulling him back.

'No! Don't move!' she whispered. 'Whatever you do, don't move! It'll kill him! You need to trust me!'

He wanted more than anything to ignore her, to help Knud, but he knew he was out of his depth. He had to trust her. Astrid loosened her grip and Jarl backed up against the wall.

Inching forwards, Astrid looked over at Knud, her eyes adjusting to the dark. Curled around him like a snake, the Angu worm had him trapped, its stony skin pulsating as it tightened its grip. Knud's face was red and terrified and he struggled to breathe, his hands scratching around in panic.

Reaching the Angu worm, so close her knees were almost touching its sides, Astrid stretched out her hand and grabbed Knud's. Knud screamed out as he felt someone take it in the darkness, but Astrid held it firmly so he couldn't pull away.

Jarl suddenly saw a faint, blue glow in the darkness ahead of him, which slowly got stronger. He could just make out the shape of one of Astrid's hands holding Knud's, the blue glow from her other hand partially illuminating the cavern. He could hear dozens more worms in the nearby tunnels, rattling threateningly but not approaching. The blue light wasn't hurting them, but something about it was making them stay away.

Astrid fixed her eyes on Knud, urging him to look at her. Slowly he calmed, and bit by bit, the Angu loosened its tail. Jarl noticed that Knud's breathing was no longer pained and heavy but that Astrid appeared to be struggling. Each of her breaths was deep and short.

'Good! Almost there! Don't move!' she whispered. The worm had almost completely unravelled and began to slide into one of the many worm holes speckling the wall. Within seconds, it had disappeared.

'Are you ok?' Astrid asked gently. Knud nodded, but his legs suddenly gave way.

'My legs! It grabbed me by my legs!' he said, peering down at his steel boots that were dented from the Angu's powerful jaws, the only thing that had stopped them from being mutilated. The rest of him, his arms and hands especially, were visibly bruised.

'We need to get back outside,' Astrid whispered, hearing the other worms in the nearby tunnels shuddering as they approached.

'I can't see anything,' Jarl muttered, doing his best to keep his voice as low as possible, but it resonated against the cavern walls and vibrated through the tunnels. Several of the worms slithered out and approached them slowly. Jarl grabbed Knud and pressed his hand over his mouth to stop him from screaming.

Nobody moved. Knud whimpered as he felt one of the Angu slide by, its stony skin making a scraping sound on the steel of his boot.

Astrid reached out to Jarl and grabbed his arm, then inch by inch, guided him through the darkness. Jarl had a firm grip on Knud's arm, and together, slowly, they made their escape. Every few steps they stopped and listened, and when one of the worms slithered around their feet in a circle, Knud shook like a leaf but didn't dare move.

For a moment, Jarl felt Astrid let go of his arm when a second worm appeared, and he closed his eyes, praying Knud wouldn't start screaming.

There was a loud clatter in the distance, like a stone hitting the wall further down the cavern. The Angu around their feet unwound themselves and slithered away, and Astrid's hand reached out in the dark again and led them away.

Jarl felt a breeze above him, and looking up, saw a faintly lit vertical tunnel. A little reflected moonlight was enough for Jarl to be able to make out the rough outline of Astrid's face and the worried expression on it.

He looked up again at the tunnel and although he could see ridges further up, there was no way they could reach them.

'Don't move!' Astrid whispered, stepping back from the moonlight and retreating into the darkness. She took a breath and ran towards him, leaping up as high as she could, using Jarl's shoulder as a stepping stone. Her hands just about reached the edge of the first ridge and she hauled herself up, securing her feet against either side of the tunnel's walls. Catching her breath, she peered down at the others. Even if Knud used Jarl for a step-up, there would be no way for Jarl to join them.

Reaching up to her face, Astrid unwound the veil from around her neck and lowered it down the tunnel towards them. Jarl motioned to Knud to climb it and he quickly did as he was told, struggling at first. Astrid pulled on the veil as he climbed and grabbed his hand to help him manoeuvre past her. As soon as his feet were securely against the tunnel walls, Astrid dropped the veil back down for Jarl, her eyes widening as she saw one of the large Angu sliding towards him. Jarl reached up for the veil and gripped it firmly, ready to climb as fast as he could. Astrid braced herself.

'Jarl! Watch out!' Knud hollered from above them, seeing the worm circling. Astrid glared at him, urging him to be silent.

Jarl fixed his eyes on Astrid's face, not trusting himself to look at the Angu, worried he would instinctively lash out if it came too close.

Feeling his eyes on her, Astrid gripped the sash tightly, looking past Jarl and at the Angu worm. She was certain that Jarl was looking at her like every other stranger did when they first saw her face - with disgust and horror. But when her eyes caught his for a moment, she was shocked to see that she was wrong. Jarl was looking at her like he couldn't even see the scars, his blue eyes fixed on hers. Looking only at her eyes.

After circling him several times, the Angu worm slid away, and Jarl climbed the sash frantically. Astrid reached down and took his hand, helping him climb past her into the tunnel above.

Halvard and Skad yelped with relief as soon as they saw Knud's bright red hair emerging from the earth. They reached down and hauled him up before turning back to help Jarl.

Seeing none of them turn to help Astrid, Jarl turned back and reached down the tunnel for her, took her hand firmly in his and pulled her out. Halvard and Skad saw her face and grimaced, Halvard gasping loudly, revolted by the sight. Astrid quickly wrapped the sash veil back around her neck and clipped the end over her face, then picked up her wolf-skin and strolled back to the clearing.

Back around the fire, Jarl saw just how powerful the Angu worm's grip had been. Knud's left boot was heavily dented.

'Let me see,' Astrid said gently. She knelt down in front of Knud resting her axe on the ground, unstrapped his boot, and took his foot in her hand. The skin was red and already bruising around the ankle. 'This should help,' she whispered, smiling under her veil. Her hand glowed blue as she ran her fingers over the skin. The redness vanished with her touch. Halvard gasped in shock as he watched what she was doing, the air crackling with magic.

'How did you do that?' Knud asked, amazed, staring up at her in awe.

'Doesn't matter,' Astrid replied. 'Never wander off again.' She moved her hand to the edge of her veil to check it was fixed firmly in place and then moved away from the fire, leaving her hammer axe on the ground beside him.

Halvard, with his hand on his sword, looked like he was about to draw it at any moment and attack her.

'Where are you going?' he asked, his tone a mixture of suspicion and disgust.

'I want to check we're the only people around,' she replied, not looking him in the eye. 'I think Knud woke the dead with his screaming.'

The snow had stopped falling a few minutes earlier but a thin, white blanket covered the canyon. It was deathly silent, the moonlight illuminating everything, the sky having cleared completely. Only the moon and stars remained up above.

Jarl sat down next to Knud and peered down at his now healed ankle, then turned to flash Skad a questioning glance. Skad ignored him.

'She's a witch!' Halvard hissed

Skad snorted. 'She's not a witch.'

'You should get to sleep,' Jarl said to Knud, fondly ruffling his fingers through Knud's curly, red hair, his heart still racing from their adventure in the tunnels. 'Don't ever scare me like that again.'

'I'll try not to,' Knud replied, the last traces of fear still etched on his face. He pulled out his sleeping blanket and laid it out near the fire, then lay down and hugged it around him. Within minutes he was gently snoring. Jarl was amazed that he could go to sleep so easily after what had just happened.

He settled down just a few feet away and watched Knud like a hawk, half expecting one of the worms to pull him down into the ground again. He glanced across at Astrid's hammer axe on the ground and picked it up, running his fingers over the emblem on the axe head, his attention caught by the pattern of thorns entwined around a thistle. Jarl was sure he had seen the pattern somewhere before, but couldn't place where or when.

'Something's not right about that woman,' Halvard said from the other side of the fire. 'Did you see her face?'

'She saved Knud's life,' Jarl muttered, not bothering to say anything more. That was all that mattered to him.

'That's a face only a mother could love!' Halvard went on, not even hearing what Jarl had said. Skad chuckled and Jarl looked up at them, disgusted. He got to his feet and grabbed one of the burning torches from the fire, then walked out after Astrid with her hammer axe in his hand. He followed her small footprints in the snow until he saw her in the distance.

'Thank you,' Jarl said as he approached her, handing her the axe. She took it from him and fastened the leather wrist strap to her belt before turning back to look at him.

'Your friend doesn't trust me.'

'No, he doesn't,' Jarl replied, not seeing the point in lying to her.

'Why? Why don't dwarves trust...other people?' she asked, her tone making it sound oddly personal.

'Some people just fear what's different.'

Nodding, Astrid turned away and held her head up to the moon. 'You should get some sleep. We'll leave at dawn,' she said, walking off again to circle the camp.

Jarl strolled back to the fire and spread out his own sleeping bag close to Knud's. He tossed a few more logs into the fire then settled down and closed his eyes.

He awoke a few times during the night and instinctively looked up to check that Knud was still there. Each time he glanced across at Astrid who sat with her legs pulled to her chest and the wolf-skin wrapped around her, its head over hers, making her look like a wolf in the firelight. Her green and grey eyes glinted in the red light of the embers.

Make Me Strong

37 years ago...

'Wake up!' Skad barked from the top of the stairs. 'Bring the axe, don't bother with the bow. I won't teach you to use that thing!'

Still groggy from sleep, Astrid sat up, rubbed her eyes and stumbled to her feet. Skad looked in disgust at her charcoal-covered blanket and the smudged drawings of her parents on the floor of her room. She carefully stepped over them and padded down the stairs after him. Dag was fast asleep on his bed by the fireplace, and she followed Skad outside and closed the door quietly behind her.

Skad, ignoring her, led her into the forest, and when he reached one of the many glades further up the mountain, he turned to face her. Astrid stood perfectly still as he observed her for a few seconds. She held Arnbjörg's hammer axe tightly in her fist.

'You're too young to use that,' Skad said, walking forward to grab it. Astrid's grip on the handle tightened and she glared at him.

'I want to use it!'

'You can't. It's too heavy.'

'I can get stronger!'

'You're too weak!'

Like a fire had suddenly been lit inside her, Astrid's eyes flashed with determination and she pushed Skad away.

'I'll get stronger!' she said again, clenching the axe and holding it tightly at her side.

Skad glared back down at her. 'Fine!' he spat.

He stood in front of her and spread his feet apart, instructing her to do the same. 'Stand firm! Legs apart! The axe is making you fall over! You need to balance the weight with the rest of your body!'

Astrid spread her feet and tried to balance herself. Not having the strength to hold it in front of her, she rested the hammer axe head against her chest.

Skad moved towards her as if to attack and Astrid stumbled back and fell, the heavy axe toppling her over, hitting her chest and winding her.

'See? It's too heavy. Now put it down.'

'NO!'

Frustrated, Skad moved to take it from her, his hand pressing firmly over hers. Astrid grabbed the handle and swung it at him, for a brief second seeing red. The blunt end of the axe caught the corner of his brow bone and scraped the skin away, removing half of his eyebrow in one swipe. Skad pressed his hand over his face in pain.

'I'm sorry!' Astrid said in horror. She dropped the axe and moved towards Skad, her hand extended and glowing.

'Don't...touch me!' Skad hissed at her, glaring at her with disgust, brown blood seeping between his fingers.

'I can help,' Astrid whispered.

'I don't *need* your help!'

Skad lowered his hand and Astrid winced as she saw what she had done.

'I can heal it,' she said quietly, holding her hands together nervously.

He ignored her. 'You want to use that thing? Fine! Pick it up!' he snarled, spreading his feet apart and taking his stance again. Astrid picked the hammer axe up again and held it in front of her.

She managed to miss the first sweep of his axe but wasn't fast enough to step back in time and dodge his second attack. He swept her legs out from under her with one kick of his leg. and Astrid fell heavily to the ground.

'I'm not going to be soft with you! I know you want to learn how to fight, so I'll keep knocking you down till you learn how to stand up!'

Getting to her feet, her breath knocked out of her from the fall, Astrid held her axe in front of her again. 'I know,' she replied. Skad easily knocked her down again. Astrid got up again, her face fixed in a determined glare.

'I *will* be strong!' she muttered to herself, taking each fall and picking herself up, over and again. 'I *will* be strong!'

* * *

Astrid strolled into the hut and sat down opposite Ragi. The goblin looked up at her curiously.

'Is the dwarf still with you?'

'Yes,' Astrid said, her hands hanging by her side, barely having the strength to raise them. The muscles felt as if they were on fire.

'Don't tell him about me,' Ragi warned. 'If he doesn't like you, he'll probably kill me.'

'I'll kill him first if he tries!' Astrid said, and Ragi laughed, despite knowing how serious she was.

'I have no doubt you would. He's a miserable creature.'

'You saw him?'

'I was watching from the trees. I don't like him.'

'I don't think I do either.'

'Then ask Dag to send him away,' Ragi replied indignantly.

'But he can teach me to fight,' Astrid said, shrugging her shoulders.

'I'll teach you to fight!'

'He's a dwarf though.'

'And I'm not,' Ragi muttered.

'I...I didn't mean it that way!' Astrid spluttered. 'I just want to know more about dwarves. And elves. It's not that I don't like you!'

Ragi just looked at her, and Astrid stared at the ground, ashamed.

'Dag told me it's your birthday this season,' he finally said. He reached into the large wooden chest behind him and pulled out a long, thin bundle wrapped in green silk. 'Open it,' he said, passing it to her.

Astrid's hands shook as she struggled to undo the twine wrapped around it, every muscle sore and weak from exhaustion.

'Let me do it,' Ragi said gently. He untied the twine then slid the silk package back towards her. 'Go on! Unwrap it!' He couldn't stop an enormous grin spreading across his face when she saw what was inside.

There were three daggers, the largest of which looked like a small sword. The second, half the length, was thinner than its predecessor, and the third was so small that the blade - an oval shape that tapered out into a needle-like end - was only the length of Astrid's hand. All three of them had a leather scabbard to protect them, the leather plain and polished to a shine.

'And there's one more thing,' Ragi said excitedly, pushing the daggers aside and reaching for a small, black velvet bag. He placed it in Astrid's hands.

'I gave this to Dag for your parents. He gave it back to me when...' His voice trailed off. 'Anyway, I think you should have it. It would have gone to you anyhow, one day.'

Astrid opened the bag and tipped the contents into her hand. A ring tumbled out and split into two. One was a jasmine flower, made of silver, with white diamonds set into the centre of the flower heads. The other was a thistle made of a dark copper, with red rubies embedded into it.

'They both fit together, see?' Ragi said, placing them next to each other. The rings slid together and held fast with a 'click'.

Astrid said nothing for a few moments, swallowing and rubbing at her eyes, determined not to cry.

'Why are there two?' she asked, knowing exactly why, but she needed to say something out loud to stop the tears from falling.

'One for you, the other for the one you love...one day.' Ragi smiled. He took the rings and slid them onto a strong, steel chain, then placed it carefully over her head.

'Thank you Ragi!' she said, pulling the goblin into a hug. He tried to escape but Astrid held him tight.

'Ok! Ok! That's enough!' he said, and Astrid let him go. 'Now don't lose them. Took me months to make them, and metal this good is hard to find.'

'You made them?'

'Yes. I used to be a blacksmith. I'm still very good!'

'I've never seen you making anything.'

'That's because my forge is further up the mountain.'

'Thank you,' Astrid said again, opening the sheath of the smaller dagger and running her finger over it.

'Careful! They're all very sharp,' Ragi warned, and Astrid winced as the blade sliced her skin. 'Sharp!' Ragi repeated. Astrid sucked at the blood and put the dagger down.

'Why is it so small?' she asked.

'That one goes around your ankle, or in your boot. It's small, but perfect for hiding. That little thing has saved my life more times than I can count.'

'And this one?' Astrid asked, holding up the middle dagger.

' It wraps around your left arm; quicker to reach it. Perfect for when trouble is too close.'

'And this one is for my belt?' Astrid asked, holding up the last and longest of the daggers.

'Yes. Wear it so your left hand can get to it as quickly as possible. You should know how to use them with either of your hands. It's better to be prepared for everything.'

Astrid strapped down the daggers in their correct places and stood up. She reached for the handles and pulled them out, one by one, admiring how firmly they stayed in their sheaths but came loose the minute her hand touched the handles.

'Will you teach me now?' she asked, a dagger in each hand, looking up at him excitedly. Ragi laughed at her enthusiasm.

'You're too tired now. You can barely hold your arms up! Come tomorrow before Skad wakes up and I'll teach you.'

*　*　*

Astrid groaned in pain. Her arms felt as if they had turned to stone overnight, they were so heavy and difficult to move. She tip-toed over to the stairs and saw Skad move a little in his sleep by the fireplace. She slowly backed into her room.

The top step of the stairs to her room always creaked loudly. If she woke him now he would be in an even worse mood, and she would have to wait another day to train with Ragi.

She crept to the far end of her room and shifted the thatching, creating a small tunnel jutting out onto the roof. Before she climbed through she grabbed her blanket from her bed, and once outside, draped it over the hole. She would have to take some straw from Felix's stable later and make a better covering for it, but today it would be fine and the blanket would stop the cold air getting inside. The minute it rained there would be trouble; nobody appreciated a leaking roof, and Astrid would prefer it if nobody knew about her secret door. She had helped her mother thatch the roof in her old home enough times to know how to fix it herself. If she was lucky she would be able to steal the hay from Felix and mend it later that night when Dag and Skad were eating. Dag would not question why she was not eating with them and Skad would not care. It was the perfect time to do it.

With a grin on her face, she climbed down the tree and raced through the forest, tightening the straps for the daggers as she ran. When she reached Ragi's hut, Astrid saw him sitting outside and he looked up smiling as she approached.

'Ready?'

Nodding, Astrid drew two of her daggers and walked towards him. Ragi laughed.

I'm going to have to make you some more!' he said.

'Why?'

'If you use two daggers right away, you'll only have one spare. Always have spares if you can.'

She re-sheathed one of the daggers. 'Ok, I'm ready.'

He shook his head. 'And the other one.' Astrid stared at him blankly. 'The daggers won't help at all if you can't fight without them. Take them off for the moment; I don't want you cutting me accidently.'

Doing as she was told, Astrid unstrapped the daggers, feeling slightly disappointed that she couldn't use them. She spread her feet apart and bent her knees.

'That's good, but you're too stiff.'

'Skad said...'

'Skad's a dwarf! He relies on brute strength! It's fine to be strong, but you need to be able to move quickly. It's far more important.'

Ragi stepped towards her and smiled as she leapt back, her feet naturally pointing as she did so, almost as if she were dancing.

'You move like an elf!' He smiled, and Astrid's face dropped.

'That's what Skad said.'

'It's a good thing,' Ragi assured her. 'You have both your mother and your father in you, so use both. Skad might be stronger, but he's slower. You will always have speed on your side. Strength will come with age. Now take your stance.'

Astrid moved more onto the balls of her feet, her hands held out at her sides as if she was about to walk along a tightrope.

'That's better! Now relax your muscles more. You won't be able to move as quickly if you're this tense.'

'I can't help it! Everything hurts!' Astrid moaned, and Ragi's eyes softened.

'Listen. After you've trained with Skad, I want you to go up to the hot springs. It'll help with the soreness.'

Nodding, Astrid tried to relax. The muscles in her back and upper arms felt as if someone had tied them into knots.

'Can I fight like this with Skad?'

'I wouldn't, not yet. Wait a while till you're better than him. It's the best way to fight. Make your enemy think you're weak and then destroy them!'

'Is that what goblins do?' Astrid said, smiling.

Ragi grinned at her and nodded. 'Pretend you're weak and take everyone by surprise.'

* * *

'Where have you been?' Dag asked, as Astrid strolled into the house. He was cooking another one of his horrible concoctions and she tried not to wrinkle her nose at the smell.

'I went to the hot springs.'

'Did Ragi take you?'

'No, I went by myself. Where's Skad?' she asked, glancing around. His belongings were strewn around his bed near the wall, but there was no sign of him anywhere.

'I don't know. Went hunting I think.'

'He won't go near Ragi's hut, will he?' she said worriedly.

'Ragi? No, besides he can take care of himself.' Dag dipped his spoon into the pot and tasted the soup. 'Come and try.'

Astrid struggled to look enthusiastic as she took the spoon from him and dipped it down into the simmering pot. But no matter how hard she tried, she couldn't stop her mouth from twisting into a revolted grimace as she tasted it. Dag's face dropped.

'It's terrible.'

'No! No! It's just very hot,' Astrid lied. She dipped the spoon back in, blew on it, and put it into her mouth. Dag almost managed a small smile at her attempt to make it look edible.

'I'm not a very good cook, Astrid. I never was. I'm sorry.'

Knowing it was useless now to try and lie, Astrid put the spoon down and turned to look at him. 'You're trying though, Dag!' She smiled. 'But this soup is just a little...salty.'

'They're all too salty.' He lifted the pot up and carried it outside, and following him, Astrid watched as he poured it onto the grass. Looking up, she saw her blanket hung over the rope that Dag had strung between two trees as a washing line. The charcoal marks had gone. She pulled it down, smiled, and buried her face into it, inhaling. Suddenly, she felt her stomach drop.

The smell had gone, replaced by a tang of water and clean cotton. All the memories and the sense of security that were wrapped up in it had been washed away by Dag's good intentions.

'Come help me cook, goldheart!' Dag called over, strolling back inside.

Tears stung her eyes. Holding the blanket close to her chest, she walked back into the house and climbed the stairs to her room, then opened the wooden box Dag had given her. She held her nose as close to the opened bottle top as she could, and the strong scent of the jasmine oil filled her nostrils. Sharp images flooded her mind; her mother's old songs, her father dancing with Sylbil outside the house, Sylbil laughing, having to bend her knees slightly to rest her forehead against his.

Astrid popped the cork back into the bottle and replayed the images again and again until they grew foggy and distant.

'You still have this,' she whispered to herself, reaching into her tunic and pulling out the rings Ragi had given her.

Opening the bottle again, Astrid wiped a small amount of oil from the bottom of the cork onto her fingers and dabbed it onto the blanket. She quickly folded it, placed it on her bed and walked downstairs. Tonight, if she slept, the smell, though different, would still be there. She would still have something old and familiar to cling to as her eyes closed; something to hold her safe and keep the nightmares at bay.

Danger

'Get up!' Astrid whispered.

Jarl awoke with a start, instinctively turning to check that Knud was alright, then breathed a sigh of relief as he saw his flame-red hair sticking out from under the blanket that was curled around him like a cocoon. Astrid crouched down on the ground close to him, the veil still over her face and the wolf-skin still wrapped around her.

'Wake the others,' she said, before getting up and packing together their supplies and leaving them in a heap by the ponies. She stood silently as Jarl woke the others, watching him.

Jarl took a moment to check Knud's foot. There wasn't a single trace of the skin having been crushed in the Angu's jaws and Knud stood on it as if nothing had ever happened. Jarl turned to Astrid, the question crossing his face, but neither of them spoke. When

Astrid moved away, he strolled over to the ponies and began packing the supplies onto their backs.

'Why on earth couldn't you do that?' Halvard grumbled at Astrid as he walked past her. She ignored him and ran ahead, the wolf-skin cloak bouncing on her shoulders.

Normally Jarl would have ignored any comments Halvard made first thing in the morning; the dwarf did not like to be woken this early and sleeping on the ground always made him rude and snappy. But it was crossing a line even for Halvard to make such a petty comment when she had saved Knud's life barely twelve hours earlier.

'Don't talk to her if you're going to be like that,' Jarl snapped. Halvard looked up at him, surprised. 'She saved Knud's life!'

'And I'll wager she'll end up killing all of us before this journey is over,' he said, riding ahead.

'Hey! Outlander! How long till we leave this canyon?' he called over to her, his tone condescending.

'A few hours,' Astrid replied.

Jarl rode beside Knud, determined to keep him in his sights for the rest of the journey. Knud flashed him a cheeky grin before looking ahead, his eyes fixed on Astrid.

'Did you see her face?' Knud whispered. 'I wonder how she got so many scars?'

'She saved your life, Knud. You should thank her. Don't mention the scars.'

Knud jumped down from his pony and ran alongside Astrid, who slowed down to a brisk walk to enable him to keep up. Her eyes flitted between him and the pony and Jarl watched them from a distance.

'Thank you,' Knud said quickly, unsure of how to apologise and so saying the words as quickly as he could, not realising it made him sound like he didn't mean it.

Astrid grinned under her veil, her eyes lighting up as she did so. Something about the little dwarf made her laugh.

'Did your uncle make you say that?'

'Yes, but I wanted to say it,' Knud clarified. 'And he's not my real uncle. I just call him that because he was my father's best friend.'

Nodding, Astrid moved to start running ahead again and Knud said the first thing that came to mind in the hope it would make her stay and talk for a while.

'You're really beautiful!' he blurted out, and Astrid stopped in her tracks and turned to look at him. Knud flashed her a wide grin. 'Even with the scars.'

Jarl watched as Astrid suddenly turned and strode ahead. He was too far away to have heard what was said, but he could tell that Astrid had somehow been offended.

'What did you say to her?' he asked, riding up beside Knud.

'I just told her she was beautiful,' Knud said, 'even with the scars,' and Jarl growled at him.

'One day,' he said, 'that mouth of yours is going to get you into serious trouble.'

For the next few hours they rode in silence. Astrid easily ran ahead of them but doubled back every few minutes. The path of the canyon slowly rose and wound up the last tall rock face. Eventually they reached the top, relieved to be able to travel through the thick forest that surrounded the canyon. A faint path weaved through miles and miles of old, gnarled trees, some of it almost completely obscured by moss and thick, green grass. They rode at a gentle trot, relaxing a little now that they were out of the canyon.

Looking ahead, Halvard noticed Astrid had disappeared, and he peered through the dozens of tangled branches that obscured the path ahead. For a second he thought he saw her perched up on one of the branches, and a few seconds later swore he saw a large, black wolf in the trail ahead.

'Jarl look!' he shouted, pointing down the path. Jarl turned to see Astrid, her wolf-skin bobbing on her back as she ran.

'What?'

'I saw a wolf!'

'It's just her cloak!' Skad replied, snorting. 'I'm seventy-five years older than you and even I can see that!'

Glaring at Skad, Halvard rode ahead, passed Astrid, then turned back to look her up and down. Astrid glanced up at him from under her veil, her green and grey eyes glinting at him.

Shaking his head, Halvard rode a little further ahead.

'You're going too far!' Astrid called out, but he ignored her and broke into a canter.

'Idiot!' she muttered under her breath.

Suddenly hearing the snap of a branch in the distance, Astrid stopped, reached up into her sleeve and grabbed the dagger strapped to her arm. Jarl and Skad saw the blade catch the light and Jarl took Knud's reins to stop the pony walking forward.

'What's wrong?' Skad asked. Astrid raised her hand and motioned at him to be quiet, lowering her hood and closing her eyes. She crouched down, one hand resting on the ground, her fingers spread against the earth like a spider, and her other hand holding the long thin dagger as lightly as if she were holding a feather.

'Halvard!' she barked. 'Get back here!'

Turning his pony, Halvard looked around. Several birds hopped along one of the branches near him; nothing even remotely indicated that they were in danger.

'Get down from the horses!' Astrid whispered to the others. 'Do you have any food?'

Jarl pulled his bag in front of him, reached inside and grabbed the last cake that Holmvé had made. He unwrapped it from the muslin and passed it to her. Astrid took it, walked towards Halvard and hissed at him to get down from his horse. Halvard shook his head but did as she'd said, then casually strolled back to the others.

'I have food!' Astrid called out into the forest. Halvard scoffed, looking over at Jarl as if expecting him to do the same, but he flashed him a look which quite clearly told him to shut up.

'My friends and I only want to pass through the forest. I give you my word no harm will come to the creatures who live here. We have enough food for the journey.' Astrid walked up to a small, stunted tree at the side of the road and rested the cake on one of the branches that extended from it.

'Well...she's mad!' Halvard snorted. 'Will we be giving all our food to the trees now?'

'Halvard...look!' Jarl hissed at him through gritted teeth. Halvard looked back towards Astrid, the smirk on his face wiped clean in an instant. Two dark green eyes stared at him from the much larger tree behind the one Astrid had placed the cake on. Astrid bowed slowly towards it and Jarl, Knud and Skad did the same. Halvard quickly followed.

Jarl and Knud looked up and saw a tall monster extracting itself from the tree. Its long legs were made of stone and it had large, cloven hooves for feet. Two smaller trees ripped up from the ground and transformed into hands. The fingers closed around the cake and lifted it up to its face, which was covered in long grass and vines. Its face curled up into antler-like horns where several birds perched. The creature sniffed loudly at the food before tossing it into the forest behind it. The birds flew after it in a flurry of feathers.

Jarl stared in awe and stayed completely motionless, certain that the creature was about to bring its large, heavy hooves down on top of Astrid and crush her to death. Astrid didn't flinch as it slammed a foot down on the ground next to her. The ground shook violently. What a marvel this creature was; its entire upper body made of knotted roots and vines, like muscles overlapping each other.

It leant its head down towards her, and Astrid looked confidently into its eyes. The monster slowly reached down and removed her veil. It started and stepped back for a second, shocked by her appearance, before reaching with its other hand towards her face. While gently stroking the side of her cheek with its rough wooden finger, it gave a low, sympathetic growl.

'We will not hunt till we have passed your borders,' Astrid said gently, reaching up to its flat face and stroking it, with a wisp of a smile on her lips. The large creature slowly stood and looked over at the others before motioning towards the path with its long arm.

Astrid bowed one last time, re-attached her veil and turned to walk ahead. The others quickly followed her.

The creature watched them warily, Halvard and Skad especially.

'How did you know it was there?' Halvard asked.

'Next time I'll let you walk ahead,' Astrid replied, ignoring his question. 'I cannot protect you if you will not let me.'

'How did you know it was there?' Halvard repeated.

'I heard him.'

'Heard him?' Halvard asked, confused.

'I heard his heartbeat.'

* * *

'No worms here?' Knud asked, nervously looking over at Astrid as he laid out his sleeping blanket.

Astrid smiled under her veil and shook her head. 'No. None here. They like stone, not mud.'

'Do we have to worry about that tree thing?' Halvard asked, and looked guardedly out at the dark forest. The light was fading by the second. The sun set a few minutes ago and the dark had already begun to take over.

'No. The Leshy don't break their word, provided we keep ours. We'll have left his territory in a few days' time, then we can hunt.'

'Seeing as 'he' didn't technically say anything, I'm still worried.'

'Don't worry. I'll protect you,' Astrid replied, not meaning to sound condescending, but judging by his face, Halvard had taken it that way.

'I don't need you to protect me, *human*. I could kill that creature if it attacked me.'

Not caring to argue with him, Astrid stood, picked up her hammer axe and walked away. She pulled the wolf-skin head over her own for warmth.

'Where did you get that hammer axe?' Halvard called after her.

Astrid stopped in her tracks.

'I've seen that emblem before. It's dwarven, The House of Hvass.'

'Halvard, stop it.' Skad warned.

Halvard was irritated that the old, grumpy dwarf who never stood up for anyone was now suddenly defending the human woman. 'Why? We know nothing about her, and what kind of human parent calls their child Astrid? Why would a human call their child a dwarf name?'

'Halvard!' Jarl and Skad shouted at him simultaneously.

Jarl was shocked at his friend, and Astrid stiffened at the mention of her name and glared back at Skad. Her eyes looked like they might burn a hole straight through him. She slowly turned her gaze back to Halvard.

'I'm not your friend. I am your guide. That is all you need to know,' Astrid said quietly, her voice restrained. She quickly turned and walked into the forest.

Halvard turned to Jarl. 'There's something wrong with that woman. She's not normal.'

'Nobody who protects strangers for free is normal.' Skad laughed at him.

'We're paying her,' Jarl interrupted. 'When we get there.'

'And let me guess…one hundred, two hundred Fé?'

'Two hundred and seventy five,' Halvard replied.

'Phsht! That's for free. I charged four times that amount in my day.' Skad laughed, rolled out his blanket and lay down.

'Jarl, I'm telling you we have to leave. Skad can protect us. That woman is trouble.'

'I can't protect you!' Skad laughed from the floor, and settled his bag behind his head like a pillow. 'I always took the Austr road. I never took this route. I've never liked this side of the Riddari Mountains. She knows it far better than I do.'

Halvard growled in frustration, turned and punched at the air. 'I say we put up with her till the Salt

Monasteries and then pay her. We will then leave her and find someone there to take us the rest of the way.'

'Halvard just go to sleep. You're not thinking clearly.'

'You're not listening!' Halvard shouted louder, and even Skad looked up from where he was trying, despite his nerves, to sleep. Halvard's voice echoed through the dark forest.

Looking up, Jarl stared as Astrid hung from a branch of a tree above them by her knees. She pressed a rag over Halvard's mouth and held it there for a few seconds. Halvard tried to struggle but something soaked into the rag made him queasy and he finally passed out. His eyes rolled back and he dropped to the ground. Jarl successfully caught him before his head hit the floor.

'What did you do?' Jarl asked, worried that Astrid had harmed him.

Skad just laughed and turned his back to the group under his blanket so he could sleep.

Astrid dropped down from the branch and tossed the rag into the fire. A burst of blue and green flames glowed from it as the fire consumed it. 'He's fine. The effect will wear off soon. I saw him eating some mushrooms earlier; he must have picked Red 'shrooms.'

'No, they were brown. I saw him eating them,' Jarl said, confused, and looked to Halvard who snored loudly on the ground in an undignified heap.

'They're called Red 'shrooms because they make you see red,' Astrid explained calmly. She gripped Halvard under the arms and dragged him away from the fire. She tossed his blanket over him for good measure. 'He shouldn't eat the food here. It might look familiar but a lot of it is poisonous. He was lucky. If he were any other species he'd be dead.'

'He's an idiot,' Jarl grumbled.

Astrid agreed with him, a small trace of laughter in her voice.

'I'm sorry for what he said,' Jarl apologised. 'He didn't mean it.'

'You're wrong,' Astrid replied. Her eyes held a hint of sadness. 'The Red 'shrooms make you angry, but they don't make you lie. He meant every word.' She silently walked away.

Jarl very nearly went after her, but decided against it. Moving over to his bag, he pulled out his own blanket and sat by the fire. He wrapped it around his shoulders and looked into the flickering heat. The air was colder now and the moon, fully risen, shone its cold white light everywhere.

Astrid always did this, walked away and patrolled the area, only to return when she thought they were all asleep. She sat down and wrapped her wolf-skin around her, conscious to sit as far away from the ponies as possible. She remained as motionless as stone, only her green and grey eyes swivelled and glinted in the yellow firelight.

Halvard or Jarl would normally wake a few hours before dawn and take watch, but Jarl knew Astrid would never sleep near them. In fact Jarl had never seen her sleep in the whole time they had been travelling together. She was inclined to wander off as if to patrol the area again, returning just before the dawn.

There was something about her that Jarl couldn't help but be intrigued by. For all the air of mystery and danger surrounding her, there was also something underneath all of that which he couldn't quite pin point. A strange mixture of sadness, kindness, and a desperate need to be around people, yet all the while fearing them. She was brave and kind, and that fascinated him.

Secret

37 years ago...

'I'm leaving tomorrow,' Skad said loudly across the table. Astrid and Dag looked up at him in surprise. 'I'm not spending the winter here, I'm going back to Bjargtre. I'll be back in the summer for two months next year.'

It was all Astrid could do to hide the small smile that crept up from the corners of her mouth. To be rid of him for some time was an appealing thought. Quick as lightning she looked down at her food and dropped her spoon in the soup.

Skad noticed the little twitch as she tried to hide the smile. 'Don't be too happy or I'll train you even harder when I get back,' he snapped.

'Don't talk to her like that,' Dag said gruffly. 'She didn't do anything.'

Skad growled his displeasure at being silenced and left the room with an air of embarrassment.

'Astrid, leave me for a moment,' Dag said gently, and turned to her with a forced smile. 'I need some time alone.'

Astrid left immediately, walked outside and closed the door. She headed towards Ragi's hut.

Skad was ahead and she approached him. Normally he was good in company, and kept his snide comments to Astrid's training sessions, avoiding her for the rest of the day and at times even avoiding eye contact during meals.

Today, however, she had let her feelings slip with a smile that showed her pleasure at him leaving. She had let frustration with him and the long, early hours training with Ragi show with just that slight smile.

'Don't humiliate me like that again, Brojóta burðr.' Skad snarled and knocked her to the ground without warning. He laughed down at her, and for a brief moment she saw red. She retaliated and snapped her ankles to either side of his right leg and twisted her whole body to the side. She effectively threw him to the ground, a smirk prominent on her face as she did so, though the emotion was short lived. Skad lay there and looked like he was about to murder her, with rage in his eyes.

She couldn't lie to herself; it had been immensely satisfying to knock him down. With an urge to retreat to a safe distance, she got to her feet and walked away.

Deeper in the forest, she smiled as she saw Ragi sat with a stone pestle and mortar, grinding some of the hazelnuts he had dried over the last few days. He scooped up a handful of them and spread them onto a sheet of coarse cloth that had been stretched over a wooden frame to keep it taut. Once done, he placed it out in the sun to dry over a series of raised planks he had built alongside his hut.

'Can I help?' Astrid said. Ragi smiled as he saw her and stepped aside. He poured more hazelnuts into the mortar and passed her the pestle. 'Ragi...what does Brojóta burðr mean?' she asked casually. Ragi reacted as if she had smacked him across the forehead with the word.

'Where did you hear that?' he asked in shock.

'Skad said it.'

His upper lip curled and Ragi snarled. His green eyes turned slightly yellow around the pupil, and stretched upward with an appearance like that of a snake.

'It's a horrible word, Astrid. Next time he says that, tell Dag.'

'But what does it mean Ragi?' Astrid asked again, her curiosity piqued. She refused to back down and insisted he tell her.

'It means...unwanted child,' Ragi lied.

Astrid's eyes grew wide. She was shocked and hurt. There was something he was hiding from her and that was unlike him.

'What does it really mean?'

'Rape. It means rape child,' Ragi finally said, and looked down at his feet. Deeply ashamed that he had had to explain such a disgusting slur.

'Skad thinks my father -'

'No! It's just a cruel word dwarves use for half-bloods. Skad doesn't think anything about your parents. He doesn't know them, he's just cruel.'

'Do the goblins have a word like that?'

'Yes...yes we do,' Ragi confessed, and the tips of his ears turned red with embarrassment. 'So do the elves. We all do.'

'Why? Why do you all...hate me?'

'I don't hate you!' Ragi said, and took her hands in his. 'You're my little wild child.'

'Why? Why don't you hate me?' Astrid asked.

Ragi was appalled that she would even ask such a thing. 'What do you mean?'

'Everyone else hates me. Why are you different?'

'Everyone else doesn't hate you. If your parents had just been commoners I don't think anyone would have cared. But Sylbil, your mother, was royalty, she should have been queen. There were many people who would have seen what she did as a betrayal of her race. And Arnbjörg was second cousin to Vígdís. Most people wouldn't care, it's just because of who your parents were.'

'They were brave,' Astrid whispered, pride and sadness in her voice.

'They were! Immensely brave! It would have been very hard for them to leave you,' Ragi said fondly, and gently rested his hand on the side of her face.

'I wish they hadn't,' Astrid confessed, bowing her head in the knowledge that Ragi would be shocked to hear her say such a thing.

'They loved you! That's what you do for people you love. You give up your life for them!'

'It's mean.' Astrid growled, her eyes blurred with tears, but she refused to let them run down her face. 'They shouldn't have left me alone!'

'You have Dag, and me.'

Astrid smiled and wiped at her tears with a sleeve. 'I'm sorry. I'm just being silly.' She paused for a moment, swallowing back the sadness. 'Oh, I knocked Skad down today,' she said, changing the subject.

Ragi raised his eyebrows so high they were very nearly lost in his hair line.

'You didn't.'

'I did! Knocked him right on his butt.'

Ragi burst out laughing, his laugh a quite terrifying cackle. His ears lifted up and his eyes glinted at her. 'I wish I'd seen it!'

Astrid giggled and picked up the pestle. She ground the hazelnuts some more.

The sun started to set and she ground them a little faster so Ragi would be able to spread the produce out on the cloth trays he had made before the last of the sun disappeared.

'Why do they hate each other?'

'Who?'

'The goblins. And the elves and the dwarves.'

'The goblins said the dwarves attacked them and destroyed Angh-'

'Angh?'

'An old city. I don't think it existed, if I'm honest. My tribe said it was in the Riddari Leggr but I've heard other people say it was in the Outlands.'

'Where's that?'

Ragi sat down, reached for a stick nearby and began to draw in the dirt. He sketched out a rough map of Ammasteinn on the dusty ground. Astrid crouched next to him and watched with interest.

'These mountains here are the Riddari,' Ragi said, and drew a mountain line which stretched across Ammasteinn. 'If the mountains are the shape of a horse, the Aldwood is in its stomach, and the Riddari Leggr are here, where its legs would be.'

'Where do your people live?'

'Here, above the Riddari in the north, and there are a lot of us near Lake Krewa near Bjargtre.'

'If I went there would they hate me?'

'Don't ever go there, Astrid,' Ragi said firmly. 'Goblins don't even trust goblins who aren't from their tribe, they would kill you.'

'Because I'm a half -blood?'

'Because you're not a goblin.'

The sun had completely set, and Astrid heard Dag call for her in the distance. She stood up and smiled at Ragi. 'So I'll go to the human lands.'

'They'd... probably be curious.' Ragi smiled.

'I should ask Dag to take me.'

'Why? He's not human.'

'He's not? Astrid asked, confused. She had assumed that since he did not have pointed ears that he was human.

'No, humans have darker skin. Dag is...actually I don't know what Dag is,' Ragi said in surprise. 'He's not an elf, and he's not a dwarf...'

Dag's calls for her became insistent enough for Astrid to say goodbye. She hugged Ragi quickly and ran off, grinning cheekily, before he could scold her for hugging him. Ragi shook his head at her but smiled as soon as she was out of sight.

Reaching the house, Astrid smiled as she saw Dag but looked around warily.

'Where's Skad?'

'He's inside. Are you alright? Skad said you hurt your head a little today, tripped and fell?'

'I'm alright,' she said, and tried not to sound too cheerful. She thought nothing of Skad's sudden interest in her injuries. 'Is he ok?'

'Who?'

'Skad...I..I accidently knocked him over.'

'I don't know. He seemed angry, as usual.'

Astrid tried not to grin at Dag's remark and slowly walked towards the house. She stopped and took a deep breath before she entered. If Skad was angry before, he would be furious now. She opened the door and walked cautiously inside.

Skad looked up from the table and glared at her, a flask of Dag's ale in his hand. His grey eyes looked terrifying in the firelight.

Astrid closed the door firmly behind her and stepped up to the table. She did her best not to flinch at Skad's glare.

'I'm sorry...I didn't mean to trip you,' Astrid whispered, frightened that the proud dwarf might suddenly decide to leave.

As much as she hated his cruel words at times, what he had taught her made her feel strong, less helpless. In a sad way, he was the only tie she had to her father. It was better to have him and tolerate his insults than have another small tie to her parents severed.

Skad rose and crossed to her. He straightened his back so that he towered over her, and glared down at her. He leant forward till his head was barely an inch from hers.

'Fight dirty like that again and I'll beat you to a pulp!' he hissed.

Astrid wrinkled her nose at the stink of ale on his breath, but her eyes remained fixed on his. For a brief moment his grey eyes reminded her of Arnbjörg.

'You are a Goðgá, a damned Brojóta burðr, and if you do that again I will leave! You can let the old fool teach you how to fight.'

'I'm sorry!' Astrid repeated.

Skad stood quickly as Dag walked into the house, a bundle of fresh firewood in his hands.

'Everything ok?' he asked, flashing the pair a suspicious glance.

'Everything is fine,' Astrid lied.

* * *

Astrid held her blanket around her and looked up at the light the moon had left on the slanted ceiling as it shone through the hole she had created in the opposite side of the roof. She had made a little thatch overhang to protect the hole now, and Ragi had even made her a small door which could fit over it with a lock. She had fitted it a few days ago.

Of course, Dag hadn't noticed the hole. The old warlock tended to be completely oblivious to things such as that, and rarely ventured into her room. A fact Astrid greatly appreciated.

Astrid reached up and played with the wind catcher she had made earlier that week. It consisted of brightly coloured feathers, a few eggshells and small pieces of beaten copper she had scrounged from Ragi. It wasn't even close to the one that had hung in her old room, but it was close enough.

On the wall at the end of her room she had sketched out the final drawing of her parents. The dozens of trial drawings were still scribbled onto her floor, most of them smudged now. Astrid had not bothered to clean them away. The eyes she had painted with some of Dag's brightly coloured inks that she had *borrowed* when he wasn't looking.

Downstairs she could hear Dag talking with Skad, both of them forgetting for the millionth time that she had her mother's hearing. She pulled the blanket over her ears so as not to hear them, determined to ignore them, but she sat up quickly upon hearing her name.

'You should stop being so hard on Astrid,' Dag said, his tone more suggestion than command. Skad instantly took offence that the old warlock would question his training methods.

'I train students how I see fit. I've always trained them this way. If she's too weak, I have many students in Bjargtre I can teach instead.'

'I'm just saying she's a child.'

'So? She'd better get used to it. If she ever leaves, you won't be there to mollycoddle her. She'll have to protect herself or die. My money is on the latter.'

'Don't even joke about that!' Dag said quickly.

'I wasn't joking. How do you think people are going to react when they see her? She's a half-blood. A *royal* half-blood at that, and she'll just draw more attention to herself dragging some stupid weapons around.'

'Astrid is never leaving.'

Astrid felt her heart drop as Dag said the words. She was shocked and dismayed by them.

'She's staying here with me, where I can protect her.'

'Then what's the bloody point of me teaching her if you're going to be around? Am I just her cheap entertainment?'

'She wanted to learn how to fight.'

'Then she's smarter than you. At least she knows she'll be fighting for most of her life. The child will *always* be an outsider.'

Astrid closed her eyes and pressed her nose into her pillow. She inhaled the smell of jasmine and curled up into a ball, pulling the blanket around her like a nest. Even as sleep finally crept over her, she couldn't stop thinking over what she had just heard. She played the two possibilities over and over in her mind.

If Dag made her stay she would be trapped. Stuck in this forest that seemed separate from normal time, broken away from the word, and in a way, never growing.

If she did leave, what would she find? A world she could escape to, or another nightmare? An endless circle of hate for being the product of two people who had loved each other?

'I will always be an outsider,' Astrid whispered to herself.

Fireflies

With a loud howl, Jarl was ripped from his sleep. The sound tore through him like a knife and he jumped to his feet, sword drawn. Skad did the same. Knud sat up and looked over at Jarl, frightened. Halvard scanned the area from where he had been taking watch by the smouldering fire. He readied an axe in his hand.

The sun hadn't risen, and the sky started to turn from dark blue to purple, while the horizon turned to shades of pink and red.

'What was that?' Knud asked. He kicked off his blanket and stood up.

'A wolf! Where the devil is Ast...the Outlander?' Halvard shouted, looking around him.

Another loud howl to their right set them on edge and they all saw the shape of a large gangly wolf run through the trees, accompanied by a flurry of fireflies.

'Where is Astrid?' Skad shouted, and looked around him frantically. He almost sounded worried.

'Doesn't matter where she is,' Jarl said quickly, and Knud flashed him a shocked look. 'She'll find us. We have to leave.'

Halvard kept a watch while the others quickly packed their things. Knud wrapped his sleeping blanket up into a roll and tied it at the top of his rucksack. He pulled the bag onto his back and watched as Jarl, Skad and Halvard did the exact same thing before quickly mounting their ponies. They were all set to ride in the opposite direction of the howls, when Jarl noticed that Knud's pony was missing. Jarl permitted Knud to ride his, and ran alongside it as fast as he could, his hands on the reins. The ponies were frightened out of their wits, and all of the riders struggled to keep them from bolting in fear. Knud held on to the pony with all his might, his fingers wound into its mane. Thankfully, before long, the howling grew fainter.

Jarl looked back and saw that the firefly swarm that had been chasing the wolf suddenly appeared behind them, their glowing tails burning the trees as they flew.

I'm slowing them down, Jarl thought to himself, and let go of the reins. He ordered the others to ride ahead.

Knud slowed to a halt.

'I'm not leaving you!'

'Go! Now!' Jarl bellowed at him.

Skad quickly pulled at Knud's reins and Knud struggled and shouted, screaming his lungs out, begging them to not leave Jarl behind.

Jarl watched them disappear into the forest and took a deep breath. He lowered his sword and the fireflies bore down on him. Their wings beat together so loudly it sounded like a large beast of the forest growling. A smaller swarm darted to ground level for a moment as a rabbit ran for cover. They circled in a flurry of bright lights, and the rabbit shrieked as its fur was set alight by the intense heat produced by them. It fell to its side and squirmed in agony before going still. The fireflies settled on the corpse and began to eat at it with their small but powerful jaws.

Jarl stood still and lifted his head proudly, awaiting the moment they would strike. There was nothing he could do, nowhere nearby he could hide. No matter how fast he ran, there was no way to outrun something that could fly that fast.

Without warning, Jarl felt arms around him, and then something wet suddenly being wrapped around them both in one quick movement. Astrid's face was barely an inch away from his, her breathing heavy, and panting.

'Don't move,' she whispered, her hands raised, holding the top of a black sheet she had wet in a nearby stream and had wrapped around them. Her fingers were the only part of her exposed. The fireflies buzzed around them, charring the wet sheet but unable to burn the occupants. Astrid winced each time one of the swarm settled on her fingers and burned them.

It was then that Jarl noticed her veil was gone, and recognised the material around them.

'Your veil.'

'It comes in handy,' Astrid replied. She turned her face away from him, nervous at his proximity, his hands dangerously close to her waist.

The fireflies, however, still circled them, their light glowing through the veil like demonic stars. They were so close that they could hear their jaws snap, and their sharp little feet rubbing together alongside the flutter of wings.

Astrid bit her lip in pain as more of the fireflies singed her fingers. She closed her eyes and bowed her head so that Jarl couldn't see her expression. Her head almost rested against his chest and she gritted her teeth.

Jarl looked up and saw that her hands were shaking and knew that the fireflies were burning her fingers again and again, evidenced by the smell of burning skin wafting down towards him.

'Just a few more minutes,' Astrid whispered, more to herself than to Jarl. She clenched her fingers together more tightly.

The light around them changed as the sun rose, but still had not yet breached the horizon. Several of the fireflies sensed the approaching daylight and started to leave, but most of them stayed on the wet veil. Steam began to rise from the material; the heat from the fireflies had begun to dry it.

Jarl, as close as he was to Astrid, could see just how deep the scar across her lips ran, just below her nose, where it cut through the fleshy part of her upper and lower lip. The scar had healed some, but it left a pink groove down the centre.

'Come on,' Astrid whispered, aware that the steam was starting to carry the faint smell of burning cloth.

The veil began to slip and Jarl quickly reached his arms around her and grabbed it before it slipped away and exposed them to the fireflies. Astrid shivered at his touch, his strong arms against either side of her waist.

She's frightened! Jarl thought to himself, shocked. Quickly, he moved his arms apart so that they did not rest on her sides.

Astrid looked up at him for a second, a thankful look in her eyes before she looked back down again.

The steam around them now held the unmistakable smell of burning and Jarl heard the veil start to crackle under the heat of the fireflies.

'What do we do?' he asked as calmly as he could.

'Wait for the sun to come up,' Astrid replied. 'They don't like the sun.'

Inhaling sharply, Jarl felt a large firefly, which had been perched on the veil behind his head, burn through it, and the smell of smouldering hair filled the veil cocoon.

'Don't move,' Astrid whispered, and fixed her eyes on his. Jarl did the same and tried to focus on her eyes and not the fact that his long, thick hair was about to burst into flames.

'Any moment now,' Astrid said, her eyes looking away from his for a moment to watch the light of the rising sun start to shine through the veil.

Suddenly, like a silent order had been given, the fireflies rose as one from around the veil in a glowing wave, and flew in the opposite direction of the oncoming rays of sunlight. Finally the sun peeked out from over the horizon.

Jarl and Astrid breathed an almost synchronised sigh of relief.

Astrid lowered her arms and opened up the veil, only to drop her arms around Jarl's neck. She then used the veil to extinguish the risk of his singed hair catching fire.

Jarl reached behind his head and quickly took the veil from her hands. He placed it against the back of his head till he was sure everything was put out. After a time he dropped the veil to the ground and felt the back of his head, relieved to feel that only a little of his hair had been burnt.

Astrid stepped back and visibly shivered. She turned away from him and looked at her hands. Everything from her fingertips to her knuckles was a patchwork of red, burnt and blistered skin, and her fingers shook with the pain.

'Let me see,' Jarl said gently. He turned her to face him and took her hands in his. Astrid moved as if to pull away, but not enough for her hands to move from his.

Jarl checked her hands and wondered how she had found the strength to hold them still during the attack, let alone hold the veil over them. Just the thought of how painful it would have been made his own hands itch.

'Can you heal them?' Jarl asked. 'You healed Knud!'

'No, they will heal by themselves,' Astrid said quickly, pulling her hands out of his. 'I don't waste Jakkito on myself.'

'Jakkito?' Jarl asked, unsure of the strange word. Astrid's accent had changed to a strange soft tone as she had pronounced the word.

'We should leave.' Astrid silently cursed herself for the use of Axetī. A wave of relief washed over her as she realized Jarl had not recognised it as an elven word. 'It will be hard to catch up with them if we wait any longer.' She picked up the scorched veil and wrapped it around her waist once more, then her neck, before using the end section to cover her face. She finally tucked the sides into the edges of her turban.

'What about that wolf?' Jarl asked, turning to look around them warily.

'It's dead. Fur is not the best with fireflies.'

'You don't say. Your cloak is damaged,' Jarl said, pointing at her wolf-skin. Most of it was badly singed.

'We should leave,' Astrid repeated, and ran ahead in search of the others. Jarl followed her, each of them tracking the marks the ponies had left on the ground. They came across Knud's missing pony; the creature lay dead on the ground, most of it eaten down to its bones, the rest of it smouldering.

* * *

'Stop crying!' Skad barked at Knud.

Knud ignored him, with a sniff and a rub of his eyes.

'We need to go back!' Knud shouted at him. 'We can't leave him.'

'We *did* leave him,' Skad fired back, remorseless. He slowed the pony into a gentle trot.

Halvard rode beside him with his head bowed. 'We shouldn't have,' he mumbled.

'He was smarter than you lot,' Skad replied loudly. 'At least he knew there was no point in everyone getting burned to death.'

Halvard shook his head at Skad, a disgusted grimace on his face.

Knud tried not to cry further but was unable to stop himself.

'Oh for goodness sake,' Skad growled, and hopped from the pony. 'I'm surrounded by women. Stop crying Knud. You're worse that Astrid.'

Knud snapped and suddenly threw himself at Skad. He clawed at his face, his curly red hair flying loose.

'I'll kill you. I'll kill you!' Knud howled and kicked and punched at Skad who easily threw him off and onto the ground.

Knud fell with a loud thud onto the floor, the wind knocked out of him.

'Grow up!' Skad shouted down at him, his voice echoing through the forest around them. It startled several birds that quickly scattered and flew into the treetops out of harm's way. 'Jarl is dead. Get used to it. Everyone dies eventually.'

Hearing a twig break loudly underneath a heavy foot, Skad turned and Jarl's fist caught him squarely on the jaw. Skad was knocked to his knees and spat blood from his mouth.

'Don't you touch him again!' Jarl growled at him.

Skad looked over Jarl's shoulder and saw Astrid in his shadow, her eyes shining. He knew immediately that she would have a satisfied smile on her face under the veil.

Jarl walked to Knud and helped him to his feet, and Knud threw his arms around him, which nearly knocked him to the floor. 'I thought you'd gone!' Knud half laughed, half cried.

Jarl knelt down so he was at Knud's head height and ruffled his hair. Knud rubbed the tears out of his eyes and grinned.

'I promised I wouldn't,' he said.

Skad spat again, this time in disgust, and stood.

Each of his companions glared at him. 'Good grief! You lot would be dead without me!'

'No, we'd be dead without Astrid.' Knud smirked.

Skad glared over at Astrid who just stood silently behind them. Her eyes observed but she remained silent.

'Oh that's right...Astrid! Because she's always been so good at protecting people,' Skad jeered.

Jarl got the sense that whatever Skad had said had been like a knife to Astrid's chest. Her eyes flinched as if in pain for a second, but she ignored him and walked ahead. She expected the others would follow her.

'That's it. Walk away like you always do.'

'Shut up,' Jarl ordered , ready to lay another blow to Skad's face if the old dwarf did not do as he was told.

Skad, surprisingly, obeyed him, and they all slowly walked after Astrid.

Halvard offered Jarl his horse, but he instead walked side by side with Knud and rested his arm over his shoulders.

Knud flashed Astrid an overjoyed smile as she turned to look behind for a moment. Her eyes lit up as she smiled back at him under her veil.

Jarl looked up and caught her eyes just before she turned to look ahead again.

'Thank you,' Jarl said quietly, once they had caught up with her.

Astrid nodded her head and turned away, preferring to look down at her hands. 'Another scar,' she said quietly to herself, None of the others heard her. She smiled to herself and closed her hands despite the pain it caused to move it.

'Outlander!' How long till we reach the Salt Mines?' Halvard called over to her.

'The monasteries. They're called the Salt Monasteries,' Astrid called back to correct him. She looked to her left and saw the tall ridge of the Riddari Mountains, which they had been walking along for the past few weeks through the canopies of the trees. 'Another three days, hopefully. Depends how quickly we can walk now that there's only three ponies left.'

* * *

The weather had suddenly gotten so much colder and the sun disappeared behind fast approaching clouds the minute it hit noon. Astrid pulled her cloak around her and felt the burnt patches in the fur.

Next to her, Jarl and Knud were sharing the same pony, Jarl still with his arm over Knud's shoulders. Skad and Halvard rode slowly behind them, Skad looking like he had tasted something bitter, his face twisted into a nasty scowl. Astrid felt his eyes glaring at her back as they walked ahead.

'Does Skad have to come with us?' Knud whispered.

'I can't stop him,' Jarl said, his tone of voice implying that he would like to.

'Maybe Astrid can stop him!' Knud grinned and glanced over at her from the corner of his eyes.

Looking down to her hand, Astrid winced, the skin starting to ooze slightly. While she had no problem with bearing the pain - she had endured much worse - she knew if she left it much longer it would start to affect how well she could protect the others. And that was not something she was willing to compromise.

'We should stop for a moment,' Astrid said, turning to face them. 'Rest for a bit.'

Clambering off the ponies, Skad and Halvard went about collecting firewood, all of them cold. Jarl passed Knud the flint. 'Go on. Light the fire.'

'I don't have a sword.'

'Here, take this,' Astrid said, passing Knud the mid-sized dagger Ragi had made her. 'Keep it for the moment. You shouldn't be without a weapon out here.' She turned and walked away into the forest.

Knud waited until Skad and Halvard had arranged the firewood into an upstanding triangle. Jarl tossed small pieces of kindling at the bottom and Knud quickly ran the blade Astrid had given him down the flint. A burst of sparks shot from the edge of the dagger and lit the kindling, and Knud smiled excitedly.

'Great...maybe next time he can use the flint to fight! Scare them away with the sparks!' Skad laughed, and strolled back into the forest to collect more firewood.

Astrid walked as far into the forest as she dared, worried that the moment her back was turned something would happen. Spotting a small hollow in the ground not far from her, she walked towards it, the ground falling low enough for her to be able to stand in it without her head being visible to anyone standing in the rest of the forest.

She knelt down on the ground and took a deep breath, pulling her wolf-skin cloak around her. Her burnt hands held its claws and stabs of pain shot through her nerves as her hands pressed against the wolf-skin. Astrid gritted her teeth.

'Don't scream!' she muttered to herself, closing her eyes.

Like a flower's petals closing for the night, the wolf-skin shuddered slightly before curling around her. The hairs flexed and swayed, and the wolf's head slid down over Astrid's face, its eyes opening. Its legs shook in pain, the burnt patches suddenly turning pink and raw as the skin came to life. The wolf's grey and green eyes flickered as it clawed at the dirt, its pain making Astrid feel as if she were resting on burning coals, searing every rational thought away and leaving only pure animal instinct. She wanted nothing more than to howl in pain, just as she had earlier that morning when she had stopped the swarm of fireflies approaching the others as they had slept.

Astrid focused her energy on the wolf-skin, willing it to regenerate, her wolf form whimpering as it did so.

Shaking the skin off, Astrid breathed a sigh of relief. Another few hours and it would have been too damaged to wear again. Although it was much like any animal fur in appearance, as soon as she wore it, the skin throbbed with life. It could be hurt or killed just like any other living wolf, and if the skin got too damaged, it would be useless.

'Astrid?'

Looking up, she stared in horror at Knud who was peering down over the edge of the hollow at her, a bundle of firewood at his feet. His face with shocked, his skin ashen.

He saw me!

Five Questions

'Astrid?' Knud repeated.

'Knud...please...please don't tell the others!' she begged, holding her hands out and sitting down on the ground incase Knud though she might leap up and hurt him. She didn't want to frighten him. 'I can explain! Just come down and I'll tell you everything!'

A sudden glint appeared in his eyes and Knud turned back for a second to look at the others in the distance. The fire was fully burning now; the firewood could wait. He jumped from the edge, landed next to Astrid in the hollow, and sat down on the ground in front of her.

Taking a deep breath, Astrid quickly weighed her chances.

She could run away and return later, denying that she had ever been there and blame anything Knud claimed he saw on an overactive imagination.

No...that won't work! The Red 'shrooms had already shown her that Halvard didn't trust her; he would instantly side with anything which portrayed her in a negative light. Skad...he would take neither side, stepping back to observe the chaos, and Jarl...what would Jarl think?

It wouldn't be right! To lie would hurt Jarl and Knud, and neither of them deserved that. But if she told Knud, would he keep her secret?

You have to risk it!

'You were a wolf!'

'No. The skin is. I can use the skin to take the form of a wolf, but without it I can't change into anything.'

'Where did you get it?'

'Five questions! You can ask me five questions and then you never mention it again! You never tell anyone! You have to promise,' Astrid said firmly, hearing Jarl calling out for Knud in the distance.

'Any five questions?'

'Yes any!' Astrid replied, panicking, as Jarl's voice became louder.

'Good!' Knud said, and quickly clambered out of the hollow and ran up to Jarl as if he didn't have a care in the world. Astrid waited for a few more minutes until she was sure they had both gone, then made her way out and attached her veil firmly over her face, not wanting her expression to give anything away. She didn't know if Knud would hold up to his end of the bargain, or if he could even lie convincingly. The less emotion her face showed, the better.

* * *

Jarl looked back at Astrid, surprised that she wasn't racing ahead like she usually did. Knud waited for an hour or two before falling back and walking next to her.

For all his naivety, Knud was far from stupid. In the last two hours he had run over every possible question he could ask Astrid, knocking off the questions that might be answered anyhow in the course of the journey and whittling it down to only the questions he was burning to know the answers to.

'How did you get that skin?'

'That would be a story, not an answer,' Astrid replied indignantly, regretting having promised five questions so easily.

'Then answer it with a story!' Knud grinned, refusing to back down.

'Not here. I'll tell you tonight when we stop. Ask Jarl if you can go out with me on the patrol. I'll answer you first question then.'

'We could walk ahead now,' Knud suggested, impatient.

Not entirely sure if she could trust him, Astrid agreed, and Knud raced up to Jarl.

'Can I walk ahead with Astrid?'

'No. She likes to be alone, Knud, you know that.'

'She said it was alright.'

Jarl turned to look at her and Astrid nodded. 'Ok then, but don't bother her.'

'I don't trust her,' Halvard muttered as they walked out of earshot. Jarl rolled his eyes at him, annoyed with his persistent distrust of her.

'You've said that already,' Jarl said, tired of arguing with him.

'If she'd spotted those fireflies sooner, you wouldn't have been in danger in the first place!'

'I could say the same to you!' Jarl retorted, and Halvard looked away.

'I'm just saying there's something strange about her. Humans can't use magic! And her eyes, they scream of witchcraft!'

'I think they're beautiful,' Jarl said without thinking, his face as shocked as Halvard's as soon as the words left his mouth.

'They're unnatural,' Halvard said, trying to ignore what Jarl had just confessed.

Ignoring him, Jarl strode ahead.

'Ok. Are we far enough away now?' Knud asked Astrid, glancing at the others.

She nodded. 'I was given it by a Vârcolac called Una-'

'Vârcolac?' Knud interrupted.

'Is that another question?'

'No!' Knud said quickly.

'Her family had been captured by goblins. Most of them were skinned alive before I found them. I think the goblins thought that if they took their skins, they could turn into wolves. It doesn't work like that,' Astrid said, a haunted look in her eyes, remembering the terrible things she had seen that day. 'I managed to save some of them. Una was very sick by the time I got her out. By the time we got to the Aldwood she was dying. She passed her gifts to me and gave me her wolf-skin.'

Looking over at Knud, she decided to not make him pay for more information by giving up another question. The question he was dying to ask her was practically written on his face.

'When a Vârcolac gives up their powers, they die. You can take their skin but it's useless without their birthright. They have to will it to you or it doesn't work.'

'She died to give it to you,' Knud whispered, shocked and fascinated at the same time.

'She was dying anyway,' Astrid said matter-of-factly. 'And she was happy; her family was safe and there wasn't any chance of the goblins following us into the Aldwood. Now...any more questions?'

Taking a few moments to think, Knud looked at his boots as they walked, his face twisted into a knot.

'Why are your eyes two different colours?'

Stopping in her tracks, Astrid stared at him, feeling like a long hand had reached into her chest and crushed her lungs, stopping her from breathing.

'Why do you want to know that?' she asked, her voice nearly breaking mid sentence. Knud looked at her worriedly.

'I've never seen anyone with eyes like that before.'

'I'm sorry Knud, I won't answer that,' she said firmly.

For a moment Knud looked like he was about to argue with her, but to her surprise, he didn't.

'Ok...will you give me two more questions then? On top of the four left?'

Growling under the veil, Astrid nodded, rubbing her fingers together nervously, suddenly feeling very frightened and exposed. Memories flooded through her head, each one like a fresh stab to her chest.

Please! Ask me something which will make me think of something else!

'Where did you learn to fight?'

Smiling, Astrid took a deep breath. This one she could answer.

'A friend of mine called Ragi taught me. Skad did too, and later, a human called Aaren.'

'I don't like Skad,' Knud growled.

'Neither do I!' Astrid laughed. 'He's a miserable git!'

'He is, isn't he?' Knud said, walking beneath a large pine that had half fallen across the path. It was leaning perilously on its side with its branches entangled with those of nearby trees, and its roots emerging from the earth.

Suddenly, with a creak and a groan, it gave way, crashing into Skad and his pony. Skad just about managed to throw himself backwards to avoid it.

Astrid raced over to them, relieved to see that the pony was dead. Its back legs had been snapped by the branches that pinned it to the ground. If it had survived, it would have been in so much pain that they'd have had to have killed it to put it out of its misery.

Skad, on the other hand, was very much alive, screaming at them through the thick foliage that covered him to get him out. Astrid reached him just as Jarl clambered over from the other side.

Pushing the branches aside, Astrid saw that his lower legs were pinned down under one of the larger branches, his left leg in particular caught at an odd angle. She looked up and flashed Jarl a worried look.

'Are you just going to stare at me or help?' Skad yelled up at them.

Astrid pulled her hammer axe from her belt and chopped away at the branches that prevented her from reaching down to help him.

'Cant you move your feet?' she called down. Skad swore, his feet flinching as he did so.

'I guess he can,' Jarl muttered.

Grabbing one of the larger branches, Jarl and Halvard crouched down below it, propped their shoulders beneath it and tried to lift it. The branch over Skad's legs lifted by a few centimetres but not enough for Astrid to pull him out. After a few more attempts they finally stopped, unable to lift it up high enough.

'It's too heavy!' Jarl muttered, panting.

For one very brief moment, Astrid considered either leaving Skad behind or cutting off his trapped legs to free him. Looking up at her, a small trickle of fear flashed across Skad's face, her eyes reflecting what she was thinking. Skad was terrified that now he was utterly helpless, she might act on her hatred of him.

'Knud?' Astrid said, turning to the small dwarf. 'Stand behind Skad, and when we lift the branch high enough, I want you to pull him out.'

Nodding, Knud did as she'd asked. He crouched down behind Skad and linked his arms through Skad's and wrapped them around his chest.

Astrid propped herself under the branch, and the three of them pushed on their feet as hard as they could, taking the weight of it on their shoulders. Finally, it lifted just enough to enable Knud to pull Skad out from beneath it.

Screaming, Skad gripped his left leg. His right appeared to be fine, but his left was twisted at an odd angle.

Astrid stood back and watched as Jarl checked Skad's leg, a small smile creeping up her face. They were only a few days away from the Salt Monasteries, and in this condition he would not be able to travel with them the rest of the way. She would only have to put up with him for a few more days.

'You don't need to look so happy about it,' Skad spat up at her.

'I need some bandages,' Jarl said, knowing he did not have anything of the sort in his bag. 'Some strips of cloth, anything.'

'You could use that damn veil of hers,' Skad said, glaring at her. Astrid ignored him and slipped off her cloak and handed it to Knud so she could take her bag off her back. Knud tried not to look like he was in awe as he stroked the fur like it was alive.

Astrid pulled two thick bandages from her bag, both of which looked like they had been reused repeatedly, the once cream coloured cloth now a light brown colour, some patches darker than others.

'You can use these,' Astrid said, passing them to Jarl. He plucked a thick branch from the ground and sliced off the protruding twigs and leaves with a dagger, using the branch to make a splint.

'You couldn't give me clean bandages?' Skad grumbled, looking at them in disgust.

'Would you prefer I used a dirty, torn up cloak?' Jarl snapped back at him. Skad's constant bad attitude was pushing him to the edge of tolerance.

'I don't want to get any elf diseases,' Skad muttered.

Halvard saw a look of fear cross Astrid's eyes. She quickly turned away and strode off with Knud following her, the wolf-skin cloak in his hands nearly tripping him as he walked.

'Do you have to be such an asshole all the time?' Jarl said, deliberately tightening the bandages a little too much and making Skad yelp in pain.

'She's stubborn! She deliberately gave me old bandages!'

'Be pleased she gave you bandages at all!' Jarl said, standing up. He stepped back and let Halvard help Skad onto his pony. 'I wouldn't have.'

* * *

Keeping her eyes on the ground, Astrid avoided all eye contact with Halvard, feeling his gaze on her as she walked back into the camp they had set up for the night. Two dead rabbits and a stoat, strung together, hung from her hand. Her arrow had hit them squarely in the forehead; they were dead before they even saw what was coming.

Jarl had wanted to hunt for food as he usually did, but Astrid had insisted that he stay in the camp with the others, desperate to get away to calm herself down and focus on something other than the worry that Halvard might discover what she was, or that Skad might have another slip of the tongue.

She had tucked her bow under her cloak as she walked back, not wanting Halvard to see anything which was elven. He was suspicious enough as it was.

For the moment, everything else was in her favour. She was short, too short for an elf. But she would have to be extra vigilant over the next few days. If Skad let anything else slip she swore she would break his other leg in retaliation. Reacting to him earlier would only have acted as an admission to guilt, which Halvard would have jumped on immediately. Ignoring Skad's remarks had been the only logical course of action.

As frightened as she was, the chance to be around her own kind was exhilarating, an odd combination of terror and euphoria. She was terrified that they would discover she was a half elf but she was overjoyed to find that she had so much in common with them. They were physically very strong like her and had the same kind of stoic personality. Even something as silly as knowing they enjoyed some of the same foods made her feel wildly happy.

For so long she had avoided any contact with either the elves or the dwarves, but right now she felt accepted, even if it was in a small way, and the feeling was addictive.

Sitting down a little away from the fire, Astrid began to skin and gut the stoat and the rabbits. Knud offered to help but Astrid shook her head. 'Not now,' she whispered, and Knud nodded and walked away.

'Have you ever travelled with elves?' Halvard asked, his hands extended to the flames of the fire, his voice a little too casual.

'Once,' Astrid replied, worried that remaining quiet would only make him more persistent. 'A few years ago.'

'Why?' Halvard asked disgusted. 'Why would you help *elves!*'

The feeling of acceptance disappeared and Astrid tightened her grip around the knife and skinned the rabbit more aggressively.

'Why would I help *dwarves!*' she snapped back. 'I help who pays me!'

'We haven't paid you yet,' Halvard pointed out.

'I prefer to be paid on arrival,' Astrid said quickly. She pulled the skin off the rabbit and tossed it to the ground, making a mental note to bury it later, like she often did.

'You've always been a sucker for helping people,' Skad laughed, somehow making it sound like an insult.

'Good!' Jarl said quickly, seeing a glaze moving over Astrid's eyes as she stopped what she was doing and turned the knife in her hand like she was ready to plunge it into something other than the rabbit she was gutting. 'None of us would have made it otherwise.'

And again the feeling was back, and again Astrid was completely unsure of how to react. It was such an alien feeling to her, something she had always craved but was never prepared to receive. How was it that something that came so naturally to other people felt so abnormal to her?

I am abnormal! Always will be!

'You can finish it,' Astrid said, getting to her feet and tossing the half gutted rabbit to Skad, its entrails spilling out onto him. 'About time you did something useful.'

Leaving the camp, Astrid walked away slowly, reaching up to her left ear out of habit, her hair and the wolf-skin hiding it.

'Astrid?' Knud's voice said behind her, his voice quiet and worried.

'Not now Knud. No more questions for the moment.'

'I wasn't going to ask any questions. I just wanted to know if you were ok.'

Smiling, Astrid turned to look at him. His skin looked so much paler in the moonlight, which had managed to squeeze past the thousands of leaves above them.

'I'm ok, Knud.'

'Knud!' Jarl's voice called, and Astrid looked up, startled to see him walking towards them.

He thinks something's not right about me! He thinks I'm not normal!

'Knud. Go and stop Skad from cooking. I'd like to *not* eat ash if I can,' he said.

Knud strolled back to the camp, and Jarl turned to face Astrid, not entirely sure what he wanted to say, just knowing he wanted to say something.

'He won't be able to travel. He'll have to stay at the Salt Monasteries.'

'I know,' Astrid replied, almost laughing under her veil. An uncomfortable silence ensued as neither of them could find the words to say anything more. Astrid wasn't sure why her stomach was winding itself into knots.

Jarl finally spoke. 'Your hand...'

'It's fine. Doesn't hurt as much now,' Astrid said, looking down at it and flexing her wrist as if to prove her point. The skin was still burnt and scabs covered most of it. Her veil hid any expression that might have said otherwise. 'The monks can help me when I get there. They've seen worse!' She laughed and Jarl smiled at the sound.

She has a beautiful laugh! he thought to himself, turning to walk back to the camp and hearing Skad arguing with Knud about who was taking charge of the cooking.

'Knud's cooking,' Jarl said firmly, reaching the fire and yanking the rabbit from Skad's hands. 'Knud, don't burn it.'

The Salt Monasteries

The relief they felt when they finally saw the Salt Monasteries in the distance was almost indescribable. Images of warm food, soft beds, and far more importantly, toilets that didn't involve a bush and a shovel, flashed across their minds.

They had been hiking up the many winding paths leading to the Salt Monasteries for three days, the air gradually thinning as they climbed. Jarl was surprised at the lack of oxygen, and how tired it had made him feel, assuming that being from Bjargtre he would be used to it. But as he had soon found out, the Hiddari part of the Riddari Mountains were considerably higher than the Riddari Hǫfuð where Bjargtre was built. The mountains here stretched up at least three times higher into the sky. On the third day they had even woken to see clouds forming further down the mountain. The sunrise was truly magnificent from so high up, the sky a burst of red, yellow and orange flames, the light shimmering on the backs of the pure white clouds.

Thankfully, it was not snowing, though the wind was bitterly cold. At night it cut like razors on any exposed skin. The rocky terrain made for some very uncomfortable sleeping and Jarl's back was ready to cause him a great deal of permanent discomfort if he didn't find a more level surface to sleep on soon.

Astrid seemed to be the only one who slept just fine. In fact, now that Jarl thought about it, he couldn't remember ever having seen her actually sleep. Astrid was always up and alert at all times: tending the fire, collecting wood, or searching the perimeter.

'I know you say I'm too young, but can I have some ale when I get there?' Knud begged, his feet sore and tiredness cutting down the already small filter between his mouth and his brain.

'Ale!' Skad laughed. 'You want to have Daru wine if you're at the Salt Monasteries. They're famous for it.'

In front of them, Astrid rolled her head from side to side, the stiff vertebrae in her neck clicking back into place loudly. Skad instantly recognised it as a way of her restraining any physical signs of her frustration. She had done it many, many times during the years he had trained her, and even now, thirty years later, he still remembered.

'He's not having wine,' Jarl said firmly, and Knud's face dropped.

'Please! I'll only have one!' he begged, running up next to Jarl and trying to skip alongside to annoy him, hoping it would convince him to let him have a drink. It didn't work. Astrid laughed at the expression on his face as Jarl said no again.

*　*　*

Reaching the large wooden doors of the monastery, Astrid pulled at the large hand-shaped, rusted metal knockers. The huge, heavy doors opened after a few moments and a tall human walked out. Astrid smiled under her veil as she recognized him. The monk was a good foot taller than her and had to bend down to hug her.

'Erin!' He laughed, stepping back to look at her. 'Well...I would say you've grown but we know that isn't true!' He laughed again and Astrid beamed at him and bounced on the balls of her feet.

'Will you let a few weary travellers stay the night?' she asked, her eyes shining, happy to see her old friend again.

'No, I'll turn them away!' the monk said jokingly. 'Of course!' he said, and took her hand and led her through the door, the others following behind. Halvard and Jarl were shocked to see her behaving so differently, bouncing up and down like a child.

Walking inside, they saw a large bricked courtyard, the tiles on the ground a deep terracotta red, the walls painted pure white. The pillars that held up the balcony around the courtyard were made with both red and white bricks, which had been laid to create a beautiful spiral pattern. Almost everything around them was a striking contrast of the two colours. Several monks and travellers sat in the centre of the courtyard, absorbing the little warmth the sunlight offered so high up in the mountains.

'If your friends would like to follow my brother, he'll take them to the hot springs,' the monk said, gesturing to one of the other monks nearby. Knud practically ran up to him at the mention of it. Skad and Halvard followed him with a little less obvious enthusiasm, and Jarl held back for a moment.

'How long will we be staying?' Jarl asked Astrid, waiting for her to walk with him and the others.

'A week,' the monk said firmly, and Jarl glared at him. *I was asking Astrid!* he thought.

'A week,' Astrid repeated. 'We all need to rest,' she said calmly, turning and walking off with the monk. Jarl was shocked to see her leaning her head against him as they strolled away, the monk moving his arm around her fondly like she was a little child.

'It's good to have you back, Erin!' he said.

'It's good to be back!' Astrid replied, smiling.

*   *   *

Breathing a deep contented sigh, Astrid stepped down into the hot spring bath, still wearing her clothes, her wolf-skin and shoes neatly placed by the wall. The gentle current that flowed from one end of the bath to the other washed away the dirt and mud that had collected on her clothes. She leant back and let herself float on the surface of the water.

There was something about this side of the Riddari, and the bitter cold which always found its way into her joints. The Red Mountains, when she had been with Dag, had been cold during the winters, but it had never been a cold which settled into the marrow. And along the Riddari, even in the summer the cold would wait till the dark of night to freeze any travellers to their core, making the journey all the more uncomfortable. That, along with the incessant drizzle that came and went like the wind, made it without a doubt her least favourite place to travel through.

After removing her veil, Astrid submerged her head below the water and opened her eyes. Small bubbles drifted past her in the flow of the water. She reached behind her and began to undo the long plait of hair wrapped around her head, removing the four, needle-like steel sticks pinning it in place. Her long black hair drifted around her like seaweed, the ends of it almost reaching the backs of her knees.

Hearing someone walking outside the door, and a gentle knock, Astrid lifted her head above the surface.

'Yes?'

'Erin, the Abbot would like you to come sit with him when you're done. You have to tell us all about your adventures!'

'I will!' Astrid laughed, and waited for him to leave before dipping her head back under the water and tucking her hair behind her ears. Her left ear was visible, the tip of it gone, cut away by a serrated blade. The edge was still rough and angry, still sore even after so many years.

Running her finger over it, Astrid opened her eyes beneath the water, trying to distract herself by observing how the light looked through the water. The salt lamps on the walls gave off a fire-like glow. The steam from the bath dissolved the salt and made it trickle down the walls onto the floor, and eventually into the water. Astrid could taste it.

It's good to be back! she whispered, lifting her head out of the water.

It was good to be Erin once again.

* * *

The clothes were new, she could tell; the fabric too stiff and making her feel uncomfortable. She didn't like new clothes, they were too fresh, there was no history to them, and as such, didn't move with her when she walked.

After washing her clothes in the baths and hanging them up to dry, Astrid had taken some of the spare clothes that the monks always left folded for travellers to use.

The simple beige robes were made of three layers. One simple robe reached to the wrists and the ankles, split up the sides to the hip. A pair of sturdy wide-leg trousers were worn underneath, with a rope for a belt, and finally a thick woolen cloak was worn over everything else with a simple red sash around the waist, the sleeves wide and thick.

She wrung out her long hair and pinned it in a loose bun with the four steel pins. Her hair was still wet but she did not want to appear disheveled in front of the Abbot. She could let it down to dry later.

As she stepped out of her bath cubicle, a fresh mountain breeze blew down the corridor. She gazed up at the cloudless sky and smiled as the sun warmed her face.

She was on the second floor of the Monastery, the floor reserved only for close friends of the monks. Astrid was one of the few people with such a privilege.

'Erin!' One of the monks called out, and Astrid smiled at him, her veil gone and her face exposed. None of the monks minded or even seemed to notice the marks on her face. 'The Abbot is waiting!'

Following him, Astrid glanced around her, happy to see the abbey was still the same as when she had last visited. Clean; everything was clean. The monks, though simple in their dress and surroundings, were meticulous when it came to presentation and hygiene. The floors were scrubbed daily, their hair was always trimmed short, and brushed. Their clothes were always clean and above all, they were always working on something. Time was not to be wasted, they said. It passed so fast.

And for humans it was all too true! Some of the monks she knew so well had a crown of silver hair on their heads already, their hair having been raven black the last time she had visited. It scared her, how quickly the humans died.

Walking into the large hall, the monk pushed aside the thick, heavy sheet curtains that served as doors during the day for the great hall. The walls inside were lined with two tables on either side of the walkway; only one large table was laid out across the hall directly in view of the door. The old Abbot looked up and smiled, and Astrid did her best to not run up to him, a wide smile spreading across her face as she slowly and respectfully approached. She stopped and bowed in front of the small table laid out for her in the centre of the room. Several bowls were filled with a much wider variety of food choices than the other monks had been offered.

The Abbot motioned for her to sit down and eat, and Astrid did so, reaching towards the steaming soup bowl. All the monks had their eyes on her, waiting impatiently for her to finish her food so the Abbot would ask her about her travels.

Finishing the soup, Astrid put the bowl down quietly, grinned at the monks' eager faces and looked up.

'You look tired, Erin. Maybe you should rest before telling us about your adventures?' the Abbot said. His voice sounded sincere, but Astrid knew he was only saying it to tease the others. Their eyes looked at her pleadingly, like little children dying to be told a new and exciting story.

'I can rest tonight. I have many stories you will like to hear!' The monks shuffled in their seats excitedly.

'Some I don't think I will like,' the Abbot said gravely, pointing at her severed left ear. Astrid reached up and touched it out of habit, like she always did when she was self-conscious.

'Elves,' she said simply. The Abbot's face dropped, dismayed.

'Why?' he asked

'I was in Waidu; it was my fault. I should have stayed away from the elf inns, but I couldn't help myself. I wanted to see what they looked like. They saw me standing by the doorway and I was about to leave, but some elves walked in and pushed me into the middle of the room. They thought I was a dwarf, then they saw my ears-'

'Stop!' the Abbot said quickly, seeing Astrid was starting to knot her fingers together nervously. 'Tell us something else. Tell us about your travelling companions.'

Astrid told them everything, from leaving Einn to the Angu worms, right up to the moment when Skad had his legs broken by the falling tree. The Abbot asked what she thought of each of them.

'Skad. You know what I think of him.' Astrid growled, shook her head, and quickly moved onto another topic before she had the urge to stab something. 'Knud is the young boy with the red, red hair. He's a little devil!' She laughed. 'A clever little devil! He doesn't know when to keep his mouth shut, but he knows how to use his brain!'

'And the dwarf with the sour face?' one of the monks interrupted. The Abbot flashed him a disapproving look, but said nothing.

'Halvard. He's Jarl's friend, though I don't know why. Halvard is always so angry and sour, and he doesn't trust me. Jarl is the opposite, he trusts me and he's kind. Especially to Knud. He loves that little boy,' she said, her face softening.

'Is Knud his son?'

'No. He's his best friend's son; or so Knud told me.'

'And the dwarves, what do you think of them now?'

'I don't know what to think of them,' Astrid admitted, looking down at her food. 'If they were all like Skad or Halvard, I would not want to know them. Halvard hates me just because he thinks I'm human-'

'Human?' An old monk next to the Abbot laughed. 'You're far too pale to be human! Is he blind?'

Astrid chuckled. 'He thinks I'm from the north. If he found out I'm a half-elf, I don't know what he would do. But if they're like Knud...or Jarl, then I think I would like them. Jarl especially. He's brave.'

'And the others aren't?'

'They are...' Astrid admitted resentfully. 'But they don't smile. He does, he smiles and he's kind. They aren't. If I thought all dwarves were like Halvard or Skad I would hate them all.'

* * *

Jarl was restless. Only five days had passed but it was more than enough for him. He was anxious to get on the road again, knowing that the next part of their journey was where the real danger would present itself.

The Salt Monasteries was an outpost on the edge of the wild. The pass running alongside the spine of the Hiddari Mountains was notoriously treacherous, the region plagued by erratic weather and more than likely now, by goblin swarms too. He did not like to wait around for something that worried him, preferring to face it head on, as soon as he could.

Also, in the five days they had been at the monastery, he had not seen Astrid even once. Not that he'd been actively looking for her, and to be fair the place was enormous, a large section of it built underground into the mountain, something that Jarl liked a lot, making him feel more at home. What worried him the most though, was that they were not the only travellers to be staying at the monasteries. A small party of elves were staying there too.

Thankfully the elves were sleeping in different quarters; the monks were well aware of the cultural hostilities between the two races and didn't want any fighting to break out. And neither did any of the travellers. The monks were kind and welcoming, and did not tolerate any form of fighting among their guests. Nobody wanted to be kicked out onto the mountainside, which was something the monks were not adverse to doing if they found anyone causing trouble.

Walking back into the dormitory that he and the rest of the group were sharing with a few other human merchants, Jarl lay down on his bed and closed his eyes in an attempt to sleep, figuring that it was probably the fastest way to pass the time. The sun had set an hour ago and the salmon-pink glow of the salt lamps adorning the walls were making him sleepy.

Seeing his uncle closing his eyes from the bed opposite, Knud snuck out of the room and walked down the hallway towards the great hall, hoping he would either find Astrid or some Daru wine. He straightened his back and tried to walk in a firmer manner, knowing the monks would refuse him if they suspected he was drinking without permission.

Reaching the hall, Knud smiled as he saw a monk in the far corner serving wine from a large copper basin. There were only a few people sitting around, most of them monks. A few stone tables with wooden legs stretched the length of the hall and several salt lamps burned on the walls, emitting a warm, pinkish glow.

Walking up to the monk serving the wine, Knud confidently asked for a cup of it, and the unsuspecting monk passed him a filled goblet of the dark purple liquid. Knud strolled over to the table and sat down, lifted the wine to his lips and tried to drink it as if he had done so a hundred times before.

At first the bitterness took him by surprise and he grimaced at the taste, placing the goblet back on the table. Then slowly, the sweet under taste kicked in and a warm, fuzzy feeling spread from his mouth to his fingers and toes. Knud lifted the goblet again and took another sip, the taste becoming more addictive with each gulp.

Before he realised it, he had finished it all. He stood to ask for another, but realising his legs were wobbly, he quickly put the goblet down and tried to walk out of the hall, his steps shaky.

'Your uncle is going to kill you if he finds out!' a soft gentle voice said behind him, and Knud turned around, almost falling over in the process. He saw Astrid standing behind him, her veil and wolf-skin gone, her clothes freshly cleaned.

'Aaaaastriiiid! Such a pretty name!'

With her head wrap gone he could see her long, flowing black hair, the stubborn wavy curls held back from her face by two small plaits on either side of her head. Knud saw that the scars on her face extended down to her neck, one long, thin mark that looked like it had been made by a whip cutting through her brow and the bridge of her nose. The Dip scars were the most brutal of the marks, the scars almost trenches in her skin.

Not sure what to say, Astrid watched him, amused, and then a worried look flashed across her face as she realised how drunk he really was. Taking his hand firmly, she led him up the stairs into the upper levels of the monastery, Knud nearly falling over several times and Astrid having to help him.

She pulled him into the main dining hall and left him by the door. Slowly, she approached the Abbot and bowed respectfully before asking him for some charcoal cakes. The Abbot looked over her shoulder and burst into laughter as he saw Knud swaying by the door. The other monks laughed too, as Knud's eyes started to spin in a circle.

'I'm sorry! My friend is young and foolish, but I don't want him to get into trouble with his uncle.' Astrid grinned, and the Abbot passed her a bowl of small charcoal tablets the size of peas. Astrid took a few and walked back to Knud, insisting he swallow them. She handed him a goblet of water when he did.

'You're too young to drink Daru wine!' She laughed as he pulled a face, the charcoal cakes starting to dissolve in his stomach and absorb the wine, making him feel a little sick.

'Please don't tell my uncle!' Knud begged, and Astrid smiled. 'You're beautiful when you smile,' he slurred, and she tried not to blush.

'I won't tell him,' she said, her face lit up. 'You're just going to stay here with me for a few minutes till the charcoal starts working, and then you're going to go back downstairs and promise me you will not take another drink without your uncle's permission.'

'Oh thank you!' Knud said, stumbling forward and hugging her. Astrid tried to push him away, but Knud was still too drunk to care, his body too heavy, as he hugged her more tightly.

'I promise I won't ever drink again!' he said, and Astrid pushed him away.

'Don't make promises you can't keep, Knud,' she said, leading him over to the stairs. "Come and sit down.'

Knud lowered himself unsteadily to the top step and Astrid joined him, neither of them noticing the four figures watching them from the other side of the adjoining courtyard.

'You told me that Jarl isn't your real uncle,' Astrid said, knowing that in his present state she could ask him anything she wanted, and in all likelihood he would remember nothing the next day.

'No. He's my father's best friend. My father was killed by goblins. One day I'm going to become a great warrior and kill them all,' Knud managed to say, slurring half his words.

'Not all goblins are bad, Knud,' Astrid said softly, her eyes distant. 'There are goblin families just like yours, their best friends and fathers killed by dwarves, or elves.'

'All goblins are evil,' Knud spat. 'They killed my father.'

'My best friend was a goblin. Ragi. He was a lovely goblin,' Astrid said, and Knud looked at her in shock.

'You were best friends with a *goblin?*'

'Yes. He was very kind to me. Took care of me. I hated dwarves then as much as you hate goblins now. But no race is evil. Individuals can be good or bad. Don't let one group make you hate the rest of them.'

'Is that the Ragi who taught you to fight?'

'Yes. He made that dagger I lent you.'

'A *goblin* made that?'

'Yes, he did!' Astrid said smiling. 'And all these,' she said, pulling her foot out of her boot and showing Knud the strap around her leg with several small daggers tucked into it.

After a few minutes, Knud's wooziness began to fade and was replaced with an overwhelming urge to sleep. Astrid helped him to his feet and held his hand as they made their way back to Knud's dorm at the end of the hallway.

Suddenly, four tall strangers blocked their path: four elves, their hair a deep, dark red.

"Look!' Knud slurred. 'Their eyes are the same colour as your green one!' Astrid stiffened and dug her nails into Knud's hand.

One of the elves reached out to touch her face and Astrid flinched, hitting his hand away. The other elves laughed.

'What's the matter, dwarf?' one of them asked. 'We just want to know what you are! You're not a proper dwarf, that's for sure; too light on your feet! Not fat enough!'

Ignoring them, Astrid moved to walk around them, her eyes fixed on the floor. The elves blocked her way again.

'No! Don't leave!' They laughed, and one of them reached out for her face again and moved aside the braid that covered the tip of her right ear. There was a gasp as they saw the familiar elven point at the tip of it, and Astrid turned to face them, fire in her eyes.

'You're a mewa!'

Ignoring her anger, Astrid tried to bypass them, but again they stopped her, this time with a curious disgust on their faces.

'So where's your father from then?' one of them hissed. Astrid closed her eyes, knowing what was coming.

'What kingdom did the rapist dwarf come from?'

Knud's mouth dropped open in shock. Astrid's grip on his hand tightened and Knud winced. One of the elves leant forward to take a closer look at her eyes.

'The mewa has a grey eye! So he's from Lǫgberg! Of course he is!' the elf said. The others moved in, circling her, and Astrid fixed her eyes on the ground. Knud was amazed at how restrained she was being.

'Let me guess. She died in childbirth didn't she? Killed herself giving birth to dwarf mutt!'

'Guess he was happy!'

'No way for her to tell people!'

'Not that we didn't know already. Dwarves are all just rapists!'

Hearing a commotion down the hall, Jarl got out of bed and traipsed into the hallway just in time to see one of the elves put his hand on Astrid's shoulder. He watched from the doorway, with Halvard close behind, as Astrid gripped the elf's hand and twisted it so violently that he heard the bone snap as the elf's shoulder twisted out of its socket. He fell to the ground screaming.

Noticing Knud next to her, Jarl ran towards them. One of the elves reached out for Knud's hair to try and drag him away.

With a loud thud, Jarl slammed his fist into the elf's face, punching him so hard he almost span around twice before falling to the ground, knocked out cold. Jarl stood back to back with Astrid, the other elves circling them.

'Another dwarf...another scumbag rapi-' one of them began.

With one quick move, Astrid leapt from the ground, the heel of her foot slamming into the elf's nose, breaking it. The movement was so swift and fluid it almost looked like she had been trying to dance.

The elf stumbled backwards, the pain from his broken nose blinding him temporarily, and dropped to his knees. Astrid brought her knee up to his chin as hard as she could and the elf fell to the ground. She straddled him and punched him repeatedly, beating his face to a bloody pulp in seconds. Jarl pulled the last elf away from her as he tried to hit Astrid from behind and threw him against the wall, punching him in the gut. The elf returned a punch, hitting Jarl squarely on the jaw.

Barely flinching from the blow, Jarl retaliated without mercy, as he had been trained to do. He took each blow that the elf laid on him as if they were nothing more than a mere annoyance, and fought back with double the skill and aggression of his attacker. His jaw was set in a fierce clench as he smashed his bare fists into the elf's stomach as hard as he could, winding him before knocking him down to the ground with a knee to the face.

Feeling the elf go limp beneath her, Astrid turned on the last conscious elf. The elf turned to run as she moved after him, her eyes wide and wild and her mouth twisted into a vicious snarl, the scar over her lips making her look like an animal.

Astrid grabbed the elf by his long hair and shoved him back up against one of the pillars in the hall.

'Please don't hurt me!' he cried.

Astrid leant forward slowly, her head at his height, and drew her dagger from her boot. The elf stared at her in horror and shrieked for help.

She moved her dagger to his throat. "Shut up! she hissed, and the elf, left with little alternative, was silenced.

'You're a noble aren't you?' Astrid whispered, leaning her head so close to the elf it looked like she was about to kiss him. Except right now, Jarl could see her expression and it looked like she might bite him instead, her teeth bared. 'I met a noble once...do you like your ears?'

'My wh...what?' the elf stuttered, shivering, as Astrid ran her left hand over his ear, the blade in her other hand still pressed against his throat.

'Your ears!' Astrid repeated, smiling, the smile not reaching her cold, narrowed eyes.

'Please don't hurt me!' the elf begged again as tears dripped down his cheeks.

Astrid chuckled, a deep, guttural laugh that promised pain. She moved the tip of her dagger over his lips to stop him talking and the elf whimpered and started to cry.

'If I cut the top of your ear off, do you stop being an elf?' Astrid asked. 'Can I cut it off and keep it?'

The elf's eyes widened as she moved aside the hair hanging over her torn ear tip, exposing it.

'Please...! the elf pleaded with her again, and Astrid pushed the blade tightly against his lips again. Then, with one quick movement, she pulled her dagger away. The elf felt a small gust of air pass his ear and he reached up, screaming as he felt something wet on his fingers.

There were footsteps from above and several monks raced down the stairs.

Stepping back, Astrid re-sheathed her dagger and stood silently as the monks crowded around them, then she moved her hair back over her ear quickly, avoiding eye-contact with Jarl who was doing his best not to show his shock.

An elf! She's a half-elf!

'What happened?' the Abbot asked, but Astrid stood silently and said nothing. The elf screamed from the ground that she had cut off his ear and the Abbot stepped forward to inspect it.

'Stop screaming!' It's just a cut, you fool!' he said.

'What? It's not gone?' The elf gasped, relief on his face.

'No it's not. But you are! And your group! First thing tomorrow!' the Abbot snapped back firmly.

'But she attacked me!'

'He's lying! Jarl said, stepping forward.

Knud nodded. 'They started it. They attacked her!'

Astrid said nothing, her fists clenched.

'You will leave tomorrow and you will not return to this monastery again,' the Abbot said firmly. The elf got to his feet and opened his mouth to argue, but when the monks stepped forward in unison towards him, moving their hands onto the knives they carried in their belts, the elf scuttled away.

'Astrid, follow me,' the Abbot ordered, and she bowed her head and obeyed.

Jarl turned to look at Knud. He checked Knud's face to see if he had been hurt by the elves, and then demanded to know what happened. Knud told him everything, except for the fact he had been drinking and his conversation with Astrid.

'She's a Blanda blóð!' Halvard said, his voice triumphant. 'I knew there was something wrong with her!'

'Don't call her that!' Knud snapped. 'Don't...don't ever call her that!' Halvard was shocked that the small dwarf would dare to talk to him in such a way. 'She's my friend!'

Storming back into the dorm, Knud stumbled over to his bed and Jarl raised an eyebrow suspiciously as he watched him from the doorway.

Knud pulled the blanket roughly over himself, not bothering to get under it, and prayed that once he woke up the horrible dizzy feeling would be gone.

* * *

'It was my fault,' Astrid said quickly, kneeling in front of the Abbot with her head bowed. 'I have heard those words many times before. I should have had more control.'

Clearing his throat, the Abbot tried to ignore the pleading stares the other monks in the room were giving him. Those who didn't know him well feared that he might kick Astrid out of the monastery too.

'Astrid. You know I cannot condone how you behaved with the elves. They were our guests.'

'I know. I'm sorry.'

The Abbot took a deep breath. 'And that is all I have to say,' he said quickly. Some of the newer monks gasped, and the older monks who knew the Abbot smiled. One of them flashed Astrid a wide grin, and the Abbot gave him a reproachful look but did not disagree with him. He was half tempted to do the same himself.

He had been a young Abbot when Astrid had first come to the Salt Monasteries years ago, the second youngest Abbot ever in the history of the monastery.

All the monks had been curious about her when Astrid had made excuse after excuse to stay with them. Eventually she had stayed for over three years, only leaving for a few months once a year to return to the Heilagr forest in the Red Mountains, and to Dag, always leaving in the winter despite how hard it was to travel then.

She had changed so much since then; she was no longer the young and naive half-blood. But in some ways she was just the same. Just as tortured inside.

'Erin, if you wish to stay with us, there are others who can take them to Logberg,' the Abbot suggested. Astrid shook her head.

'Thank you,' she said. 'But if they still want me to take them, I will. Jarl and Halvard are good warriors, but the pass is dangerous, even for me. I don't want Knud getting hurt.'

'And if they don't want you to take them?'

'Then I'll still go. They won't need to know that I'm there. I said I would protect them, and I will.'

Winter

36 years ago...

Astrid looked around the forge, fascinated. Ragi showed her everything proudly, his hands lovingly running over every item as he told her about it.

Whilst almost every stone was stained black, everything was orderly and not a single tool was out of place. The coals in the forge glowed faintly. Above it was a tall chimney built into the centre of the room, and shelves and work desks lined the walls around it.

'Is this where you made the rings for my parents?' Astrid asked.

'Yes. And the daggers, I made all of it here.'

'Who taught you to make all of this?'

'My mother. Nearly everyone from my tribe was a blacksmith.'

'Your father? Did he teach you too?'

Ragi shook his head. 'No. He was dead long before I was old enough to learn,' he replied, matter-of-factly.

271

Quickly changing the topic, Astrid asked about what he would be making next, and Ragi reached up to one of the shelves near the forge and pulled out a box, opened it up, and passed it to her. Several small, perfectly circular discs were inside, their edges serrated like hundreds of little teeth. Astrid picked one of them up, surprised to feel that they were actually extremely heavy.

'What are they for?' she asked, turning it over in her hand.

'Throwing!' Ragi said, his eyes twinkling. He picked one of them up and threw it with a strong flick of his hand. The disk flew past Astrid's face with a whoosh and hit the wall behind her, embedding itself in the wood.

'Wow!' she whispered, pulling it out of the wall and passing it back to Ragi. 'Can you teach me how to use them?'

'What do you think I made them for?' Ragi laughed, passing it back to her. Astrid twirled it in her hand, feeling how it was weighted before attempting to throw it.

'So what would I use them for? I guess I couldn't use them in a fight?'

'No. These are for when you don't want to fight at all. They're smaller than the daggers, so if you hit something it's more discreet. The really good warriors in my village were trained to be able to cut a thick rope with them from over thirty feet away.'

'That's impossible!'

'For a lot of people it was. Only two people could do that, my mother and my elder brother.'

Turning to face the wall, Astrid scanned it to find a target to aim for, settling on a small chip of the clay that covered the rock walls underneath.

Just as she was about to throw it, they heard Dag yelling for Astrid at the top of his voice in the distance. Astrid put down the disk and ran outside, noticing tiny snowflakes fluttering through the air. Dag saw her and raced up to her, his face worried.

'Astrid! Where's Ragi?'

'Here,' Ragi said, walking out behind her.

'Snow storm! We have to head back now!'

From so high up in the mountain they could see for miles around, and Ragi looked at the enormous, bright white storm clouds that were rolling in from the distance, the snow falling from them like sheets of glistening silver.

Ragi collected the box from inside, passed it to Astrid and locked the door. She held the box as tightly as she could as she followed Dag down the mountain, looking back every few minutes for Ragi, worried when she didn't see him behind them.

'Where's Ragi?' Astrid called out.

'He'll be going to his hut till the storms over,' Dag called back.

For the next twenty minutes they ran as fast as they could. Dag panted heavily but Astrid ran easily, lightly leaping over the ground. The wind picked up until it was almost blowing them backwards. Astrid felt a little like she was flying, and threw herself forward as she ran, the wind holding her up for a few seconds before her feet touched the ground. She smiled, her eyes lighting up, the feeling exhilarating. The snow quickly settled on the ground and their footprints barely had chance to make an imprint before fresh snow covered them.

Reaching the clearing, Dag rushed over to the small hut built into the side of the house to fetch as much wood as he could.

"Get the pony inside!' he called out through the wind, trudging through the snow with an armful of logs.

Astrid froze, her eyes darting over to the pony at the side of the house.

'Astrid!' Dag barked loudly. 'Put Felix in the stable!'

Shocked that Dag had actually shouted at her, she slowly approached Felix, her hands shaking uncontrollably as her heart began pumping faster and faster.

It's just a pony! Astrid said to herself, trying to reach out and take it by its long mane to lead it towards the stable, but unable to bring herself to touch it. Her hand stopped in mid-air and the pony stepped forward and pressed its large shoulder against it.

Like a lightning bolt had struck her, Astrid screamed and fell to the ground, revolted that she had touched it. Her hands glowed, the snow around her melted and the grass burst into flames. Her hands clutched the floor and she shivered, her eyes wild and terrified. The sound of loud hooves and of horses whinnying rang in her ears, and she crouched on the floor and screamed at the noises and images in her head.

Dag raced around the side of the house and reached down to help her up as she yelled out, swiping her hand at him. The air around her crackled with magic.

'Get away!' she screamed, and Dag stepped back, shaking his head, his arm burning where she had hit him.

Dag quickly led the pony into the stable, climbed the small ladder leading to the rafters and pulled down as much of the straw as he could. With Felix safe, he headed back outside and locked the doors.

The winter storms in the Red Mountains were particularly vicious. A storm like this could last a week, sometimes two, and after the storm had passed the snow was often so deep that they would be trapped in the house for another few weeks until it melted.

Trudging up to Astrid who was still huddled on the floor, Dag knelt down next to her, the wind now so cold it felt like multiple whips biting at his skin.

'Astrid! You have to get up, goldheart! The storm will hit soon!'

Shivering, Astrid got to her feet holding her hands to her chest, stumbled into the house and climbed the stairs to her room. She padded over to the wooden box that held the jasmine oil, pulled her blanket around her and opened the bottle. She closed her eyes and inhaled, and a lump rose in her throat as old, comforting memories washed away the sound of the hooves in her mind.

'Please stay downstairs,' Astrid whispered, hearing Dag walk up into the loft.

'I'm sorry goldheart,' Dag muttered, sitting down beside her. 'I forgot.'

'Please go downstairs,' Astrid said again, and Dag nodded, doing as she'd asked.

You forgot? How could you forget? she mentally raged at him. *Don't you think I would like to forget?*

Astrid sniffed at the bottle again, replaying the images over and again in her mind. She tried to imagine the warm Aldwood sun on her skin, Sylbil's voice calling her to come inside the house and Arnbjörg calling back that they would only be a few more minutes. She tried to picture her mother laughing with her, helping her make a small woven basket with the coarse grass which grew near their house.

Rocking back and forth, Astrid hummed one of the songs Sylbil and Arnbjörg would sing to her each night, realising to her horror that she had forgotten some of the words. She sang them under her breath again and again until she got them perfect.

Sleep and be happy, the moon is awake.
There's light in the darkness.
Smile dear, you're safe.

Don't think of the howling,
The wolves are long gone.
No matter your fears, you're safe, you are strong.

The clouds hide the moonlight,
Don't worry, don't fear.
The moon is still there,
Will in time, re-appear
There's light in the darkness,
Don't fret, we are here.
No matter what comes,
we love you my dear.

No matter what comes,
we love you my dear.

'Did you know they wrote that song for you?' Dag whispered from the doorway. Astrid turned and saw him sitting on the top stair with tears in his eyes. 'They wrote that the day you were born. I was there. They both loved to sing so much.'

'You were there?' Astrid asked, surprised.

'Yes! I nearly missed it. Sylbil was having trouble; you didn't want to be born. You were stubborn even then!' Dag laughed, wiping away the tears from his face, and smiled at the memory. 'When you were finally born the first thing Sylbil did was start singing! They both looked so happy holding you.'

Astrid closed the bottle and placed it back into the box before turning to look at Dag.

'Why did they call me Astrid?' she asked, hoping she could use the moment to coax as much information from him as she could.

'I don't know. Arnbjörg wanted to call you Asgöta, or some other horrible name like that. He was sure you were going to be a girl! Sylbil wasn't sure and was picking boy names for you.'

'What names?'

'Asbjorn was one of them. Arnbjörg didn't like it. Finnvid was another, he hated that name!' Dag laughed. 'Oh and then there was Arlen, he quite liked that one, but for some reason he was so sure you were a girl. He was teasing Sylbil for weeks afterwards that her intuition was wrong!'

The wind howled outside and Astrid smiled, remembering the great storm they'd had in the Aldwood when the wind ripped up some of the thatch and the rain poured in. She'd watched from the fireplace as Arnbjörg and Sylbil had quickly tried to patch it up. Sylbil had raced outside and climbed onto the roof whilst Arnbjörg had clambered up into the rafters and tried to patch it up from below, both of them having to shout at each other over the sound of the howling wind. After struggling for a good twenty minutes they had finally managed to make a rough patch to stop the rain from pouring through. Both of them had laughed, completely soaked through.

'They loved laughing,' Astrid said.

'At first it was hard for them. Sylbil found it really hard at first.'

'What do you mean?'

'They had to leave everything so suddenly. When it was just them, they were very happy, but when she found out she was carrying you, she was so afraid for you. Arnbjörg kept telling her it would be fine, but she would wake up in the middle of the night screaming. She kept on having nightmares of people hurting you.'

The wind picked up speed and the roof of the house shook for a moment, but Astrid ignored it, hungry for more of Dag's stories about her parents. He never talked about them, something she wished he would do. Losing them was bad, but not remembering them was worse. At times she wished Dag was more like Ragi, whom would often ask her about them as if he was asking her about the weather, refusing to tread delicately around the topic, and in doing so making it less painful.

'Arnbjörg started making a game of it. Every time Sylbil thought about what frightened her, she had to say something she was happy about. At first it was just silly little things like that they had food on the table, but then she started to dream about what it would be like when you were born: the things she would teach you, the songs you would both sing. She started laughing a lot more. She asked me if I would teach you.'

'Teach me?'

'Languages, history, calculation. When....when I came last time, I was going to start teaching you,' Dag said, his voice cracking a little. They both sat silently for a few moments, the mood turning sad again.

'Why don't you teach me now?' Astrid suggested. 'The storm isn't going anywhere. They would like that!'

'Yes, they would,' Dag said, smiling.

Exposed

Jarl stared up at the ceiling, not sure what to think.

Knud was asleep in his bed and Jarl could smell the Daru wine in the air, the rare drink having a particularly strong aroma. But he'd decided he was not going to mention it or even let Knud know that he knew; he was far more worried about what he had just witnessed.

He slid out of bed, crept outside, and saw Skad and Halvard talking in the courtyard, Skad standing with the help of two crutches, his leg newly bandaged. He strolled over and stood next to Halvard.

'She's a half elf,' he finally said out loud and both of them turned to look at him. 'You knew didn't you?' he asked Skad. Skad's jaw tightened and he looked up at the stars.

'How could you recommend a...a Blanda blóð?' Halvard spat, disgusted.

'She is the best,' Skad replied, the words like a bitter taste in his mouth. 'Astrid mastered everything I taught her within two years. My best student was a damned half-elf!'

'So you still vouch for her?' Halvard asked, still slightly shaken by the revelation of Astrid's heritage.

'Yes! If Astrid can't keep you safe, nobody can. She is the best.'

'I think I'd rather not risk it,' Halvard grumbled, turning to Jarl, expecting to see a similar sentiment on his face. 'Jarl?'

'She's coming,' Jarl said firmly, and Halvard growled with frustration. 'We don't know the pass. She does. It would be mad to try and risk it ourselves.'

'She's a half-elf!' Halvard spat.

'And she is half-dwarf too,' Jarl said straight back. 'She has done nothing that makes me think she can't be trusted. Far from it.'

'Are you mad? Isn't having elven blood enough?'

'Don't be stupid! She can't help who her parents were any more than you could,' Jarl snapped.

'At least my parents were dwarves!' Halvard shouted, angry.

'I'm not arguing with you about this Halvard,' Jarl said firmly. 'If she will still take us, then she is coming.'

'Then at least pay her now. Anyone who doesn't take half the payment isn't to be trusted. Means they have some other way of making money. Maybe selling us out to goblins.'

'Don't be ridiculous!'

'Jarl...pay her half now or I'm going back to Bjargtre.'

Seeing the resolute look on Halvard's face, Jarl stormed back to the dorm and shuffled through his bag, swearing under his breath.

Astrid didn't deserve this. She had done nothing but protect them throughout the journey so far. She couldn't help who her parents were.

After pulling the pouch of money from the bottom of his bag, Jarl stormed out of the dorm, and Halvard watched him as he walked up the stairs to the second floor before turning to look at Skad triumphantly.

Reaching the top of the stairs, Jarl strode over to the two monks who were standing outside the great hall.

'I'm sorry, I know I'm not meant to be here, but I need to talk to Astrid,' Jarl said urgently, wanting to get the unpleasant task over and done with as soon as possible. He had no doubt Astrid would be deeply offended, but he had no choice. Halvard had to come with them. If Vígdís did listen to him and send an army back to Bjargtre, he needed someone he knew and trusted to stay with Knud.

'I'll find her,' the first monk said, pushing aside the heavy rug-like curtains that covered the entrance to the great hall. The second monk stood nearby, a scowl on his face, and glared down at Jarl.

'So, you're here to pay her off?' he asked, disgusted.

'No, just to pay her.'

'Because nobody could possibly trust a woman who has, I'm guessing, already saved your life a few times,' the monk replied.

Astrid pushed the curtain aside and stepped out from the great hall, looking at him nervously.

'Can...can I talk to you alone?' Jarl asked. The monks glared at him, then shook their heads and walked away, grumbling as they did so. Astrid knotting her hands together nervously. Her hair had come loose during the fight and half of it hung down from the bun she had pinned it in.

Seeing the pouch of money in Jarl's hands, Astrid looked down, an angry but resigned look on her face. 'I'm no longer your guide?'

'Astrid, would you mind if I paid you like you asked, when we arrive at Lǫgberg?' Jarl said suddenly, and Astrid flinched as he said her name and looked up at him surprised.

'What?'

'Halvard said if I didn't pay you now he would leave, and he needs to come to Lǫgberg with us.' For a moment Astrid said nothing, her eyes flickering with confusion. 'I don't care that you're a half elf,' Jarl said firmly, and Astrid felt a little like she had been stabbed in the throat as he said the words. She did her best not to visibly react, even though inside it felt like her stomach was knotting itself up like an ouroboros.

'Halvard won't believe you if you lie,' Astrid said finally, gulping as she said the words. 'Pay me tomorrow when we leave. I can pretend to get angry and I'll give it to the monks. He'll believe that.' She smiled and Jarl laughed at her suggestion.

'Yes, that he *would* believe!'

* * *

Pulling his bag onto his shoulders, Jarl walked out of the dorm, barely able to hide the small grin on his lips. Halvard and Knud walked behind him down the hall listening to the pouch of Fé jingling in his hand.

Seeing Skad in the courtyard as they walked past it, Jarl stopped for a moment, and Halvard and Knud walked on ahead of him towards the gate.

Skad, with a wooden crutch and several new bandages over his splinted leg, looked around expecting to see Astrid nearby.

'Going then, are you?' Skad grumbled, shifting a little on his crutch. Jarl nodded. 'Well then, make sure that mutt doesn't get you killed!' He laughed, and Jarl glared at him, repulsed.

'If you hate her so much, then why did you suggest her to us?' Jarl asked. Skad shrugged his shoulders.

'I might have a mutt which is uglier than a pure breed, but if it's better for hunting I'd take it.'

'You're disgusting!' Jarl spat, turning to walk away. Skad laughed.

'Astrid's a sucker for protecting people. It's her addiction. As long as you play on that you'll be safe.'

Shaking his head Jarl walked off, not bothering to say goodbye, and stormed through the front gate. Halvard and Knud were waiting for him outside. Astrid was nowhere to be seen.

'Twenty Fé says she decides not to come!' Halvard grinned. Several monks waited with them, a few of them unable to hide their disgust at Halvard's bet.

'Fifty says she does,' Jarl retorted.

'Done!' Halvard laughed, crossed his arms and smiled gleefully as the seconds ticked by.

Through the open door, with her veil down and wrapped around her neck, Astrid appeared. Halvard's face dropped as Jarl walked up to her and passed her the money.

'I thought it was best if we paid you half now,' Jarl said, doing his best to sound sincere, shocked as a furious look crossed her face. She glared at him.

'You can pay me when we arrive, as we discussed!'

'No, we pay you half now,' Jarl demanded, wondering for a moment if Astrid had forgotten about their plan. Her reaction was frighteningly convincing.

'Fine then!' she hissed, grabbing the pouch from him and turning to toss it over the abbey wall. Several of the monks waiting in the courtyard who had been informed of the plan yelled as they saw it hurtling down towards them. A scuffle ensued as they all leapt up to catch it. One of them yelled out a loud victory roar and danced victoriously. The other monks laughed at him.

'There! I've taken your money and I've spent it! We're leaving!' Astrid shouted, storming off down the path. A small grin spread across her face as soon as the others were behind her. Jarl stared after her in shock.

'See? That wasn't so hard!' Halvard gloated, and Jarl ignored him, walking quickly after Astrid. When he reached her, he tried to look into her eyes but she still appeared to be angry with him as she glared at the ground.

'He believed it,' Jarl whispered.

A broad smile spread across Astrid's face and her eyes flashed with happiness. Jarl breathed a sigh of relief, trying not to laugh.

'I thought you were really angry at me for a moment!'

'I wanted to see your expression,' she said, grinning. 'It was worth it!'

* * *

The descent back down the mountain was a lot easier than the climb, and with Skad gone the atmosphere was a lot more relaxed. Miles upon miles of land stretched out below them, the forest tapering out into flat plains of thick, yellow grass. Heavy storm clouds hovered in the distance.

'It's going to be hard to find food in that,' Halvard said.

'We have enough from the monastery,' Jarl replied. 'If we're careful, we'll have enough to last till we reach Waidu.'

'Maybe the elf could use some of her magic and bewitch the animals to come out,' Halvard said, his tone implying it was an insult. Jarl walked away from him and got into step alongside Knud.

He had never known Halvard to be so vindictive, but the journey had exposed aspects of his personality that Jarl found deeply revolting. It was beginning to feel like he had less and less in common with him.

For the next few hours they hiked down the mountainside in silence, Astrid ahead of them, her wolf-skin bouncing on her shoulders as she made her way along the rough path. Several rock slides covered parts of it and they had to clamber over the stones to reach the other side. Astrid practically danced over them and the others couldn't help but notice just how light footed she really was. She seemed to get more and more elven by the moment.

'An elf, a damned elf!' Halvard grumbled as he climbed over the stones, getting more and more irritated that Jarl and Knud were walking closer to Astrid than they were to him. Feeling rejected, his anger towards Astrid increased.

'Damn elf!'

A Master

33 years ago...

Astrid walked down the stairs and groaned as she heard Dag outside talking with Skad. It was the third year that he had gone back to Bjargtre for the winter; another peaceful winter without his foul temper and constant degrading remarks to put up with when Dag wasn't around.

Once again, the snow storms had trapped them indoors and Astrid had spent her time poring over Dag's old books: Astronomy, calculation, languages... Language books were Astrid's favourite, along with the many maps Dag had of Ammasteinn, the older ones in particular fascinating her. The territories and kingdoms were often wildly different from each other and Astrid was intrigued about why they had changed so much. Dag always refused to answer though; his face would darken and he'd pull the maps away from her and try to change the subject. Astrid eventually stopped asking him and looked at them in secret.

Many cities listed along the Haltija pass and the Riddari no longer existed in the newer maps, and she wondered what could have happened to have wiped so many of them away. Some of the cities had been so large that they looked like mountains at first glance.

But now the winter was over and the books had been put away. Spring had arrived, and with it, Skad.

Traipsing outside, Astrid stood quietly behind Dag. Skad stepped to the side so he could see her and she looked up at him, noticing that either she had grown considerably in the last few months or Skad had gotten shorter.

Skad made the same observation. Her long black hair reached her lower back and now she was almost as tall as he was, but without the solid build of a dwarf woman. Her neck was too long and her body too slender, and she walked lightly on the tips of her toes instead of the balls of her feet.

'You've grown.'

'Yes she has!' Dag said proudly, and Astrid smiled at his reaction. His food certainly had no part to play in it so it was quite amusing to see him responding so proudly.

'How old are you now?' Skad asked, barely concealing how irritated he felt. The journey to the Red

Mountains felt as if it had taken twice as long as last time for some reason.

'I'm nine. I'll be ten soon,' Astrid said quietly, knowing Skad didn't care and that he was just making conversation so that Dag would have no reason to get angry at him.

'Well, we can train tomorrow. Let's hope you haven't forgotten everything I taught you.'

* * *

'Astrid! Astrid get up!' Skad bellowed from the ground floor. She awoke with a start and rubbed her eyes, grunting as she rolled out from under the blanket.

And there's another thing I liked with him gone, she grumbled to herself. *A good lie in.*

She grabbed the hammer axe from next to her pillow and scrambled down the stairs to see Skad waiting for her by the door with a face like thunder.

'I'm not waiting for you any longer! Move it!'

Dashing ahead of him, Astrid stood in the clearing and felt a pair of eyes watching her. Glancing up, she spotted Ragi high in the branches of a pine tree, smiling at her.

They were both excited for this moment.

Storming into the clearing, Skad didn't even bother to say anything. He swung his heavy sword down towards her and caught her by surprise, knocking her hammer axe from her hands.

'Three years!' Skad shouted at her, swinging his sword again. 'Three years teaching you, and you still can't hold your damn axe!'

From up in the pine tree Ragi snarled, but quickly replaced it with a knowing grin as Astrid threw herself back from Skad. She spread her feet and braced herself.

'The dwarf won't even know what hit him!' Ragi laughed to himself.

Almost as if she were dancing, Astrid easily dodged Skad's next swing at her, twisted around towards him and slid under his arm. Skad turned in shock, glimpsing an excited smile on Astrid's face. She dodged his swing again and twirled around him.

She had realised last summer that she was already better than the old dwarf, but Ragi had convinced her to wait another year until she was a vastly superior fighter.

'You don't want to just beat your enemy! Wait till you can beat them so completely that they know there is no point in trying to fight back because they'll just lose. It is the best way to fight because you only fight once!' he had told her. She had waited patiently, and now patience was no longer required.

Snarling, and realising to his horror that she was toying with him, Skad began to lose control for one of the first times in his life. He swung his sword like a madman, his face reddening, his eyes wide. He felt humiliated and angry.

'Think you're better than me, do you?' he bellowed.

Astrid said nothing and ducked around him again, took the small knife which hung from his side as she did so, and tossed it towards a nearby tree. The dagger was thrown with such accuracy that it hit the centre of the trunk and stayed there, quivering.

Up in the pine Ragi burst out laughing and Skad, hearing the noise, looked around for the culprit, not thinking to look up at the tree tops.

'Just like an elf to cheat! That's not how a real warrior fights! Pick up your axe!' Skad bellowed, heaving like an angry bull.

Picking it up, Astrid spread her feet apart again and centred herself with a firm grip on the handle. Her eyes narrowed. This was going to be easy!

As he moved forward to attack her, Astrid slipped under his arm just as he swung his sword towards her. The sharp edge of the blade passed within millimetres of her face as she dodged it. Her face remained emotionless and calm, every movement executed with deadly precision.

Before Skad even realised that she had dodged his attack, Astrid grabbed him by his arm and threw him to the ground, kicking the sword out of his hands. She picked it up and twirled it around her like a baton.

'That's how a warrior really fights!' Astrid laughed and bowed mockingly. She lifted Skad's sword and sheathed it into the ground so firmly that she nearly pushed it down to the hilt. Her smile faded and she looked at him with barely restrained contempt.

'You are no longer in Dag's debt; you can leave,' Astrid said. Ragi heard her clearly even from the tree top, and as she strode away from the clearing, Ragi looked down with a satisfied grin on his face at Skad, on his back, panting in shock.

Slowly Skad hauled himself to his feet, shook his head as if he was sure he was in a dream, then stumbled over to his sword and tried to tug it out of the earth. His face reddened as he pulled at the hilt with all his might, and when the sword suddenly slid free, he fell backwards in an undignified heap.

Smiling, Ragi climbed down from the pine and strolled away from the clearing, following Astrid. He caught up with her a few minutes later.

'How do you feel?' Ragi asked, surprised to see she wasn't smiling anymore.

'Horrible,' Astrid confessed, shame in her eyes. 'I shouldn't have been so mean. He looked at me like...'

'Like?'

'Hurt! He looked hurt! I've never seen him look like that.'

'He deserved it!' Ragi said remorselessly.

They reached Ragi's hut but continued past it, up over the mountain and towards his forge. Astrid rubbed her fingers together nervously.

'He did deserve it. But I shouldn't have done it.'

'You're right. Dag should have done something.'

'It's not his fault!' Astrid said quickly. 'Skad never says anything nasty around him, and I never tell him how he treats me. I don't want him to know! I asked him to teach me to fight and he did.'

'No, you asked *Dag* to teach you! He did what he always does, buries his head in the mud and gets someone else to do what he should have done,' Ragi snapped. Astrid was surprised to hear so much anger in the goblin's voice.

'Ragi?'

'Ugh, don't mind me. Sometimes I just get angry at him.'

'Why? What's he done?'

'It's what he hasn't done that annoys me. He's a warlock! He is meant to stop people like Skad! The old fool's forgotten what he was trained to do. He's a coward! It's because of people like him that Angh was destroyed. Weak men who were happy to learn magic and be revered, but too cowardly to stand up to those who they were meant to judge.'

'What do you mean?' Astrid asked, confused.

'Those maps Dag has, the old ones. That was Ammasteinn before The Purge. Everyone had different stories about how it started or who started it, but the result was the same. The goblins were pushed into the northern plains and the elves and the dwarves fought-'

'But Dag couldn't have been there.' Astrid interrupted, not sure how to take this new information. 'He's old, but he's not that old!'

'Dag is at least three thousand years old, Astrid,' Ragi said calmly. 'He would have been around five hundred years old when it happened; a fully trained warlock.'

'Ragi, what's wrong?' Astrid asked, sensing something else beneath the sudden anger at Dag.

'My father and two young sisters were killed, twenty-nine years ago today.' Ragi snarled. 'Dwarves; I don't know why they attacked. My mother always thought it was as revenge for a raid a nearby tribe had run. The dwarves didn't care that we weren't the same tribe. We were goblins, so it was all the same to them.'

'I'm sorry.'

'Don't be. Just ignore me. Sometimes I have to get angry or I'm afraid I might burst.'

'I want to leave!' Astrid said suddenly, stopping and turning to Ragi. 'I've wanted to leave for a while now. I want to see elves and dwarves! All those beautiful places in Dag's books!'

'A lot of them aren't beautiful anymore,' Ragi said, but Astrid ignored him.

'I can fight now! They can't hurt me anymore! I want to see my parents' homes...their people, the places they would have known!'

'They *will* hurt you Astrid,' Ragi said, his voice serious. 'Even if they don't know who you are, to the dwarves you will always be an elf, and to the elves a dwarf. You'll be miserable.'

'Where can I go then? I can't stay here anymore.'

'No you can't,' Ragi agreed, pausing for a few moments to think. 'You should go to the human lands.'

'Would they like me there?' Astrid asked, and Ragi laughed at the question. Even now, she was still so desperate for acceptance. It would be charming if it wasn't so heartbreaking to see.

'Some would, but you would be an outsider. Some would be fascinated, others afraid.'

'Would you come?' Astrid asked, deadly serious. Ragi was taken by surprise. 'It would be nice to have a friend with me. Dag would never come...'

'No, he wouldn't,' Ragi agreed. 'When you want to leave, yes, I will come with you.'

Conversations

'I'm sorry, but we can't light the fire here,' Astrid said.

Halvard faced her, his hands on his hips. 'Why not?'

'There's no cover. If there are any raiders they'll see us. Most of them like to hunt at night.'

'Do you want us to freeze to death?' Halvard yelled. 'What about food? Can we cook food?'

'I brought food so we don't have to cook,' Astrid said, reaching into her bag and pulling out one of several small parcels wrapped up in black muslin. She passed it to Halvard who opened it up hungrily, grabbed one of the flat oat cakes and passed the rest to Jarl and Knud. Jarl waited for Knud to take the food he wanted before helping himself, then passed it back to Astrid and flashed her an apologetic look for Halvard's behavior.

They sat on the grass, pulling their cloaks around them, trying to get warm. Knud shuffled closer to Jarl as the wind picked up and started to howl. Astrid took off her veil for a moment to tighten it around her neck and head. Some of her long hair had come loose at the back and she quickly wrapped it away under the veil.

'How long do these plains last?' Jarl asked as he ate.

'Two more days. There's a small forest after that, there's a place we can stay while we're there. An old friend used to live there.'

'If it's an elf friend I'm not staying,' Halvard said quickly, almost spitting out the food in his mouth.

'I don't have any elf friends,' Astrid snapped at him, her eyes flashing, her veil coming loose for a second. All her scars looked so much more pronounced in the low light. 'And if you don't like it then you can sleep outside!'

'No elf friends? I don't believe that. Your kind stick to each other like shit!'

'Hal!' Jarl shouted. 'Stop it!'

'No! No I won't! She's an *elf*!'

'I am NOT AN ELF!' Astrid bellowed, her voice deep. She thumped the ground with her fists and the grass around her burst into flames. Even the dirt seemed to catch fire for a few seconds.

All of them jumped in shock and Halvard smiled delightedly.

'Not an elf, eh?'

Getting to her feet, Astrid moved towards him, her eyes murderous. Halvard jumped up and drew his sword, pointing it at her, the tip barely an inch from her collar bone.

To everyone's shock, Knud suddenly rushed forward, wrapped his arms around her, turned to look at Halvard over his shoulder and glared at him. Astrid gasped, frightened that someone was touching her. Her hands shook but she didn't push him away.

'She's my friend! Leave her alone!' Knud yelled. Jarl moved his hand over Halvard's sword and made him lower it.

'She has magic!'Halvard hissed. Knud took Astrid's hand and led her away so that Jarl and Halvard could battle it out. Jarl had a face like thunder, and Knud knew his uncle was tired of Halvard's constant trouble making.

'So do some dwarves!'

'Are you blind? Are you all blind?' Halvard shrieked, exasperated. 'Look at her face! Look at her eyes! Everything about her screams trouble!'

'No! You're the one causing trouble! That woman has done nothing but help us and save our lives since we left. But for some reason you're hell bent on driving her away.'

Suddenly, Halvard raised his fist and hit Jarl as hard as he could, sending him spinning backwards. Spitting blood, Jarl returned the blow, landing a second one just a moment after the first blow had hit Halvard squarely on the jaw. The second blow broke his nose, blinding him temporarily, and taking the advantage, Jarl swept Halvard's legs out from under him. He crashed to the floor.

'What is wrong with you?' Jarl shouted down at him furiously. 'You've got to stop this! It's not helping anyone!'

'You're right,' Halvard muttered, slowly getting up. Jarl reached out to help him but Halvard pushed his hand away. 'I'm not helping anyone. I should just go.'

'No, Hal, you know that's not what I meant.'

'Well one of us has to go!' Halvard shouted back. 'I'm not traveling with a Brojóta burðr any more!'

In the distance, too far for Knud to hear what was being said, Astrid winced and her eyes filled with tears. She bit her lip and forced them away.

'You can hear them?' Knud asked, amazed.

'Yes,' Astrid hissed, staring angrily into the distance. 'I can hear everything. I always do.'

'You're mad!' Jarl said, glad that Knud was too far away to hear them. 'You know we need you to come!'

'Good. So she goes then!' Halvard snapped, stomping off in Astrid and Knud's direction as if to tell her. Jarl yanked him back.

'And you know that without her, none of us will reach Lǫgberg alive.'

Halvard stepped back, glaring at him. 'So you pick the elf over your own kin? Of course you would! A Vǫrn would!'

Even being so far away, both Astrid and Knud heard Halvard fall heavily to the ground. Jarl hit him so hard that he span around before he fell.

"Leave! Jarl spat.

He stood back, his fist still clenched, and waited as Halvard got to his knees, steadied himself, and stood up. He ran the back of his hand under his nose and looked down at the smear of blood on his skin. With gritted teeth, he walked over to his belongings, gathered them up, pulled his bag over his shoulders and stormed off, quickly disappearing into the darkness.

For a few brief seconds, Jarl considered running after him, but the thought was quickly replaced. It was far more important that they get to Lǫgberg, and over the past few weeks of travelling, Halvard had started to become more and more insufferable. If the worst came to the worst then it was better that Knud was left in the care of strangers than a dwarf who would wear him down and make him cynical and bitter.

Seeing the silhouettes of Astrid and Knud in the distance, Jarl strolled towards them, Knud still holding Astrid's hand and refusing to let go.

He trusts her, Jarl thought to himself, reaching them and looking down at Knud. 'Halvard's gone. He's doesn't want to come with us anymore.'

'Good!' Knud said to his surprise. 'Is Astrid still coming with us?'

'If she still wants to,' Jarl said, looking up at her. Her veil was down, her face exposed. Astrid looked at him, confused.

'Why did you let him go? He's a dwarf! I'm...I'm not!'

'He can't get us to Lǫgberg. You can.'

He took Knud's hand from hers, and Astrid flinched slightly as his fingertips brushed against her skin. Ignoring it, Jarl led Knud back to the clearing and Astrid followed behind.

She sat down next to her bag and peered through the trees. She could just about make out Halvard in the distance, walking away with his head down.

Jarl picked up the bag of food that had been left on the ground, dusted off the mud that had stuck to the bottom of it and wrapped it back up.

'I'll take the first watch,' Jarl said quietly, his eyes distant. Knud moved over to sit down next to him as the wind picked up.

Silently nodding , Astrid pulled her wolf-skin tighter around her, the head dipping down and covering her eyes. She didn't bother to reattach her veil; the thought didn't even occur to her.

After a few minutes Knud fell asleep, snoring loudly, his head resting against Jarl's shoulder. Jarl moved his cloak over his shoulders.

'The Haltija pass; how dangerous is it to cross it?' Jarl asked, looking up at Astrid.

'Very. We could try and go over the Riddari Kviðr Mountains instead of the pass, but it would probably be even more dangerous. A lot of

Frǫðleikr live there. They don't like to be disturbed. With the pass, we would only have to worry about goblins.'

'Frǫðleikr?' Jarl asked, never having heard the word before.

'That creature I gave the cake to after the Angu canyon, that was a Leshy, but he's a Frǫðleikr. A magic creature. There are a lot of them up in the mountains.'

'But you have magic. Wouldn't they trust you?'

'It's not about trust. They're old, and angry. They were pushed out of their homes in the plains and the Haltija pass centuries ago. They still remember that. All strangers are dangerous to them, and my magic is weak. I wouldn't be able to defend you.'

'You didn't look weak to me!' Jarl said, a grin forming at the corners of his mouth. Astrid looked up and managed a small smile.

'Dag never taught me magic.'

'Dag?'

'Dag Eir.'

'Oh, I forgot you were raised by a warlock. Why wouldn't he train you?'

'You've seen what happens when I get angry. I have no control over it. I would have been dangerous.'

'I'm pretty sure you are still dangerous!' Jarl laughed, and Astrid's face broke out into a full smile, the expression looking a little unaccustomed on her face.

'Why did Halvard come with you?'

'What do you mean?'

'He obviously annoyed you, I'm surprised he was your friend. You both are so different.'

'He was more Knute's friend than mine.'

'Knute?'

'Knud's father, he was my best friend.'

'I'm sorry,' Astrid said quickly. 'So you stayed friends with him out of respect for Knute?'

'You could say that. He was meant to come with us so that if something went wrong, there would be someone there to take care of Knud.'

'So you thought I would fail and let you get killed?' Astrid asked, pretending to sound offended, her eyes twinkling when Jarl looked up to quickly clarify what he had meant.

'We're going to Lǫgberg because I think Bjargtre is on the verge of being attacked, and we will lose if we do get attacked.'

'So...you are going to ask Queen Vígdís to send her armies to help?' Astrid said slowly, starting to understand why Jarl had tolerated Halvard for so long.

'Yes, and if she does, I am going to go back. I have friends in Bjargtre. I left instructions and money for them to leave if things get worse before I returned, but if Vígdís does send her armies, I have to fight for my city.'

'Why?' Astrid asked, and Jarl looked at her with surprise.

'What do you mean?'

'Why would you fight?'

'Because it's my home!' Jarl said, slightly insulted for a moment that she would ask such a question. Astrid looked away, her face a mixture of confusion. Jarl realised that the question had been a genuine attempt to understand his loyalty, not an attempt to question it.

She's never had a home; she doesn't know what it feels like.

'It's my home,' Jarl repeated, this time more softly. 'My family's home is in that mountain, it's my history. It's all I have.'

'Apart from Knud.'

'Yes.' Jarl grinned, turning to look at Knud, and laughed as he saw he had fallen asleep with his mouth hanging open. He gently moved his head onto the ground before he started drooling all over him. Knud shivered but didn't wake up.

Taking her wolf-cloak off, Astrid moved next to Jarl and laid the cloak gently over Knud. 'You'll get cold. He'll be fine without it,' Jarl said, moving to hand it back to her. Astrid stopped him, accidentally touching his hand, and flinched again.

'I don't need it. I'll be warm enough without it.'

'Why do you do that?'

'What?'

'Flinch when people touch you?'

'I don't like people touching me,' Astrid snapped, her voice defensive. 'You should sleep. I'll take the watch now.' She got up and walked away. Jarl saw she was shivering, but it wasn't from the cold.

* * *

'Knud wake up!' Astrid said gently, shaking him. Knud stirred and his eyes widened when the first thing he focused on was the large snout of Astrid's wolf-skin lying on the ground next to him, its sharp white fangs glinting.

'We've got to go,' she said, turning to shake Jarl who was next to him.

Waking with a start, Jarl instinctively reached for the dagger in his belt.

'What! It's morning? Why didn't you wake me? Did you keep watch all night?'

'We should go,' Astrid repeated, ignoring his question. 'If we're lucky, the weather will hold before we reach the forest.'

Knud passed Astrid her wolf-skin and she pulled it over her shoulders. Jarl noticed she had let her hair down and she seemed so much more relaxed now that Halvard and Skad had gone. There was a light in her eyes.

They both followed her. Jarl rolled his shoulders back, stiff from a night sleeping on the uneven ground, and cold due to the dampness that had made its way into his bones.

In the distance they could see the faint, dark smudge of the Riddari on the horizon. The cold biting wind blew down from it across miles of endless moorland. The howling wind was the only sound.

Running ahead, Knud looked up at Astrid, a grin on his face. 'I know what my next question is!'

'And what is that?' Astrid asked, amused.

'Where did you learn to use magic?'

'I didn't,' Astrid replied quickly, looking away from him and fixing her eyes on the horizon. Knud recognised the tell-tale signs that he had brought up a topic she did not like to speak about. Her eyes glazed and she pressed her lips into a tight line. 'It's just something that happens when I'm angry.'

Taking a moment to think about his next question, neither of them noticed Jarl catching up with them, walking close enough to hear their conversation.

'What is the most beautiful city you've ever seen?' Knud finally asked, hungry for stories of places he had never visited.

Her face lit up and Astrid smiled. 'Bayswater. It's not really a city, more of a collection of small towns, but it is so beautiful.'

'Why?'

'Is that another question?'

'Yes, if you tell me everything about it!'

'Ok. The sun is different there; hot. You step outside and it's like standing in front of the doors of an opened furnace. Here the sun gives light, but there it feels like a warm blanket washing over your skin.'

Looking up at her, Knud smiled, the expression on her face making him happy. She looked blissful, her face relaxed and glowing, her eyes half closed as she visualised the scene she was describing.

'The sea there is a bright blue and so clear you can see to the bottom of it. And the fish are so colorful! I don't know how to describe them...like jewels with fins!'

'Where is this?' Jarl asked, and Astrid turned to look at him, aware that he had been listening.

'Bayswater,' Knud replied, turning to look back at Astrid and expecting her to continue her story. Astrid looked hesitant but continued.

'It's in the centre of the human lands, by the sea.'

'And?' Knud asked, spurring her on. 'What do the buildings look like?'

'Most of them are painted white, but the walls that don't face the sun are painted a bright colour like red, orange or blue. A beautiful blue.'

'Like the sky?' Knud asked, and Astrid shook her head.

'No. The sky is a weak blue; the blue there is...like Jarl's eyes, but bluer!' Astrid said, looking around to try and find something which was close to the colour she was describing. Her eyes met Jarl's and she suddenly felt oddly self conscious, as if she had blurted out a secret she had wanted to keep to herself.

'And the people?' Knud asked.

'Happy, and kind. I blame the sun. You can't be unhappy when the sun's always smiling like that!'

'Do you like them better...than your own people?' Jarl asked.

'I don't have any people,' Astrid replied, looking away into the distance. 'To the elves I am a dwarf and to the dwarfs I am an elf. If I did have people it would be the humans; to them I am both a dwarf and an elf.'

'And what abou-' Knud began.

'Enough questions! You can ask me some more later,' she said quickly, pulling the wolf-head hood over her and strolling ahead of them.

Why are you telling them all this? The voice inside her head said. *You don't tell people about yourself.*

'I'm tired,' Astrid replied to herself out loud, too far away for the others to hear her. She leant her head back and closed her eyes. 'I want...I want to talk. To trust people.'

Fine then! The voice hissed back, *but you will regret this! You always do!*

Plans

33 years ago...

Walking down from her room, Astrid kept her eyes on the floor. Skad looked over at her from the door, his face hard. Dag handed him a small bundle of food for his journey, which Astrid was certain would be tossed away as soon as Skad was out of sight of the house.

'Astrid, aren't you going to say goodbye?' Dag asked, his wrinkled face smiling cheerfully.

'Goodbye,' Astrid said firmly, lifting her head and straightening her back, staring directly into his eyes with her head held high.

'Goodbye,' Skad replied, looking away, humiliation on his face. He strode out of the house with Dag close behind, the wind making the door slam behind them. Her ears twitched as she heard their conversation.

'You only just got here. You could stay for a few days before you leave?'

Astrid shook her head. As much as she loved the old warlock, he truly was a clueless old fool. Despite Astrid hiding how much she hated Skad, it was blindingly obvious to anyone that neither of them liked each other. Knowing the dwarf would never be back in her life was an incredible relief, and here Dag was trying to prolong his stay.

'Just go,' Astrid growled, turning and walking back up to her room. She slipped behind the make-shift carpet door that she had completed the previous winter, the threadwork rough and patchy but holding together well enough.

Lying on her bed, she stared at the ceiling and reached up to the wind catcher hanging from the rafters. Her fingers played with the feathers and eggshells hanging from it as a small breeze blew through the room from the secret door in the roof. She closed her eyes and smiled. Things would be different now. Skad was gone, she was a trained fighter, and Ragi had promised to travel with her. It was a frightening and beautiful new world.

'Ragi!' Astrid whispered. She jumped to her feet and ran over to the small opening in the roof. She could hear the hooves of Skad's pony in the distance and she clambered onto the roof, her bare feet and hands reaching out for the tree growing alongside it. Reaching up to one of the branches above for her sandals, she slipped them on, climbed down the tree and dashed through the forest, the flexible leather shoes allowing her to feel the ground as she ran whilst still protecting her from the sharp pine needles that littered the ground.

Reaching Ragi's hut, Astrid looked around for a moment, expecting to see him outside like he normally was. The tall pine tree that had almost fallen the previous winter had a few more of its branches cut away and a new pile of wood was neatly stacked beneath it. Ragi had been chopping at it for months, worried that at some point it could crash into the hut. It seemed stable enough for the moment, though.

Running inside, she saw Ragi lying on his bed mat, fast asleep.

'Ragi,' Astrid whispered, and he turned to look at her, his yellow eyes dazed and tired. 'He's gone!' She smiled, trying to stop herself from jumping up and down excitedly. Ragi groaned at her to leave him and let him sleep.

'But Ragi! We can go now! And I know where I want to go!' Astrid laughed excitedly. Ragi sat up, resigned to the fact there was no way he was getting back to sleep now. Not with Astrid jumping around like a spring rabbit.

'And where is that?' he asked, his voice irritated but his eyes saying otherwise.

'Bjargtre! And then onto the Salt Monasteries and then the Gold coast!'

'Bjargtre? Astrid you can't go near dwarf cites. Especially big cities. You'll get hurt!'

'I can fight now!'

'How would you feel if every dwarf looked at you like Skad did? Said the things he did?'

'I can ignore them,' Astrid replied, her face dropping slightly but still determined.

'Do you want to, though? Isn't it better to just remember the dwarves how you remembered your father?'

Her mouth clenched into a tight line and she looked at the ground, knotting her fingers together nervously. 'I can't remember his face any more. I want to see what my people look like. The cities! I want to speak Mál again like I did with him!'

'Astrid, none of the dwarves are going to be like Arnbjörg. And none of the elves are going to be like Sylbil, no matter how hard you look. They wouldn't want you to put yourself in danger.'

'If they didn't want me in danger they shouldn't have killed themselves for me,' Astrid hissed.

'Don't be silly,' Ragi snapped. 'They saved your life. Those cowards who tried to kill you can't ever touch you! Don't you realize how powerful that magic is?'

Astrid said nothing. Too many angry and confused words ran through her head to be able to speak any of them and make an ounce of sense. Glaring at the ground, her fingertips crackled with magic and started to glow a light orange.

'I'm not saying this to make you sad, Astrid,' Ragi said gently, sitting down in front of her. 'Also, I can't go with you if you go to Bjargtre. They'd insult you but they'd kill me.'

Looking up, Astrid shook her head, ashamed that she had not thought about how Ragi would be treated. 'So if we just went to the Salt Monasteries and then onto the Gold coast, would you come?'

'I'd have to hide my face, but yes, I would come.' Ragi smiled.

'Hide your face? How? Do you have a mask?'

Ragi chuckled. He walked over to a small chest at the foot of his bed mat and opened it, then pulled out a long black sash. The sash reached from one side of the hut to the other, three times over, the material thin and tough.

'I could make a tent out of this!' Astrid laughed, holding the end of the sash with an amused look on her face.

'That's the point,' Ragi said excitedly. He took it from her and started to wrap it around his waist, the sash going around him several times before he began to wrap the remaining part around his neck and head. The end of the sash had a loop of string attached to it, which he pulled over his head. The string wrapped around his head and held the end of the sash in place from one ear to the other, covering his face from the bridge of his nose downwards.

'I can still see your eyes!'

'Ah!' He reached back into the chest and pulled out a leather mask that he slid down over the front of his face. With Ragi's yellow eyes peering through the thin slits of the stretched leather, he looked like some kind of terrifying snake.

'You can't wear that, Ragi! You'll scare someone to death!'

'I know!' Ragi laughed. 'I'll have to make a new one. Maybe I'll make it look human.'

'What is it for?' Astrid asked, taking it from him and looking at it, intrigued.

'On the plains we wear these before fighting. It helps to terrify the enemy.'

'What if we went to the plains?' Astrid suggested. Her face lit up and Ragi's face dropped.

'I will never take you there. They'd kill you.'

'What if I hid my face with that mask and the veil?'

'Astrid, I'm not ever going back to the plains,' he said angrily. His eyes flashed and his pupils thinned. Astrid passed the mask back to him.

Then without warning, the pine finally gave way, its roots loosening from the earth and sending the trunk smashing down into the hut.

* * *

Reaching up to her head, Astrid felt something hot and warm trickling down her skin, her left eye blinded for a moment as the blood from the cut in her forehead spilled into it.

'Ragi? Astrid whispered, struggling to breathe and feeling something heavy pinning her down across her chest. 'Ragi!'

Barely three feet away from her Ragi opened his eyes, his hands shaking as he tried to look down at his legs, but he was unable to see past the thick pine branches that blocked his view.

'Astrid, don't move,' Ragi choked, each of his breaths a horrible rasp. 'Just don't move!'

'Why?'

'Just wait for Dag to come looking for us.'

'That could be hours!' Astrid replied, panicking. She took a deep breath and tried to free herself, shuffling uncomfortably on the floor.

'Stay still!'

Astrid ignored him and pulled herself out from under the pine branch, her left leg sending a flash of vision-blurring pain with each of her movements. She pushed through it, dragged herself out and turned on her side. The light wicker roof of the hut had fallen between her and Ragi, and she crawled forward and pushed it aside.

Seeing her face come into view, Ragi didn't need to ask what she saw. Her expression told him everything he needed to know.

'Go get Dag, goldheart,' Ragi whispered. 'He can help,' he lied, starting to feel the cold sensation from his stomach spreading upwards along his spine. 'Astrid! Get Dag!

'No, no I have to get you out!' she said, moving towards the branch impaling Ragi through his gut.

'Don't touch me!' Ragi yelled, his eyes wide, his pupils so thin Astrid could barely see them. 'Astrid...you can't do anything.' A strange feeling spread from his spine towards his head.

Reaching for his hand, Astrid closed her eyes, a terrible pain bursting from her stomach the minute she did so.

'Astrid, stop! You can't mend this! Go find Dag!'

'No! You're just saying that so I won't be here!' Astrid screamed, trying to take his hand again, but Ragi pulled it away.

'Yes I am, goldheart. You don't need to see this!'

'I'm not going!' she said, crawling up next to him. She took his hand and Ragi, getting weaker by the second, gave in and let her hold it. His skin was turning grey and pasty.

'Astrid, please don't stay here,' he whispered. 'Dag would let you hide away till the day you die. Don't let him. Leave!'

'But you said you'd go with me!' Astrid sobbed, her lips trembling. 'I don't want to be alone!'

'I'm afraid you're going to have to get used to it for a while, goldheart!' Ragi chuckled, the chuckle turning into a cough. The inside of his mouth was speckled with flecks of blood. 'But it won't always be lonely, the Outlands are full of people. You'll find new friends.'

Seeing his pupils starting to dilate, Astrid reached for his face and pressed both her hands on either side of it, screaming from the pain as she tried to absorb as much of Ragi's as she could, refusing to allow him to die.

'No! No you stay with me!' she shouted. Ragi opened and closed his mouth, trying to say her name, but the blood caught in his throat making a horrible gargling sound.

'Ragi! Ragi!' Astrid shrieked, her hands glowing bright blue and her fingertips reddening. The skin dried and cracked under the pressure of trying to hold death back and her stomach felt as if she had a red hot poker burning its way through it.

'Astrid!' Ragi gargled, reaching up and weakly pulling her hands away from his face. 'Leave!'

Slowly, with her hands shaking, the glow around her fingers faded. Astrid moved Ragi's head into her lap and she stroked his face gently. He closed his eyes as his face relaxed, his breathing weakening, until he finally let out one long, pained breath. Everything went still.

Klaire de Lys

'Sleep and be happy, the moon is awake.
There's light in the darkness.
Smile dear, you're safe.'

Helpless

Knud was freezing, the damp having gotten into his bones. He pulled his cloak tighter around him and rested his head on his knees.

'Knud! Here, eat this. It'll help keep you warm,' Jarl said, passing him something which looked like a compressed piece of bread. Knud took it from him and bit a small piece, his hands shaking.

They had finally reached the forest edge but the dampness seemed to only have intensified as soon as they reached it, trapped under the trees' thick canopy. Their clothes felt heavy on their backs and they had stopped for a moment in a hollow to rest. Knud looked like he was about to collapse at any moment, exhausted.

Seeing him shaking, Astrid pulled off her wolf-skin cloak and placed it over his shoulders. Knud flashed her a grateful smile and pulled it as tightly around him as he could, tucking his feet and head under it so he looked like a big ball of fur.

'Thank you,' Jarl said, his breath turning to mist in the cold night air.

'He needed it,' Astrid replied, a small smile on her lips. Turning her head, her eyes warily scanned the forest around them. It was too silent. Silent was never good.

Goblins could be stealthy when they wanted, creeping up on their prey like a mist, preferring fast and sudden attacks. They would rush in, kill as many as they could, and then leave before they suffered too many casualties. It was a brilliant strategy for the goblins but it made life very difficult for anyone who wanted to try and travel through the pass, having to stay alert and ready at all times. It was exhausting both mentally and physically.

'We should leave soon. I know Knud's tired, but I can carry him. The house I mentioned is about a mile from here. We can stay there for a few days if we need to,' Astrid said quietly.

'What is this place?' Jarl asked.

'An old friend used to live there,' Astrid said flatly, implying that was all she wanted to say on the matter. Jarl took the hint.

'Can he rest for a bit longer? Then we can go,' Jarl said. Astrid nodded, hearing the faint snores from within her cloak.

Jarl sat down next to him, moved his arm over him and pulled him close to keep him warm. Knud snored more loudly and Astrid grinned at how comical he looked.

Suddenly she felt her ears tingling and heard the sound of light scuffling in the undergrowth a few feet away from them. Turning to face the sound, she pulled her dagger from her boot and held her hammer axe in her other hand. With her knees bent, she was ready to attack. Jarl heard her draw her dagger and looked up, his own hand moving to his weapon.

For a few seconds there was silence. Jarl pulled Knud to his feet, waking him, and stood in front of him protectively.

'Run!' Astrid whispered.

He didn't need to be told twice. Jarl practically dragged Knud along behind him as they ran, the young dwarf struggling to keep up with them, his tired feet catching on the many tangled roots that covered the ground. He tripped and stumbled clumsily forward, doing his best to keep up, but failed miserably. When he fell for the second time, slowing them down once again, Astrid ordered him to climb onto her back. Knud did as she'd asked and Astrid ran ahead again as if Knud weighed nothing at all.

'It's not far,' Astrid said under her breath to Knud who was holding onto her so tightly he was almost strangling her.

Glancing around her as they ran, Astrid tried desperately to recognise her surroundings, so much of the forest having changed since she last travelled through it. She sighed with relief when she saw an old twisted tree ahead of them, the relief turning to horror as she saw a goblin drawing his bow from the corner of her eye.

Smirking, the goblin released the arrow and Jarl stared in horror, time seeming to slow down as it shot towards Knud.

'KNUD!'

Not even having to think, Astrid turned to face it. Jarl bellowed in shock as she reached out fast enough to grab it. The arrow head cut through the skin between her thumb and index finger, her grip temporarily slowing the arrow down, but not enough to stop it piercing her shoulder. Astrid grimaced in pain.

For a few seconds nobody moved. The goblin stared in disbelief and Astrid looked up, their eyes meeting for a moment. She had yellow eyes like Ragi's and her hair was pulled back into tight braids with several silver tribal bracelets wound into it.

'I'm sorry,' Astrid whispered under her breath, and with one fluid movement, Astrid turned the arrow in her hand to her bow and shot it back, shooting the she-goblin straight in the forehead.

'Come on!' Astrid shouted, racing ahead. She reached the oak, whispered something under her breath and a door appeared in front of her. She threw it open and Knud scrambled down from her back and ran inside. Jarl sprinted past her and into the tunnel and flashed Astrid a worried look as he passed her. Blood gushed from the torn skin on her hand and the superficial wound on her shoulder. Astrid closed the door as soon as they were all inside.

'Where are we?' Knud asked, reaching out in the darkness. Everything was pitch black.

'We're safe,' Astrid panted back, her heart pounding as she heard goblins shrieking outside and the sound of multiple pairs of feet scrambling over the tree above them.

'Can they find their way in?' Jarl said worriedly, his deep voice echoing in the tunnel.

'No. This place is protected with magic. They'd kill themselves if they tried to get in uninvited,' Astrid said.

'How did we get in then?'Knud asked.

'I know the password,' Astrid replied, as if it was obvious. Jarl could tell from her tone of voice that she was smiling. 'I just don't want them to know we're here or they'll try and starve us out.'

Of course they will! Just like they're trying to do with Bjargtre, Jarl thought.

They all turned and stared as a faint light began to glow at the end of the tunnel. Astrid walked towards it and the others followed until they reached a large room that looked as if it had been hollowed out by hand. Roots covered the walls and a few of them had started to make their way across the floor. Astrid snapped a few that had grown across a cupboard in the wall.

Everything smelt musty and old. Hundreds of faces were painted onto the wall behind the tree roots, and faded eyes stared out at Jarl. Something about them made him feel distinctly uncomfortable.

Astrid opened the cupboard door, the old, rusty hinges making it creak. 'Food?' she asked, pulling out a few sealed jars. She sat down on the floor and grabbed a handful of nuts from one of them before passing it to Knud, ignoring the fact that her hand was still bleeding.

Knud scooped out a handful of nuts and ate them as quickly as he could.

Jarl put down his bag and hammer axe and knelt down next to Astrid. Taking her injured hand in his, he turned it over gently to look at it. Astrid flinched but didn't pull away.

'We need to clean this,' Jarl said quietly. 'The arrowhead was probably poisoned.'

'It wasn't,' Astrid replied, trying to stop herself from shaking but her body refusing to do as it was told. She pulled her cloak tighter around herself, trying to pretend that it was the damp that was making her shiver. 'Besides, Dip venom doesn't hurt me anymore.'

'Anymore?' Knud asked, sensing another story about Astrid's adventures coming up.

'If you drink it in small doses you become immune to the poison. A little like hemlock,' Astrid said, moving to pull her hand way but Jarl not letting her. 'It's a slightly painful process but it's worth it.' She turned to Jarl. 'Don't worry about it. It'll scab soon.'

'It'll scar if you leave it.'

'It will be a good scar,' Astrid said, slowly pulling her hand out of his, her fingers tingling where his skin had come in contact with hers. She suddenly felt stupidly light headed and her stomach was in knots. She lifted her hand to her mouth and sucked away the blood.

Jarl reached into his bag and pulled out a tunic, then ripped a piece into a thin bandage.

'Jarl, I'm fine, really,' Astrid protested.

'No! You just saved Knud's life. Again! You're going to let me bandage that hand!' Jarl said firmly, taking her hand in his again. This time she didn't flinch but set her jaw tightly, trying not to wince as Jarl pressed the bandage over it to stop the surprising amount of blood flow.

With her hand in his, he noticed just how strong she was. Her fingers, though long and elf like, were coarse and tough, the skin of her palm as weathered as his, though slightly softer.

The bleeding finally slowed and Jarl wrapped the bandage firmly, being as gentle as he could. Taking advantage of the moment, his eyes ran over the beautiful ink pattern of her tattoos. Stemming up from her nail bed, the white thorn patterns twisted over her hand as organically as if it were a real rose bush, the thorns circling the bottom of her index finger more tightly than on her other fingers. A beautiful large black rose stretched from the gap between her thumb and index finger and reached her wrist, the arrow injury almost having cut through the skin the tattoo was inked on.

'There!' Jarl said, tucking the end of the bandage in and letting go of her hand. 'See? It didn't hurt that much.' He smiled, looking oddly nervous, his smile wavering.

'Thank you,' Astrid whispered, looking down at her hand and flexing her fingers, the bandage holding fast. She nodded her head to the hallway. 'Nobody can get in through that so you won't need to keep watch.' She dragged her bag next to her to use as a pillow so she could sleep half sitting up, then pulled her wolf-hood over her head and closed her eyes.

Jarl hovered by the door. He trusted what Astrid had told him but knew he would not be able to sleep well knowing nobody was on watch. He pulled his cloak around him and held his hammer axe in his hand, staring down the hallway with his head resting against the wall behind him. Knud, having fallen asleep a few moments ago snored gently, and when he turned to look at him, he found himself looking at Astrid instead. She was curled up like a cat, her hood pulled so far down over her face that only her lips were visible.

I wonder what Holmvé would think of her? he thought, smiling as he imagined her reaction. The scars on her face would shock Holmvé at first, but he had no doubt that as soon as she spoke to her, the old dwarf would adore Astrid and admire her bravery.

Astrid would hate Bjargtre! And people like Áfastr Gull would hate her! Clenching his fists, Jarl turned away from Astrid and glared back down the passageway. Áfastr would be brutal, of that he was sure. In fact there were very few dwarves in Bjargtre who he could think of who would treat Astrid with anything other than contempt. They would shun her publicly, make snide remarks behind her back, which she would undoubtedly hear perfectly. Just the thought of it made him angry.

She deserves better! She should be loved by her people! He suddenly felt horribly empty at the thought that once they reached the outskirts of Lǫgberg, she would leave them. Leave him.

Ask her to come back with you! the small voice in his head suggested. *If she covers her ears and if you find dwarf clothes for her, nobody will know she's a half dwarf!*

Slowly. the beginnings of an idea began to form at the back of his mind. Looking back over at Astrid, his eyes gleamed. She would get to see a dwarf city! Her people! And he would get a few more months to travel with her.

* * *

She was sitting in the kitchen again, and Sylbil and Arnbjörg were humming together as they worked on the thatching on the roof. Looking down at her fingers, Astrid saw her tattoos were gone. She reached up to her lips and felt for the scar, smiling as she felt that it was gone too. It was a dream, she knew that, but it was a good dream. She was inside the house. Her dreams were always good when she was inside the house. So long as she stayed inside, bad things wouldn't happen. For a moment she considered going up to the top rooms and her heart leapt at the thought of seeing their faces again.

But she decided against it. Their faces would be foggy like they always were, or worse, their faces would morph into the faces of other people like last time when Arnbjörg's face had morphed into Skad's. It was better if she just waited down here. Maybe if they came down she would be able to see them.

'Astrid!'

Turning around, Astrid saw Ragi, and the still mildly conscious part of her brain told her something was wrong. Ragi never appeared in her dreams here. When she dreamt of the Red Mountains, yes, but her dreams of the Aldwood had never included him.

'Ragi? What are you doing?'

'Still running wild child?' Ragi asked, climbing up into the rafters and smiling down at her with a thistle

and a jasmine in his hand. He pulled the petals from the jasmine and dropped them over her. They floated down like feathers.

'Running?'

'You're afraid! So you're running!'

'No, I'm taking Knud and Jarl to Lǫgberg.' Astrid smiled, trying to climb up into the rafters so she could sit down beside him. Ragi disappeared in a puff of smoke and his voice echoed through the air as he hummed the song she had sung the day he had died: There's light in the darkness. Smile dear, you're safe.

Suddenly, she felt someone holding her hand and she looked down to see Jarl next to her, taking her bandaged hand and wrapping it some more. He was smiling, humming as he wrapped it around and around. Astrid turned to face him, a strange feeling in her chest, like her heart had grown hundreds of wings and was fluttering around inside her, leaping each time he looked up at her with his sky blue eyes.

'Why do you flinch when people touch you?' Knud asked behind her, and Astrid turned to look at him.

It's just a dream! You can say anything in a dream!

'I'm frightened they'll hurt me!' Astrid said.

Knud watched as Jarl continued to wrap the bandage and Astrid suddenly realised that she was running her fingertips along Jarl's hand as he held hers.

Why are you doing that? Stop that!

'Why don't you mind us seeing your face?' Knud asked. Astrid looked at him, her mind ordering her to pull her hand away from Jarl but her hand refusing. It felt as if it was made of lead and not attached to her body.

'You don't mind my face, nor does Jarl,' Astrid said. 'I covered it because I didn't want Skad or Halvard to see it. It made them stare. I hate people staring at me!'

'Why doesn't Jarl mind?' Knud asked, and Astrid thought it was strange that he was asking her but not questioning it. It was a dream after all.

'I don't know! He's always been kind to me.' Astrid smiled.

Suddenly, Jarl moved his hand and rested it against the side of her face. Astrid felt her heart jumping up into her throat and she was unable to look away from his deep blue eyes that were fixed on hers. He stood up and stood in front of her. Astrid remained seated on the chair, staring up at him as his face slowly lowered towards her, his lips moving in to kiss her...

* * *

Astrid woke up screaming and Jarl and Knud nearly jumped out of their skins as she sat bolt upright and hit out at the empty space in front of her.

'What's wrong?' Jarl asked, reaching out to hold her arms.

Astrid shivered violently and pushed him away. 'Nothing! Nothing! Just...a bad dream!' she said, rubbing her face and getting up. Overwhelmed with an urge to run, her eyes darted around the room. She shook her hands as if they had dirt on them that she couldn't get off.

'Astrid? What's wrong?' Jarl repeated. He stepped towards her but she took a step back.

'Nothing!' she replied, almost snapping. 'Nothing.'

Sitting back down, Astrid leant her head against the wall, trying to shake the image out of her head. Her cheeks were bright red. 'I'm sorry, I didn't mean to wake you,' she said to Knud. 'Go back to sleep.'

Knud settled back down again and she turned to Jarl, avoiding his eyes.

'I'll take the next watch. You get some rest.' Jarl nodded and they passed each other in the passageway. Astrid walked down it until she reached the door and sat down cross-legged in front of it, resting her head on the ground for a moment.

What on earth was that? she hissed at herself, confused at the sudden rush of emotions and feelings that were flooding her mind, all of them new and frightening. She felt excited but frightened. Her stomach was in knots and she felt oddly light-headed. A little sick. *Stop it! Stop doing that! Why are you doing that?*

Looking ahead, Astrid focused on the small hand print embedded in the back of the door and forced herself to run her eyes over it again and again until she could visualise it perfectly, pushing all other thoughts away.

'That's better,' she whispered to herself, finally able to close her eyes without seeing Jarls face, his eyes shining at her.

Whatever that was, it's not going to happen again.

Always An Outsider

33 years ago...

Astrid said nothing as Dag filled the grave up, but stood silently by his side clutching the velvet pouch with her parents' rings in it. Her eyes were red and glazed.

Ragi's hut was behind them, the tree still lying across it. Dag barely moved the tree when he dragged Ragi's dead body out from underneath it. Everything was broken, in disarray.

Looking up at Astrid, Dag put the shovel down and stood silently by the mound, the clouds above them rumbling as small flecks of rain began to patter through the leaves.

'We shouldn't leave his hut like this,' Astrid said quietly, her voice hoarse and raspy. She turned to the hut and moved towards the axe leaning against the side.

'Goldheart, we should leave it,' Dag said, and Astrid turned to look at him in surprise. 'It's not our business to move anything.'

'Yes, yes it is!' Astrid snapped, glaring at him. 'He's our friend! We can't leave his home like this!'

'Ragi's dead now. There's no point in moving anything,' Dag replied, his manner so apathetic that Astrid couldn't help but gasp. She stepped away from him in disgust, shook her head and picked up the axe then climbed over the crumbled roof and hacked at the nearest branch, cutting through it in one swipe before moving on to the next one.

For a moment Dag's hands began to glow, and Astrid stopped and watched him as he mentally wrestled with his dilemma. Eventually, he turned and walked away. Astrid glared at him before hacking at the tree some more. Tears stung her eyes as the rain picked up and began to pour down, drenching everything around her in seconds.

Leave old man! Leave like you always do! Coward! What's the point of living in this world if you won't be a part of it?

After several minutes, Astrid stopped what she was doing, realising it would take her days to cut through the tree. With the rain pouring down it was becoming harder to keep her footing on the ground. Clenching her fists, she looked down at her hands. Her fingertips glowed a bright orange, like small tongues of flame licking their way over her hand.

With her eyes firmly fixed on the tree in front of her, Astrid placed her hands on the bark of the trunk, refusing to close her eyes and focusing on the wood. Ragi's voice echoed in her head as she replayed every memory she had of him in her mind, forcing out every sad image and only letting the memories which made her happy play in front of her.

Like a fast growing weed, the light around her fingertips grew and spread over the pine, covering it in a yellow, cocoon-like glow. Then, closing her eyes, Astrid pictured the moment the tree had come crashing down, and the look in Ragi's eyes as the light was pulled from it.

With a terrible roar, the entire tree was consumed within seconds, the wood and pine needles crumbling and twisting in the flames of her magic, and the heat that bellowed from what remained of the tree turned the rain into fog and blew away in the breeze.

Opening her eyes, Astrid looked down. The pine was gone and only the broken line across Ragi's hut showed where it had once been. Rubbing at her eyes, Astrid crawled out of the hut and sat down next to Ragi's grave, pulling the black velvet bag out of her pocket. She dug at the loose soil with her fingers and tipped the two rings into the hole before covering them over.

'You should have them,' Astrid whispered. 'I'll never need them.'

* * *

Sitting by the fireplace, Dag watched the door, his hands wrapped around the hot mug of nettle tea. It was nearly midnight and although Astrid still hadn't come back, he couldn't bring himself to go out and look for her. She was broken again, her eyes with the same lost expression as when he had found her in the Aldwood. He hated that expression. It made him feel so utterly lost and helpless. In fact now that he thought about it, mostly everything about raising Astrid made him feel lost.

There were no set rules or codes of behavior when it came to raising her, and he hated that. There needed to be rules; he hated the guesswork and the constant fear that he was somehow doing something wrong. Life had been so much easier before her.

With a loud slam, the front door was thrown open by the wind and Astrid walked in, completely drenched, and closed the door behind her. She had a bag of Ragi's in one hand and the long black sash he had shown her earlier in the other.

'Astrid?'

Saying nothing, Astrid went to her room, stepped out of her wet clothes and changed into the only spare set she had.

'Astrid?' Dag called up again.

Opening Ragi's bag, she glanced around her room, looking for anything she would want to take with her. She reached for the wooden box Dag had given her containing the jasmine oil before moving away from it.

There's no point remembering. It just hurts you. Leave it!

She tied the black sash around her like Ragi had shown her, wrapping it several times around her waist, then draping it around her neck like a loose scarf a few times before finally moving the last stretch over her head like a hood. She closed the bag, with Ragi's daggers tucked away neatly at the top, pulled it over her shoulders and picked up her hammer axe and her bow and quiver.

Hearing Dag moving around downstairs, Astrid opened the door, half considering leaving through the secret hole in the roof but deciding against it. Dag, for all his flaws, had still raised her. At the very least he deserved a goodbye.

Stepping back in shock, Dag stood aside from the bottom of the stairs to let her pass.

'You're going?'

'Yes,' Astrid said firmly.

'Where?'

'I don't know. The human lands.'

'Astrid, you'll just get hurt!' Dag begged. 'No matter where you go, people will always treat you like an outsider! Stay here!'

'Why?' Astrid snapped. 'Because I won't get hurt? Ragi's dead! The people I love die! That's just what happens to me!'

'I can protect you here!'

'I don't want protecting!' Astrid screamed, and Dag stepped back in shock. 'I'm tired of people protecting me! I'm tired of people dying!'

'You can't stop people dying, Astrid,' Dag replied gently, reaching out to take her hands in his. Astrid pulled away.

'I'm going to try,' she said, a determined look lighting up her eyes, a small idea taking root at the back of her mind. She moved towards the door.

'Astrid, no matter where you go, people will always treat you like an outsider. Stay here! Please!' Dag begged.

Turning to look at him, feeling tears welling up in her eyes but refusing to cry, Astrid opened the door and walked outside. *I'm done crying!* The rain poured down so heavily it was almost a continuous waterfall of water.

Stopping for a moment, Astrid turned back to him, and the old warlock looked at her disbelievingly, still clutching his tea.

'I'll be back in the winter,' Astrid said over the sound of the wind and rain. Then turning, she ran from the house, gradually picking up speed until she was running at full pelt, her feet barely touching the ground. As she leapt through the forest she took a deep lungful of air.

Get used to it, the stern voice in her head whispered. *You'll be running for most of your life.*

Questions

Waking up, Jarl looked over at Knud out of habit. He was passed out against the wall, his mouth hanging open and his bright red curly hair sticking out in all directions. Astrid was nowhere to be seen and after getting to his feet, he strolled down the passageway. She was sitting at the end with her head leant against the wall.

'Astrid?'

She looked at him, suddenly feeling her cheeks flush, thankful that the passageway was too dark for him to see.

'Yes?'

'Are you alright?' he asked, sitting down next to her.

'I'm fine!' Astrid snapped. 'Sorry, I...I'm fine.'

'How long was I asleep?'

'A few hours.'

'A few?'

'I'm not sure exactly. I haven't gone outside.' She smiled, hearing Knud's snores, and her grey and green eyes caught the little light in the passageway. 'We can leave when he wakes, he's still tired.'

'He's managed this journey so much better than I expected,' Jarl said, not noticing the slightly alarmed look on Astrid's face. She felt her cheeks flush again. 'I thought I'd have to carry him after the first few days.'

'You might have to still. I don't know how bad the Haltija pass will be. Last time I came, the skirmishes between the goblins and the humans in the pass were only just starting. and I have no idea how bad it will be now. There's a small village between here and the pass. I have friends there who I can ask about it.'

'If I'd thought about it, I would have left Knud in the Salt Monasteries. It would have been safer for him.'

'Don't worry, I've travelled through worse places than the Haltija pass.'

'He likes you. What does he talk about with you? He keeps talking with you for hours!'

'It's just a game,' Astrid said quickly, thinking of how best to lie to him. 'He tells me something about Bjargtre and I tell him something about the human land. Stops him from talking my ears off!'

'What has he told you about Bjargtre?' Jarl asked, laughing.

'Not much. It's in a mountain.'

'As are all dwarf cities.' He laughed again.

'I tend to talk more than he does.'

'Really? I would think it would be the other way around.'

Shrugging her shoulders, Astrid smiled. It felt good just to talk like this, and there was something about being in the dark which made her lower her guard, like the rules she enforced on herself in the day time didn't apply.

'It's easy to talk to him.'

'Normally he's the one talking,' Jarl said. 'And I suppose Halvard wasn't the easiest of people to talk to, nor me for that matter.'

'Halvard wouldn't have been happy if I'd talked to you. Brojóta burðr's would only give you strange ideas after all,' Astrid said sarcastically. 'Sorry, I didn't mean to insult your friend.'

'It's not an insult, it's exactly the kind of stupid thing he would say.'

'I've not met many dwarves...' Astrid began, her voice hesitant. 'But the few I have met, I don't understand why they hate...people like me. Or even some of their own kind. I met a dwarf once and he wouldn't speak to another dwarf in the same group as him because the other dwarf was Ósómi. I don't know what that word means.'

'Was his hair short?' Jarl asked. Astrid nodded her head.

'Really short. It looked like it had be shaved off recently, even his beard. I'd never seen a dwarf with such short hair.'

'Osómi means disgrace.'

'So he did something wrong?'

'No, not necessarily. Halvard's father had his head shaved for publicly disagreeing with the King. It's the worst thing you can do to a dwarf aside from killing him,' Jarl muttered, anger in his voice. 'Halvard's father killed himself and his wife after trying to kill Halvard. He was so ashamed, he thought it was better for his family to be dead after being made an Ósómi.'

Turning, Jarl saw Astrid's shocked face staring at him, her mouth hanging open. He thought perhaps she was starting to understand Halvard's constant sullen behavior a little more.

'Status and birth is very important to the dwarves,' Jarl explained. 'Too important, especially to most of the nobles.'

'Aren't you a noble?' Astrid asked.

'Yes. But my family lost their reputation a long time ago,' Jarl said sadly. 'I guess I don't care as much because I don't have a family around me to care.'

'I'm sorry,' Astrid replied. She was tempted to ask him what had happened, but restrained herself. *If you ask him, he'll ask you about your family,* the voice in her head whispered.

'What, you're not going to ask me what happened?'
Jarl asked jokingly. Astrid shook her head.

'If you want to tell me you can, but I won't ask. I
don't like when people ask me, so I won't ask you.'

Jarl said nothing for a few moments. 'Would you
want to see Bjargtre?' he finally asked.

'What?'

'Bjargtre. Would you like to see it?'

'Why are you asking that?' Astrid said defensively.
Jarl was just able to make out her face in the dark. Her
brows were bent into a tight arch.

'Because if everything goes well in Løgberg, I
would like for you to travel back with me,' Jarl replied,
and Astrid felt her heart beating inexplicably faster.
Worried Jarl might be able to hear it, and not knowing
what else to do, she coughed.

'You've kept us alive so far. I can't promise Knud
that I'll come back, but I do know I'm more likely to
survive if you come with me. And it would be nice to
have a friend with me.'

If Astrid had been unsure of how to react before,
she was now utterly speechless as a torrent of emotions
flooded her head and chest.

'I don't know...I'd have to think about it,' Astrid
said, somehow managing to keep her voice emotionless.
'I think if I went you might end up having to protect me,
and I'd rather not have my other ear cut off!'

'I'd kill any dwarf who tried to touch you,' Jarl said. 'Besides, we can hide your ears easily enough. With your height, anyone would think you were a dwarf!'

'Not with my eyes,' Astrid muttered. 'My eyes always give me away.'

'Your eyes are beautiful.'

Astrid turned to look at him, his own blue eyes looking into hers. 'Your eyes are the first thing I noticed about you!' He smiled.

Astrid couldn't move; she felt hypnotised. She realised that Jarl was the first dwarf she had ever met who had always looked at her straight in the eyes. He hadn't even seemed to notice her scars.

'Astrid?' Knud said suddenly behind her and she nearly jumped out of her skin in shock, her heart beating like a drum.

'Knud! You're awake!'

Nodding groggily, he sat down between them, his red hair looking orange in the low light and sticking out like a wild thorn bush in all directions. 'When are we going?' he asked, yawning.

'Now you're up, as soon as we have everything together,' Astrid replied, feeling slightly annoyed that Knud had woken when he did, but strangely relieved too. She was both worried and excited about what Jarl might have said next.

You idiot! The little voice inside of her hissed. *You cannot feel like this about him! Look what happened to Mātīr and Faðir. What on earth makes you stupid enough to think that falling in love with him wouldn't end the same way? Or worse.*

But then another little voice, a quiet and gentle voice, whispered back.

'I'll think about it,' Astrid said, turning back to Jarl. He nodded but said nothing, and continued to sit quietly in the dark with a small smile forming at the corners of his lips.

* * *

Slowly opening the door, Astrid stepped outside with an arrow drawn on her bow, ready to fire at the first sign of danger.

Behind her, Jarl and Knud waited in the passageway, Knud holding the goblin dagger she had lent him and Jarl with his sword in his hand.

Looking around, Astrid closed her eyes, letting her ears do the work. Jarl didn't need her to call them out, because a few moments later he saw her shoulders relax and the familiar glint in her eyes when she turned to look at them. They stepped outside and the edges of the door disappeared as soon as it closed shut.

'Where are we going now?' Knud asked.

'I have some friends who live in a small village just before the Haltija pass. We can stay there for a night or two. I need to know how bad the pass is.'

'How long will it take to get there?'

'Another two days, one and a half if we hurry.'

'What friends?'

'Humans.'

'How did you meet them?'

'Is that a question?' Astrid asked.

'Yes!'

Walking alongside them, Jarl listened, Astrid not minding in the least that he could hear. She realised to her surprise that she quite enjoyed the audience.

'I met them when I was travelling with some merchants from the Gold Coast to the Salt Monasteries. They joined the caravan, and after we reached the Monasteries I took them out here since we were both heading in the same direction. I think they'll still be here.'

'You think?' Jarl asked.

'Humans don't live for long, and I haven't been back in over a decade, but I hope so.'

'How old are you?' Knud asked.

'Is that a question?'

'No!' Knud said, deciding it would be better to save his last one.

'Yes it is!' Jarl said quickly. Astrid looked at him surprised. 'I would like a question!'

'You have to give something in return,' Knud pointed out, and Astrid turned and flashed him a look. Knud quickly shut his mouth, the sentence fading out as he finished it.

'A question for a question?' Jarl suggested, and Astrid nodded. 'Very well then, how old are you?'

'I'm forty-seven.'

'So young!' Jarl exclaimed. 'I thought you would be at least one or two hundred!'

'Why would you think that?'

'Because you look like you're my age.'

'How old are you?'

'One hundred and twenty-five.'

Astrid couldn't help bursting out laughing as soon as Jarl finished speaking, a loud and full laugh like it had been repressed all of her life. Her whole face lit up.

'Sorry! I didn't mean to laugh!' She giggled, wondering why she was even giggling in the first place. 'I've just spent so much time around humans I'm used to their ages!'

'I suppose to humans I would be an old man.' Jarl grinned. 'Wrinkled and bald!'

'You'd more likely be dead!' Astrid laughed morbidly. 'That's so strange. You're seventy-eight years older than me!'

'It's not that old.' Jarl said. 'I'm a young dwarf. There's a couple hundred years still left in me!'

'My turn to ask a question now!'

'No, you already asked one!' Jarl said.

'No I didn't!'

'You asked my age!'

Realising he was right, Astrid shook her head, smiling. 'Very well, what's your question?'

Taking a moment to think, Jarl looked at her and Astrid felt her cheeks getting hot. She reached to her veil and moved it to cover her face. Jarl reached out and stopped her, gently holding her hand back. Astrid stopped in her tracks.

'You don't have to wear that. Halvard isn't here to make comments.'

'I prefer to hide my face,' Astrid muttered, pushing past his hand and attaching her veil.

'Not around humans you don't.'

'What?' Astrid asked, turning to stare at him. Jarl looked back at her, his eyes glinting.

'I know you only wear that around us, or your face would be lighter where the veil hides it. Especially if you travel to Bayswater and the Gold coast,' he said calmly, not even a shadow of doubt in his voice. He knew what he said was true and Astrid stared down at the ground.

'I don't like people asking questions about the scars,' Astrid finally said, continuing to walk ahead, Jarl with her and Knud a few feet away, pretending he couldn't hear every word they were saying.

'Then I won't ask any questions about them,' Jarl said firmly.

Slowly she reached up to her veil and pulled it away. 'What is your question then?'

* * *

Sitting down in the grass, they all breathed an exhausted sigh, Astrid's a little less obvious. Knud flopped to his side in a heap and pulled his bag under him like a pillow.

'Knud wait! You need to eat something!' Astrid said, pulling him up and passing him a few of the oat cakes the monks had given her. 'If you don't eat now you'll be even more tired tomorrow. Just have half of the cake and I'll be happy.'

Snatching it from her hands, Knud ate it as quickly as his exhausted body could manage. Even his jaw protested as he chewed.

'There. Finished. Can I sleep now?'

Astrid had barely nodded her head when Knud dropped like a rock back onto his bag, curled into a ball and closed his eyes. He was asleep in seconds.

'I'll take the first watch,' Jarl said.

'No. I like taking the first one.'

'Will we reach this village by tomorrow?'

Looking down the plain for a moment before she answered, Astrid shook her head. 'No. We walked too slowly today. We'd have to walk far too quickly for

Knud to keep up if we wanted to reach the village by sunset tomorrow.'

'You were asking too many questions!' Jarl laughed, pulling his bag next to him as if about to go to sleep, but instead he sat up to talk to her.

'If you didn't want me to ask questions you shouldn't have offered to answer them!' Astrid said. 'Tomorrow it's your turn!'

'Good!' Jarl grinned. 'I have a lot of things I want to know.'

Smiling, Astrid got up, realising to her horror that she was walking a little more lightly on her feet. They almost felt as if they wanted to dance.

Why are you doing that? Stop that! The little voice hissed. Astrid tried to shake the smile off her face but she couldn't, as hundreds of invisible strings pulled at her facial muscles. Each attempt at erasing the smile just made the strings pull back harder, made her smile larger. She remembered Knud asking where her favourite place was.

Today...today it was here, she thought.

Yes, Bayswater was beautiful beyond belief. But today she had felt like the void inside her that she tried so often to hide had been filled a little. Jarl had told her so much about Bjargtre, Lǫgberg and the dwarves, answering every question she had asked him. She had listened, fascinated, as he told her about the culture of her father and her own heritage, visualising as best as she could the great stone halls carved into the mountain, the hundreds of people bustling through the tunnels, the smell of stone. It had been a good day.

*　*　*

'Jarl?'

Waking, he looked up at her, realising to his horror that the sun had already risen.

'Astrid! Why didn't you wake me for the watch?'

'I'm a half elf,' she replied, quite shocked at how easy it had been for her to say those words in front of him. 'I can go for days without sleep.'

'You should have woken me,' he muttered, getting up. 'I'll take the first watch tonight.'

'Very well,' Astrid replied, not caring to argue.

Waking Knud, Astrid helped him to his feet. He rubbed his eyes and stared in awe at the sunrise, the sky a brilliant mixture of fiery orange and pink. A few dark purple clouds hovered on the horizon, their edges glowing as they attempted to block the sun.

Shivering, Knud pulled his cloak around him, rubbing his hands together. 'When will we get to this village?'

'Tonight if we walk quickly. You see that ridge?' Astrid asked, pointing into the distance. Knud shook his head.

'Our eyes aren't as good as yours,' Jarl said, smiling.

'It's not that far!'

'I just see the plain, and the mountains,' Knud said. 'It can't be that close!'

'It is!' Astrid assured him. 'If we run we can make it by sunset.'

'Ugh...running,' Knud muttered. 'I can't run that fast.'

Hearing a low hum behind them, Astrid turned around, her ears twitching nervously. 'Can you hear that?'

'Hear what?' Jarl said.

'Get on my back!' Astrid said quickly, turning to Knud.

'What?'

'Do what she says!' Jarl ordered, seeing the look on Astrid's face. He took Knud's bag from him and slung it over his shoulder along with his own. Knud climbed onto Astrid's back and they ran as fast as they could, away from the high pitched yelps and snarling that they suddenly heard behind them.

Looking back, Knud felt his heart jump into his throat. A pack of Dip wolves were slowly catching up on them, their long thin bodies leaping over the grass, their red and silver eyes getting closer and closer.

'Astrid!' Knud yelled, frightened.

'Keep running!' Astrid yelled at Jarl, whose heavy boots kept catching on the tufts of thick strong grass and began to slow him down.

'Astrid! The wolf! Use the wolf!' Knud begged.

No! No you can't! The quiet voice inside her head ordered. *Think about how he'll react!*

The Dip were getting close and when Knud, turning around on her back, saw their sharp needle-like teeth glinting in the sunlight, he screamed in terror.

It doesn't matter how he reacts, the stoic voice she knew so well replied in her head. *It matters that they live. There was never any hope for you anyway. All you can do is save them.*

With a jolt, Astrid skidded to a stop and Knud was thrown from her back onto the ground. Jarl rushed up to him and, when he'd tumbled to a stop, hauled him up from the ground. He stood in front of him protectively and stared at Astrid. The Dip circled them, snarling, wary, their animal instinct sensing that they should be afraid of the green and grey eyed woman.

'Astrid!' Knud screamed, terrified. The Dip bayed around them, slowly approaching.

'No more questions Knud!' Astrid said turning to him, looking like she was about to cry for a moment. Then her mouth twisted into a snarl and she dropped her bag onto the ground.

Without warning, three of the Dip suddenly leapt towards Jarl and Knud. Jarl cut through one of them with his sword and grabbed the second by its neck with his bare hand to hold it back. Knud fell back, holding out Astrid's knife in front of him, and the Dip impaled itself on it as it leapt towards him. Jarl tossed the Dip away, its neck half crushed in his grip, and it fell on the ground, whimpering and snarling in pain, its eyes glowing red.

But then he noticed some of the Dip were stepping back and he heard a low, terrifying growl behind him. Before he could turn around, several of the Dip closed in on him. Two of them bit into his left arm, one of them managing to pierce his leather vambrace, and a burning pain shot up his arm as the teeth punctured his skin.

With a terrifying howl Astrid threw herself at the Dip, her enormous claws ripping across the face of the one attacking Jarl. She grabbed a second Dip with her teeth, sinking them into the back of its neck as it leapt to attack Knud, and tossed it so high into the air that it fell to the ground over thirty feet away, breaking its neck on impact.

Reacting instinctively, Jarl moved to attack the wolf and Knud threw himself onto Jarl's arm.

'No! Don't! It's Astrid!' he yelled.

Hearing Knud yell out the words, Astrid turned to look at them for a moment.

Staring at the wolf, Jarl noticed its eyes - a bright green and grey and so expressive, so familiar. The wolf bowed its head and turned back to the Dip who was snarling, its hackles raised.

'Get away!' Astrid's voice growled from the wolf, and she reared up onto her hind legs with her long, vicious, blood-stained claws fully extended.

The five remaining Dip bayed loudly. One of them limped, with a deep claw mark at the top of its foreleg. At first it looked as if they might retreat, taking a few steps back, and Astrid dropped down onto all fours and prowled in front of Jarl and Knud protectively, her teeth bared.

But they were starving, their ribs protruding, desperation driving them on. In an instant they dived at Astrid, their mouths open, revealing hundreds of razor-sharp teeth dripping with silver venom.

As Astrid reared up, her claws caught three of them, disemboweling them. She felt someone step beside her and Jarl's sword caught the remaining two. He kicked one of them away as it tried to bite at Astrid's leg, his thick steel boots breaking its skull.

Astrid looked up at Jarl, panting and terrified, with her claws covered in blood. She slowly stood up and the wolf-skin slid from her back to the ground. She stared at it, rubbing her hand nervously on her sleeve.

This is it. The only question he'll ask now is 'how fast can you leave'.

'Knud knew,' Jarl said gently, the complete lack of anger or shock in his voice making her heart jump into her throat. She nodded.

'You distracted the fireflies?'

Astrid nodded again.

'Thank you.'

'What?' Astrid asked, sure she had heard wrong, feeling a lump rise up in her throat. She tried to force it back down but her emotions wouldn't let her.

'He said thank you.' Knud smiled and walked up to her with an impish grin on his face. 'He's not angry.'

Opening her mouth, she tried to say something but the word caught in her throat. She gasped as if she was being strangled, the lump making it painful to even breathe. Her eyes watered and she quickly turned away, knowing she was going to cry and that there was absolutely nothing she could do to stop herself. Her shoulders shook.

Stepping forward, Jarl reached for her shoulder and slowly turned her to face him. Astrid moved her face away but allowed him to stand in front of her.

'We should go,' Astrid mumbled, a barely concealed sob breaking through her words. She was relieved at Jarl's reaction and felt dizzy from the rush of euphoria that followed. 'Did any of them manage to bite you? Knud? Are you alright?'

'I'm fine,' Knud warbled back, his voice shaky. He stared at the blood on his dagger but managed a weak smile. 'I killed one of them!'

Feeling another shot of pain, Jarl looked down at the vambrace protecting his arm. He untied the straps and lifted the double tunic underneath. There was a deep, cauterised puncture in his skin.

Astrid quickly reached for his arm. 'Sit down,' she said gently.

'I can stand just fine.'

'You won't be able to in a few minutes,' she replied, and Jarl did as she'd said. Knud's eyes widened as she pulled out a small dagger.

'Don't worry. It won't hurt,' Astrid said, smiling reassuringly at Knud. 'The venom will have numbed his arm.'

Pressing the tip of the knife into Jarl's skin, she cut around the puncture, lifting up the cauterised skin to make it bleed. Jarl was unable to feel a thing, just like she had said. Pressing her fingers down around the puncture, Astrid pushed out as much of the blood from underneath as she could. A silvery-black liquid oozed out with it and Knud's stomach lurched, his skin turning grey.

To his dismay, Jarl felt his head starting to spin.

'You're probably going to be sick at any moment,' Astrid warned him and Knud scuttled away quickly. Jarl turned away from them, bent over double and promptly threw up with Astrid still pressing down on his arm and forcing the venom back up to the surface.

'Can you feel anything in your arm yet?' she asked, as Jarl emptied his stomach again.

'No, I can't,' he finally managed to say. Knud reached into his bag and pulled out his flask of water, passing it to him.

Lifting his arm up, Astrid pressed her mouth over the puncture and sucked as hard as she could, pulling out the remaining venom. She spat it onto the ground then took a drink from her own flask to rinse her mouth.

'Ok, now I can feel something,' Jarl muttered, resisting the urge to scratch at his arm.

'You're going to find it hard to walk,' Astrid warned. She helped him to his feet and looked at his face. His skin was colourless, but he picked up his bag resolutely.

'We should get to your human friends' village by nightfall,' he said, his arm shaking as he pulled the vambrace back over his hand. He slowly walked forward, trying to hide how dizzy he was feeling, his stomach churning.

Astrid scanned the plain, worried that there might be more Dip hiding in the grass, hoping that if there were they would have the sense to stay there.

'You're not going to be sick again?' Knud asked, walking at a distance from Jarl.

'I hope not,' Jarl muttered.

'He will,' Astrid replied. 'Come on, we need to go.' She took his arm and draped it over her shoulder. Jarl protested but Astrid refused to let him go. 'Don't be stupid, or else you'll be crawling without my help.'

Ruins

'I can see the village!' Astrid said, relieved. Jarl muttered something indistinguishable. His skin was an off grey colour and he was barely managing to walk by himself, pure stubbornness being the only thing stopping him from letting Astrid and Knud help him. 'Wait here!'

Rolling his eyes, Jarl slumped down onto the ground, doing his best to keep hold of the little that remained in his stomach. His throat felt as if he had been throwing up glass shards and sand. He watched Astrid as she marched towards the village. The sun had started to set and the temperature had dropped quickly the minute the light had started to fade.

Jarl gripped his sword tightly, despite his hand shaking, the setting sun and the sound of Dip yelps in the distance worrying him.

Astrid lowered her wolf-hood to expose her face, not wanting to alarm any of the guards in the towers. She raised her hands slightly, her eyes scanning the tall stone walls.

'My name is Lilly Agviðr!' she called out. 'I'm a friend of Hellen and Peter Barrow.'

There was silence; she could hear nothing but the wind.

Walking up to the gate, her hands still raised, Astrid noticed the scorch marks and slashes that covered it. She leant forwards and pushed it open, the wood creaking and the large rusty hinges shuddering as she did so.

The village was deserted; destroyed. Every house had its roof burnt away and most of the walls had fallen in. Astrid stared at the remains of a large pyre in the centre of the village and walked towards it, her heart in her mouth as she began to slowly make out shapes in the ashes. The charred remains of bones. Human bones.

Astrid gasped, stepping back. 'No! No! No!' Her stomach churned as she noticed several small child-sized bones amongst the sprawled figures. Two skeletons curled around one of them protectively; parents trying to protect their child from the flames that had burned them all to death.

Letting out a strangled gasp, Astrid turned away, tears stinging her eyes. She ran out of the village and back towards Jarl and Knud.

'We need to leave! Now!'

Knud looked at her, confused. 'What about-'

'Everyone's dead!'

As they began to move away, Astrid heard the unmistakable sound of approaching Dip in the distance, their shrill yelps screeching across the plain towards them. The sun had fully set and the moon had not yet risen enough to light up their surroundings. Everything looked blurred in the twilight.

'The village! We have to get inside the village!' Jarl shouted, and he and Astrid grabbed Knud by his shoulders and raced forward, pushing open the heavy gates and closing it behind them. The Dip appeared and yelped and scratched outside the door, howling loudly.

Looking out of the small hole in the gate, Astrid's face dropped as she saw how healthy the creatures were. These were not like the Dip wolves they had encountered earlier that had been thin and rabid. These were healthy, cared for creatures, two of them with copper torques around their long thin necks.

'Goblins! There are goblins nearby!' Astrid whispered, looking around the village for anything they could use to their advantage, knowing it would not be long before their masters would follow.

'We could hide in the houses,' Knud suggested, marching ahead.

'Come back!' Jarl ordered, but Knud ignored him.

'If we hide in the ruins maybe...'

With a horrible snap, the strong steel jaws of the trap laid just beneath the surface of the mud closed around Knud's foot. The powerful spring closed the sharp teeth of the trap like a bear's bite, and they all heard it crunch through the bone of his ankle with the delicacy of a hammer. Knud screamed out in agony and dropped down to the floor, clutching at the trap and trying to pull his foot from it. Jarl and Astrid raced up to him.

'Get it off! Get it off me!' Knud screamed, tears running down his face. The colour drained from his skin within seconds. Jarl managed to force the trap open, his strong arms straining to hold it there, and Astrid quickly lifted Knud's foot from it. The bone was cut clean through and his foot hung by a few threads of muscle, flesh and veins. Knud's eyes rolled back and he passed out from the pain.

'Idiot, idiot, IDIOT!' Astrid shrieked. Jarl wasn't sure if she was talking to herself or to Knud. Her hands gripped Knud's foot as she tried to hold it together, the blood spurting out between her fingers.

Jarl pulled off his cloak and began to rip it into thin shreds. Astrid took the first one from him but paused, knowing what she would have to do but not quite able to bring herself to do it.

'Jarl, he's lost the foot. There's nothing I can do to save it,' she whispered. The Dip shrieks outside the gate intensified and goblin horns sounded in the distance.

'I know,' Jarl said, his face stern. 'Let go, I'll do it.'

Stepping back, Astrid looked away as Jarl took the goblin dagger Knud had dropped, and in one clean swipe, cut through the remaining muscle and tissue still connecting his leg to his ankle. Jarl flinched slightly but there wasn't a single flicker of emotion on his face. He knew what needed to be done and he did it. He wrapped Knud's foot as tightly as he could with the torn strips of Knute's cloak, and Astrid turned back to help him, doing her best to not look at the small severed foot lying on the ground.

He's never going to be able to run again! Or climb a tree! He's going to be a cripple!

Picking Knud up in his arms, Jarl turned to face the gate, hearing goblins shouting as they approached the walls of the village. 'The wall!' he shouted at Astrid. 'We have to go over the wall!'

Running past the charred ruins to the other side of the village, they quickly climbed up the rough footholds built into the stone. Jarl waited for Astrid to climb first and passed Knud to her before climbing up himself. He heard the gate open just as he dragged himself over the top.

Dropping down on the other side and taking Knud from Astrid, they ran for their lives, Knud's unconscious body a dead weight in Jarl's arms. The bandages around his severed foot were already stained bright red as the blood seeped through the strips of Knute's cloak. A cold sweat covered Knud's face.

In the village the goblins, realising they had climbed over the wrong wall, quickly ran back out of the gates, shouting at their Dip wolf scouts to chase them. The Dip hurtled through the village, their thin gangly feet pattering on the ground.

'Keep running! Don't stop!' Astrid howled, skidding to a stop herself, the wolf-skin stretching over her body. The wolf head slid down over her face and Astrid's grey and green eyes stared through it. Her claws tore up a cloud of dust from the ground as she scratched at the grass, snarling at the approaching Dip with her eyes flashing.

Ignoring her, Jarl stopped too, laid Knud gently on the ground and drew his broadsword.

'What are you doing? Run!' Astrid shrieked at him.

His face was set as hard as stone as he moved towards the approaching Dip He lashed out at the first Dip and took its head off with one swipe. The second Dip to attack died just as quickly. Jarl held Knud's goblin dagger in his right hand and the sword in his left, fighting and slaughtering them with both weapons as they approached. Astrid caught the last Dip between her teeth and crushed its head between them. Jarl sheathed his sword and picked Knud back up then ran ahead, the dagger still in his hand. Astrid followed him, back in her human form.

'The goblins. Are they following us?' Jarl panted, running as hard as he could. Astrid looked over her shoulder.

'No!'

No sooner had the words left her mouth, they heard the sound of hooves ahead of them. They ground to a stop and four goblins rode out of the darkness towards them, the lower part of their faces covered by horrifying masks that made them look like demonic animals. Each mask was unique and skillfully carved. Astrid remembered the mask Ragi had shown her so many years before.

Drawing her bow, an arrow already pressed against the string, Astrid took aim, shouting out in a strange language Jarl couldn't understand. The goblins froze the moment they heard her, their eyes widening in shock, confused and amazed at hearing their own language being spoken so fluently. Astrid repeated herself, the words slightly different this time, and Jarl suspected it was a different dialect.

Hearing more goblins closing in behind them from the village, their feet heavy and pounding on the ground as they ran, Astrid shouted out at them once more, praying they would listen to her. Ragi's face flashed before her eyes.

Please don't make me shoot you!

When the goblins pushed their ponies forward, Astrid clenched her jaw tightly and shot at them repeatedly, each arrow either hitting them straight in the forehead or directly in their heart. The goblins toppled to the ground with loud, heavy thuds.

'Grab a pony!'

Jarl draped Knud's unconscious body over a pony's back before he clambered on himself, took control of the reins, and rode ahead. Astrid raced after him, turning for a brief moment to fire the last of her arrows out into the darkness. Jarl heard a horrible screech as each one found their mark with such a deadly accuracy that none of the remaining goblins dared to follow them.

* * *

They travelled in silence as fast as they were able, Astrid still keeping her distance from the pony. The moon rose and illuminated the plain and Astrid looked behind her several times to check that they were not being followed.

The Riddari split on either side of them, making way for the Haltija pass. Astrid led the way but stopped every hour to rest her hands on Knud's face, her own face flooding with pain each time she did so. She made sure he remained unconscious, but with her hands glowing, she took as much of his pain as she could without impairing herself.

Finally, just as the sun was beginning to rise, they stopped. Astrid took Knud from Jarl and sat down on the ground. She held him in her arms resting her hand on his head again, her fingertips glowing blue with a faint tinge of orange. Tears ran down her face and her mouth pressed into an angry scowl.

'I'm sorry! I should have seen the trap,' she whispered, looking down at him.

'It wasn't your fault!' Jarl said angrily, taking Knud from her. Astrid mistook his tone and thought he was angry at her, and not at himself, and she clenched her fists, her fingers still glowing.

'We can rest for a few minutes and then we should start moving,' she whispered. She rested her head in her hands, not caring how many tears were streaming down her face.

Hellen and Peter were dead, and once Knud woke up he might wish he was dead too.

Astrid looked away as Knud opened his eyes. Groaning and groggy but feeling nothing, he gazed up at Jarl, a frightened and confused expression on his face.

'M...my leg!' he yelled, twisting his neck to look down at the empty space where his foot had been. Jarl didn't stop him and Astrid felt like her heart might break as she heard him gasp before he let out a torrent of tears. Astrid tried not to sob loudly but tears slid down her cheeks and her whole body shook.

'Astrid?' Jarls voice said softly, and she slowly turned to face him. His blue eyes looked at her so intently that she had to turn away. Unable to look Knud in the face, she knelt down next to him.

'I am so, so sorry.' she wailed. 'I should have seen the trap. Knud, I am so sorry.'

'We should go,' Knud whispered, his eyes dazed and vacant. The cheeky glint in his eyes that Astrid was so used to seeing was gone. Nodding, she stood up.

See? I told you it would end badly! the voice whispered in her head.

* * *

They had reached the other side of the pass after a solid day's ride. They'd kept as close to the mountains as they could and darted into the tree line at the first sight of goblins, but didn't enter the forest. Even Jarl was able to feel the magic which tingled off every root and stone in it, warning them it would be unwise to enter.

They hadn't been able to light a fire, worried about the unwelcome attention it could bring. They were freezing and Astrid had given Knud her wolf-skin. The cold winds from the Riddari penetrated her bones just a little more each night, despite her thick clothing.

Stopping for the night by a stream, Jarl set Knud down next to the flowing water. He knelt down beside him and carefully unwound the dirty bandages. Astrid held Knud's hand and absorbed his pain as Jarl re-wrapped his stump with the remains of Knute's cloak. She winced as she watched but said nothing. She had said nothing for days. Jarl looked up at her for a moment, noticing her expression, before he turned back to Knud and helped him hobble back to the tree line.

Knud had refused to let anyone carry him, using a stick he had picked up from the ground earlier that day to help him walk.

Jarl tethered the goblin pony to one of the roots of a tall, red pine and sat down next to Knud whom had already fallen asleep. Astrid had pulled the wolf-skin over his head to hide his face; she couldn't bear to see the paleness of his skin, the dark circles, the emptiness she knew was behind his eyelids.

Jarl looked across at Astrid who was sat with her back to them and staring out into the plain. The wind had picked up and she visibly shivered as she hugged her knees to her chest.

'Astrid?' he called out, and she briefly turned to look at him, unable to hold his gaze. She looked away, shivering as another gust of wind blew down from the mountain. 'Astrid come and sit with us. You're freezing!' She shook her head.

'I should keep watch.'

'And you can't keep watch with us?' Jarl asked, raising an eyebrow. 'Those ears of yours will hear anything approaching from a mile away. Stop being so stubborn.'

She sighed, got to her feet, walked a few paces towards them and sat down. The pony was tethered nearby but Astrid barely noticed it. Staring down at her feet, she pulled her knees to her chest again and wrapped her veil back around her head and across her face.

It wasn't your fault Astrid,' Jarl said. 'Come here. You can't help us if you die from the cold.'

For a moment she did nothing but then shuffled a little closer to Knud, still refusing to look Jarl in the eyes.

'Astrid...look at me!' Jarl said, his voice firm. Astrid slowly raised her head, grateful that the veil was hiding half of her face. Her mouth trembled as the lump at the back of her throat grew more and more painful. Her eyes stung. She was drowning in guilt.

Suddenly, Jarl lifted his hand up and reached over Knud's sleeping body to touch her face, gently pulling her veil away. Astrid, not knowing how to react, stared at him, her stomach twisting into a knot.

As he slid his rough hand against the side of her face, Astrid found herself unable to stop herself from leaning forward. He moved his hand behind her head and pulled her gently towards him, stopping when her face was barely an inch from his.

Astrid looked at him with an expression which could very easily have been mistaken for complete and utter terror, but Jarl ignored it. His hand moved back to her cheek and he ran the edge of his thumb against her lips.

'Can I kiss you?'

Astrid's breath caught in her throat and she found herself completely unable to say anything. The knot in her stomach unravelled in an instant and the feeling was suddenly replaced by another, one which she imagined was close to how it must feel to fly. She felt weightless; light headed.

Say something! Say something! both voices in her head screamed at her.

Astrid tried to do as they were telling her but every sound she attempted to make was stopped by the lump at the back of her throat. Her body was unable to decide whether it was going to laugh or cry, so she did the only thing she possibly could. She leant forward. And Jarl instantly pressed his lips against hers the minute he saw her moving towards him.

Nothing could have prepared her for the rush of emotion that followed. She felt invincible and vulnerable all at once. She kissed him back slowly, afraid that she was somehow doing it wrong. But Jarl didn't seem to mind. His hand cupped the side of her face and then slid slowly to the back of her neck.

What are you doing? the stern voice whispered in her head. *You know how this ends! Stop it! Haven't you messed up enough already?*

But there was nothing the voice could have said that would have made her stop.

'Oh shut up!' Astrid mumbled against Jarl's lips, not meaning to say the words out loud. Jarl pulled away from her. 'What?'

'Nothing,' Astrid said, still shivering but no longer cold. She smiled and her whole face lit up. Even her eyes glowed in the moonlight.

'Please stop,' Knud suddenly said, and Astrid and Jarl both looked down to see Knud staring up at them. 'That's disgusting!' he said, his face revolted. But the twinkle in his eyes was unmistakable.

Astrid turned bright red and Jarl grinned.

'Knud, I think you should mind your own business,' Jarl joked.

'Then *you* can sit in the middle!' he said firmly, using Astrid and Jarl's shoulders as a support to help himself stand. He wobbled slightly and Astrid and Jarl quickly reached up to steady him, but Knud pushed their hands away. He leant against the tree, hobbled past Astrid and lay down on the ground a few feet away from them. Then he pulled the wolf-skin head over his own to hide the grin on his face and closed his eyes.

For a few moments neither of them spoke, watching Knud until they were sure he was asleep. Astrid's face hardened as she looked at his severed limb emerging from the bottom of the wolf-skin.

'I lost someone once,' she suddenly whispered. Her eyes glazed over as her face automatically masked the turbulent emotions flooding her mind. 'A little boy from Waidu, Ned. I took my eyes off him for one minute and he was gone.'

Jarl said nothing, his arm still around her. Astrid shivered.

'I never helped a dwarf or an elf again after I lost my ear,' Astrid explained, turning to look at him, the glazed look slowly ebbing away as she met his eyes. Jarl clenched his fists as he saw the torn and jagged edges of what remained of her right ear-tip. 'I never wanted anything to do with you, but Knud reminded me of him. I felt like I could make up for my mistake if I got him to safety, if I...' Her voice trailed off, riddled with guilt. 'He'll be a cripple because of me, he'll...'

'He'll be alive because of you!' Jarl interrupted. More than anything, he wanted to pull her closer and hold her tight but he was terrified that she might pull away. Instead, he rested his hand against the side of her face and Astrid relaxed at his touch.

Oh look at you! the harsh voice in her head snarled, *next you'll be skipping around sniffing flowers and giggling like a fool! You're pathetic! I thought you were smarter than this!*

Shaking her head, Astrid suddenly moved forward and leant her head against Jarl's chest. He tentatively hugged her closer, surprised, but he didn't say a word.

'I have friends who live in the Aldwood. We can take the Three Sisters' Pass and go there first before we head to Waidu. If he likes it, Knud could stay there while we go to Lǫgberg.'

Jarl didn't say anything for a few moments, but turned to look over at Knud, and at Astrid's wolf-skin rising and falling as he snored gently.

'I don't like the idea of leaving him with strangers,' Jarl admitted, turning to look back at her. 'And he'd probably find a way to follow us, he's ridiculously stubborn.'

'I don't know how well I can protect him now,' Astrid said, ashamed. 'The pass is a lot worse than last time, and last time I was able to cross the mountains. The Frǫðleikr thought I was a wolf so they let me through. I can't do that with both of you.'

'Would your friends help us travel to Waidu?'

'They would if I asked them to,' Astrid said slowly, her tone implying it was possibly the very last thing she wanted to ask them. 'I could ask Bugual to come with us, or Loba, but they would all want to come.'

'All of them?'

'Vârcolac travel in packs. It's safer that way for them.'

Jarl said nothing. The thought that he might have to leave Knud in the care of complete strangers made him feel sick to his stomach. This was Knud, his best friend's son. His own son, almost. He couldn't leave him with complete strangers. But if Knud stayed with them he would be in a lot of pain and would slow them down. He wouldn't be able to run; he could barely walk. What if taking him got him killed?

'We would be taking the Three Sisters' Pass anyway, wouldn't we?' Jarl asked, and Astrid nodded.

'We could stay with them for a few days and give Knud time to rest. Bugual might be able to help me make a peg leg for him if you want him to come. But he would have to wait till his leg heals. At least a month.'

'We can't wait that long. If I'm right about the goblins, then Bjargtre only has a few months at the most. How long will it take to reach Lǫgberg?'

'We can reach Waidu in two weeks if we don't stop in the Aldwood. With ponies it should only take another two weeks to pass through Kentutrebā.'

After a few seconds silence, Jarl took a deep breath and turned back to look at her. 'Do you trust them?'

'With my life,' Astrid replied firmly.

'Then we should stay with them for a few days. It would give Knud time to heal, and if he wants to stay then he can. But what about you?'

'Me?' Astrid asked, confused.

'Will you come back with me to Bjargtre?' he asked, a small smile at the corner of his mouth.

Astrid said nothing, looking away for a moment, her eyes flicking over the nearby tree roots as she tried to think. The soft little voice goaded her on while the harsh voice screamed at her that she was crazy to even consider making such an important decision.

She turned back and looked into his eyes. 'Yes,' she said. 'I'll come with you.'

The End

Acknowledgements

Firstly, because I promised you years ago that I would dedicate my first story to you, I would like to thank my English teacher, Mr. Ronald Warwick. I was absolutely terrified at showing my work to anyone who wasn't family or friends, and I told myself that if you didn't like my work then I wasn't good enough and should stop writing. You not only liked it but enthusiastically encouraged me to keep going. Thank you.

To my mum, who has always encouraged me in all of my hobbies and passions, despite my constant mood swings and self doubt. Thank you for always pushing me, even when I felt I wasn't good enough and came close to giving up. I would have quit a lot of things a long time ago if you hadn't helped and encouraged me.

And lastly, I would like to thank my editor, Elaine Denning, who had to put up with my horrific, dyslexic spelling. I'm sure it probably made you want to cry at times! And thank you to Harrison Davies for formatting the book. I would never have been able to do any of this without your help.

Web Links

Website:
www.klairedelys.com

Elaine Denning (Editor):
www.facebook.com/ElaineDenning

Harrison Davies (Formatter):
www.harrisondavies.com